EUROPE:

OR ^UP A^ND D^OW^N WITH
SCHREIBER AND BAGGISH

BOOKS BY RICHARD STERN

EUROPE:
OR UP AND DOWN WITH
SCHREIBER AND BAGGISH

Richard Stern

Foreword to the new edition by David R. Slavitt

TRIQUARTERLY BOOKS
NORTHWESTERN UNIVERSITY PRESS
Evanston, Illinois

TriQuarterly Books
Northwestern University Press
www.nupress.northwestern.edu

Northwestern University Press edition published 2007. Foreword copyright © 2007 by David R. Slavitt. Copyright © 1961 by Richard G. Stern. "The Sorrows of Captain Schreiber," *Western Review,* 1953, copyright © 1953 by Richard G. Stern. "After the Illuminations," *Western Review,* 1955, copyright © 1955 by Richard G. Stern. All rights reserved.

Printed in the United States of America

10 9 8 7 6 5 4 3 2 1

Library of Congress Cataloging-in-Publication Data

Stern, Richard G., 1928–
    Europe, or, Up and down with Schreiber and Baggish / Richard Stern ; foreword by David R. Slavitt.
        p. cm.
    Originally published: New York : McGraw-Hill, 1961.
    ISBN-13: 978-0-8101-2449-3 (pbk. : alk. paper)
    ISBN-10: 0-8101-2449-1 (pbk. : alk. paper)
        1. Americans—Europe—Fiction. 2. Travelers—Fiction. 3. Travel—Psychological aspects—Fiction. 4. Europe—Fiction. I. Title. II. Title: Europe. III. Title: Up and down with Schreiber and Baggish.
    PS3569.T39E87 2007
    813.54—dc22
                                                                                    2007017840

∞ The paper used in this publication meets the minimum requirements of the American National Standard for Information Sciences—Permanence of Paper for Printed Library Materials, ANSI Z39.48-1992.

Parts of this novel were published in somewhat different form in the *Western Review* and *Prize Stories of 1954: The O. Henry Collection.*

For Gay

"Every man of character has a typical experience which recurs over and over again."

NIETZSCHE

FOREWORD TO THE NEW EDITION

David R. Slavitt

Those of us who are old enough can remember how the novelists who emerged at the end of the forties were "important," which is to say that they commanded public attention in a way that those who came after them could never quite manage to do. They were good, even excellent, writers—Mailer, Styron, Capote, Vidal, and a few others—but they were not remarkably better than the novelists who followed them and for whom the literary ecology had begun to change. It was still possible to make a splash—as Bellow and Updike did, but they were relicts, or maybe just lucky. Mostly, novelists had ceded their centrality in the discussions of the day. Wright Morris, Herbert Gold, Philip Roth, Vance Bourjaily, Nelson Algren, Frederick Buechner, Richard Yates, George Garrett, Calder Willingham, Richard Stern, and their like were lively, sensitive writers, adventurous with language and fresh and interesting in their perspectives on how we live. But public attention had turned to politics (the war in Vietnam and the civil rights movement), and the very idea of an "important" novelist began to seem slightly odd if not frivolous. There have been a few since then who have made some impression, either by fluke or by clever manipulation of the publicity machinery. But these days we are in a truly dismal reading environment in which the most important tastemaker in American literature is Oprah, which means that serious readers and writers find ourselves marooned on a semitropical island where the ship stops only rarely.

Richard Stern is one of those novelists who would have been important—without the quotes—if the audience had been good enough or had been paying any attention. He has had a distinguished career, producing one book of real interest after another and a body of work which, now that Northwestern University Press is reissuing it, we can see has been a real contribution to our culture. All of Stern's books are wonderfully well written. He can make dry and understated jokes that explode splendidly, but his talent for doing so ought not to distract us from the seriousness of *Europe: Or Up and Down with Baggish and Schreiber,* which is that Europe—or, for an American in the sixties, *otherness*—can be a crucible that refines and clarifies character. This is Henry James's great subject, after all, but Stern is much more modest and glancing. One of the pleasures I had (which students mostly won't) in reading this novel is remembering that moment when Roth and Bellow, Algren and Gold were coming onto the scene with new rhythms in their sentences and paragraphs and therefore a new kind of energy. Stern's droll but sympathetic voice was and remains a significant contribution to the atmosphere of that time.

The story is less ramshackle than it appears. Schreiber, a kind of likable nebbish, and Baggish, a much less likable hustler, go to Europe in different ways and for different reasons, and we watch what it does to them and what they do to themselves. They have some tangential and not-quite-random connections. And they each find resolutions that are not altogether the result of chance but are in suggestive ways the result of their different characters. And what is the novel, after all, but the study of character in action over time?

But to put it this way, in abstract and intellectual terms, is to betray the fun that Stern—and, I suspect, his readers, too—has with his characters as he runs these kinds of thoughts through their quirky minds. Here is Baggish thinking about Schreiber:

With that pure instinct for opportunity which, in the eyes of those who lack it, is usually called luck, Baggish saw, or rather, at this stage, felt, that Schreiber was a strait through which he would pass to his wider prospect. The feeling was, of course, an educated one; there was evidence to support it, although the evidence was far less than that on which non-Baggishes would proceed. The evidence, most of which came from Joan Poster, consisted of Schreiber's position as Chief Analyst of an Intelligence Section, his apparent wealth (he had gone to Harvard Law School, traveled, had lived in Rye and Noroton, wore expensive-looking clothes, was divorced, and had a sort of relaxed quality which Baggish took as a sign of financial independence and probably ease), his place in what was generally regarded as the chic social group in Heidelberg civilian circles (Baggish had seen him at their desirable table in the Casino), and, most of all, an air about him, which, for Baggish, cried, "Use me. Dupe me." Without malice aforethought, though without charity, Baggish moved in.

You write a passage like that, and you are entitled to a split of champagne and a nap.

A worthwhile book on its own, when viewed in the context of Stern's other works, *Europe* becomes essential reading. It shows Stern's growth since his first novel, *Golk,* and suggests something of what is to come later. I can't remember who it was who called Stern "the greatest American writer you've never heard of," but I adduce that rueful remark with emphasis on the first part of it. To bring these books back in what is almost a Jamesean collected edition is a good thing. Stern deserves the attention. And his readers will be the beneficiaries.

EUROPE:

OR UP AND DOWN WITH
SCHREIBER AND BAGGISH

PART ONE

C H A P T E R   O N E

I

Valerie Schreiber ran across the gravel road yelling "Bucci, Bucci, get over here." One of the carpenters, sitting on the second floor skeleton of the Peniman house, pointed a hammer at a pile of leaves, where, half-buried, a spine of orange fur that was Bucceroni, the old cat, glistened and shook. Valerie yanked it up and hurled it across the road. "I'm going to feed you to the crows, you rat you."

Bucceroni hauled himself off to the house, and there, on the porch, he lapped up a dish of cat meat while his mistress studied the Peniman house and decided that she would begin the evening hostilities by introducing the subject of its progress. It was one of those rare, really valuable subjects which never failed to arouse her mother, to attack, that is, for her mother, like herself, was perpetually aroused by the fat slob who had one day invaded their lives in his captain's uniform, and then, doffing it, had played that other oh-so-cute game of being her father. The invasion had taken place one week before her seventh birthday six years ago, but it wasn't until the actual day of the party that the old war hero exhibited his pure, true self by cavorting around the house with her friends, playing Pin-the-Tail, Blind-Man's-Buff and six or seven other hot-shot games, not only as if he relished them, but as if nobody else could without him. As if

3

the whole world had waited for him to get back from the war before
it could continue living. Between him and his greaseball law partner
who had tried to sneak his way into her affections by giving her this
lousy cat—whom he had prodigally endowed with his own cleancut
name—her life was one scarcely interrupted hell. That legal eagle
was chiefly distinguished by smoking, *gumming,* the fattest, foulest
cigars in Stamford, Connecticut, and by his sweet habit of pinch-
ing her friends, her grown-up friends, on the cheek and announc-
ing in the reassuring tones, which only liars use, that he was a
great friend of their fathers. The day she had overheard him called
a shyster as she tried on a polo coat down in Best's was one of
the days in her life she would not forget nor forgive: that her own
father should be the partner of a law-skirting shyster was the
equivalent of his having spent fifteen years in prison for armed
robbery. Worse, for prison wasn't a part of the discussable world.

When the Mercury wormed up the driveway, and her father called
"Hello" from the wheel, she waved at him.

"How was school, Valerie?" he asked.

"Was none, Teachers' conferences." She went to the stair well
and called up, "Dad's home, Mother."

"I'll be right down," said Florence, but she didn't move from the
bed, only turned the pillow over for the fiftieth time in two hours to
get some coolness from the other side. This time her arms wrapped
it around her ears as if she were squashing a beetle. She listened
for the noises her husband made in the kitchen as he drew out ice
trays, cracked the ice, and spooned it into the Old-Fashioned glasses,
probably before he'd dissolved the sugar and bitters in them. Or
he'd forget the bitters. His coat would be off, his collar dirtier than
a miner's, and his tie would sport a gob of thousand-island dressing
above his tie-pin; as if any civilized man under sixty wore one of
those anymore. Most and worst of all she saw his fatness, saw, felt,
smelled it so sharply that she could detach it from his form and
measure the vices it accumulated about itself. Every day he seemed
fatter to her; it was as if each pound were trying to bury whatever

little they had had together. He ate like a beast, his head sinking into the plates, grunting and sighing like a lover, befouling himself with the stickiest, ugliest components of every dish. He saw nothing that couldn't be crammed into his throat, ate without interrupting to pass a spice or answer a question, the veins romping wickedly in his temples. She held the pillow to drive out all his noises, real and imagined, and then, groaning, slid out of bed into her pumps, made up, and came down to the porch where her Old Fashioned sat on the tray next to the ring his glass had made.

"Couldn't wait?" she asked, staring at the glass in his hand.

"Good evening," said Schreiber, handing her the tray and taking a first sip of his own drink. "Anything new? I see there's no mail of interest."

"Your aunts are not remarkable letter writers. Prompt but unremarkable."

"Gretta's the worst. Cheers."

"What about?" said Florence; then, seeing Valerie drinking Coca Cola from the bottle, she added, as if still speaking to her husband, "How many times do you have to be told not to drink from a bottle?"

"That's right, Valerie," said Schreiber, and received a look of filial hatred that made him tremble.

"Did you bring the light bulbs?" asked Florence.

"Sorry, forgot."

"No wonder you have such a distinguished practice."

After a while he asked, "We going to Mother's?"

"It's Wednesday, I believe."

"You're in a particularly jovial mood, *ce soir.*"

"You always bring out the best in me, Max."

After a moment he said, "You ready for another?"

"Thanks."

In the kitchen, Valerie was drinking another bottle of Coca Cola behind the ice box. "You'll make a good spy, Vallie," he said.

"Mother hates to wash glasses anyway."

"And a statesman."

"Why don't you talk so people can understand?" she said, and put the bottle in a paper carton under the sink.

"I'm sorry. It's necessary to talk this way when you're a lawyer."

"I know. Mr. Bucceroni."

"Don't you think he's always understandable?" said Schreiber quietly, and he cracked ice cubes with the hard rubber spoon Valerie had given him for his last birthday.

They went out to the porch and sat on the red davenport facing the gravel road.

"They finished the second story today," said Valerie.

"There'll probably be six other houses up before those trees get put in," said Florence.

"They've been ordered for two weeks," he said. "As it is, we're pretty well screened from them," and he looked out as if unable to see the white crossbeams of the skeleton.

"Not quite as well as we would be if they didn't own the lot."

"Please," he said.

"I've decided to ask Mother to advance us the money to buy one hundred feet on both sides of us."

"Why not?" he said. "She might as well protect her investment."

"You sound as if we pay her rent."

"We pay through the nose. Tonight for instance."

"I wish she'd hear you just occasionally. Except she'd kill herself for being taken in."

"We'd better get dressed if we're going to go," said Schreiber, and he went upstairs leaving behind a pool of detestation which for mother and daughter covered over the issue of the Coca-Cola bottle.

2

They started for Mrs. Carroway's house at seven. It was a twenty-five minute drive along Tokeneke Road to the Post Road, over to the Parkway and Long Ridge Road and finally through a blazing green wood twelve acres of which belonged to the Carroway house.

It was the house Schreiber loved better than any other, the single by-product of his marriage he would have been sorry to lose. The oldest portion dated from the 1750s and comprised a stone cellar, wine room, and the central part of the first floor. Mr. Carroway's grandfather had added a wing and second story, and he himself had added another wing just after his marriage. This was the New England version of a Queen Anne house, white, rambling but intact, surrounded by wide lawns and gardens, built into and over a long slope which led to a trout stream a half a mile into the woods. Fifty yards from the house was a paddle-tennis court equipped with lights for the night games no one had played there since Florence's brother had been killed in the Pacific war. The house of a New England family which had been prosperous and nearly distinguished for two hundred years, it was filled with mementos of prosperity and distinction, sea chests, models of three-masters, old desks, family portraits, maps. Nonetheless, the house was brightly, rigidly modern. Its relics were distributed in nooks and passageways while the rooms strutted in the blues and greens of thick chairs and sleek lounges, silver and silk.

Mrs. Carroway governed it now as she never had in her husband's lifetime. Her father had been a Professor of Modern Languages at Amherst, and she, one of five daughters and three sons. She had married well, better than any of her sisters but the one who had married a Vanderbilt, yet her husband had been a tyrant, a man who nipped at her for thirty years to duplicate the grace of his father's home, as he himself endeavored to maintain its self-centered stability. After his death, just before that of her son, she had made a clumsy attempt to remarry, but again chose the wrong man, a luxuriating bachelor who had temporarily disguised his sole intention, which was to suck perpetually at the winey comforts of the Carroways, and who lit out at the first hint of marriage. From then on, Mrs. Carroway had made her life vivid by indulging a talent for eccentricity. Upon the stupid placidity of her nature, she imposed minor but absorbing erraticisms of dress, opinion, and action. At first, these had been displayed only before her servants as a kind of private theatrical, but in the past year she had begun to lose control of the flamboyance, until it led to isolation from nearly all her friends and relatives but the Schreibers.

Since he had returned from the Army in '45, Schreiber had become an outlet for her self-indulgence. She'd begun to think and speak of him as her son and of Florence as a pushy alien who had married above herself into the Carroway family. The aberration led to incorporating herself in Schreiber's history. If he told an anecdote about his home in Pennsylvania, she would butt in with, "You were such an intrepid boy for Hazleton. I remember how other boys used to envy the way you climbed trees." Schreiber thought of such fantasies as part of his mother-in-law's twitting of Florence, but Florence feared them and hated what she rightly suspected was their origin: her mother's wish to disown her whole cringing past.

"Put her there, partner," said Mrs. Carroway, holding her fingers out to Valerie. Over a gorgeous cocktail dress, she wore a red apron embroidered with silhouettes of Mickey Mouse and Pluto. "You're looking chipper, Max dear. Good evening, Florence. It's not too chilly to have cocktails on the porch, is it? Vallie, tell Joseph he can bring the martinis out here, will you please, dear? Bella has your dinner ready. Your little gut must be starved."

Valerie spent all her time at her grandmother's in the kitchen gossiping with the Negro couple who had served the Carroways for almost forty years. (It had been the first place on the list the agency gave them, and they had never looked for another, although they well knew that they could command two or even three times their present salary by simply going to an agency, or, even more simply, by asking Mrs. Carroway for more money. They had held, however, to an older conception of service which demanded much more than money. In this view, money was a substitute for other obligations, a means of evasion.) Bella and Joseph preserved the more formal manners of Mr. Carroway, and their ambition was to restore Mrs. Carroway to the sanity of those manners; indeed, their contracted brows were often enough to pull her out of an absurdity, and into the quiet terror of her old dependence.

Their unexamined love for Florence and Valerie roused a similar, if greedier, affection in the mother and daughter: Joseph and Bella were the richest tokens of their family arrogance, more important than the house and its contents, because Florence and Valerie were more concerned with present commands than with trophies of old commanders. For hours, Valerie would sit in the pantry alcove and cry out "Bella!" at the baked surprises on the table, and the three of them would talk about Stamford scandals as if neither age nor condition separated them.

The talk on the porch was more constrained. It began after Joseph passed the martinis, drinks for which he had been praised in a twenty-year-old ritual. "As good as ever, Joseph," and, "How does the rest of the world get on without them, Joseph?" the Schreibers said, and Mrs. Carroway, with nervous displeasure, watched Joseph smile at the comforting familiarity of the praise.

"I'm afraid I'm angry with you, Max," she said this evening after Joseph left. She lapped up the olive in her glass, gnawed off the meat and spat the pit back into the liquid, her eyes glistening with this acquisition to her vulgar trove. "You've not done such a thing to me before."

Schreiber contrived a questioning look, although he found it difficult to break through the gentle alcoholic contemplation which was already taking control of his evening.

"It's your distinguished partner," said Mrs. Carroway, and made a grimace which glinted in her white face like still whiter bone. "Your Bucceroni. The first time he's crossed my path directly."

The gross, if classical apparition of his senior partner dispelled the haze. "That's surprising. What is it?"

"A small thing to him, perhaps, but not to me. He's representing —and for all I know, you're representing—that family who moved in in back of the Chadwicks."

"The Chadwicks?" said Florence.

"Dee and Jarvis. Max knows them," said Mrs. Carroway.

Florence, who had known them all her life, said, "I didn't know the Longman place was sold." Her mother had gone on. "A fearsome clan from Minnesota or some place who took the Longman house on High Ridge Road and proceeded to do everything in this world to drive Dee and Jarvis out. Parties the whole weekend, rabid poodles running around in Dee's garden and God knows what else. Jarvis went over to speak to this fellow about it, and the very next day, a man came around and started putting up a four-foot stone wall in back of the garden and stringing barbed wire on top of it. Dee says it looks like a concentration camp, and every time she goes out there to putter, she expects to see people caught up in the wire, screaming. Jarvis called them up again last week and suggested doing something less drastic, but this Gabrielson man said the wall was the best solution. So Jarvis called Norris Williams and Norris, on a hunch, had a surveyor take a look, and sure enough, in three or four places the wall touches the Chadwick's property. They're taking it to court, and Gabrielson has called in Bucceroni. Now, Max, Bucceroni must know that I've known the Chadwicks since I don't know when. I want you to speak to him about it."

"That's not the way lawyers operate, Mother," said Schreiber, just trying to clear away the debris of talk so that he could fade back into haze. "A case is a case."

"A hundred dollar case!"

Schreiber filled his glass from the shaker. "It's funny, you people who've been around here all your lives. You don't know what it's like, starting up in a town. It's pioneering," he said. "With axes. The only person Bucceroni knew when he came into Stamford was his uncle, who's a butcher, and some cousins who were laborers, common laborers." Mrs. Carroway, who disliked speeches, slobbered in her glass. "Like pioneers," repeated Schreiber.

"And so he takes you in because you're Mother's son-in-law," said Florence as if touching a grease spot on his coat.

"And because I know a little something about property law acquired at the expense of more sweat and effort than you've ever mustered for anything. And naturally because he thought I might be an entrée." He sat down, and then threw in, somewhat over-expressively, "How little he knew."

"Max," said Mrs. Carroway, with the well-bred woman's kindly condescension to the intoxicated, "I'm not angry, and I don't ever want you to think that I don't admire you coming out of the army and taking up with this fellow—doing it all your own way. I know how hard a time you had in Rye, and I know how hard you worked, there and here. I've always tried to let you know what I think of independence. But there are limits to indulging independence and this Gabrielson man exceeds them. What would become of the world if people like this had their way? You know they go to Bucceroni because the Chadwicks are friends of every respectable lawyer in Stamford. All I want you to do is speak to him. He's probably a man of good instincts. Harriet Craigie says his wife is lovely; she was head of Civic Music a few years ago. He'll understand the nature of the case."

Although this was the first time their evening talks had touched directly upon what was called his "practice," it was not this which gave Schreiber especial pain. It was a sense, here on the cool porch, of the tiny, homicidal bloodlettings which had for years constituted their relationship. He felt the barbed trivia they summoned to deflect boredom, suppression, and self-disgust, bearing him, raddled and vetted, into extinction.

"I'll speak to him," he managed. "I'll let you know," and then to divert further thrusts at himself, he said, "Your daughter's got a proposal to make you."

"Max is always premature with the wrong things," said Florence. "After dinner, Mother," and to secure this, she went upstairs.

"What is it, Max?" asked Mrs. Carroway. "Why was she upset about telling me now?"

"She hasn't had time to think up a way of telling you that would embarrass me sufficiently. She's working one out upstairs."

"You were away too long in the war, Max," said Mrs. Carroway, and she smiled, seeing that this casual remark had hooked her son-in-law, drawn red to his face.

After a moment, Schreiber said that he had "heard a good one yesterday." Mrs. Carroway blinked angrily at the change, but she always welcomed one of the dirty stories she had begun exchanging with her son-in-law as an emblem of their new relationship. She had started a year ago with a story remembered from school days at Farmington, and, by now, the edginess of those first exchanges was planed off.

When Florence came down, she saw them huddling like tribesmen over a fire, and she shuddered. "I suppose he told you."

"I couldn't pry it out," said her mother.

After dinner, they celebrated the surprisingly tranquil presentation of the request to buy the lot, and the decision to buy it, by drinking even more than usual, so that Schreiber went to bed much happier than he expected to be.

The room in which he and Florence spent Wednesday nights was almost in the center of the house on the summit of the hill, and Schreiber liked to look down the slope, especially on nights when the moon was bright enough to illumine the decline but not bright enough to reveal its size, so that, squinting, he could imagine it as a large wooded valley. Tonight he watched a long time, and then, turning back, he saw Florence in the other bed, the pillow clutched round her head. He squinted toward her, and said quietly, "Micheline."

CHAPTER TWO

I

"An American novel today, Mademoiselle?" asked Schreiber craning around Goupin to see the yellow paperback in the pocket of his daughter's pullover. They were walking home along the Cher.

"So you see, Captain," said Micheline, pulling the book out so that he could see more than Jack London's name.

"*Le loup de mer,*" said Schreiber, just catching the last word as the book slid back into the pocket. "I haven't read it."

"London," said Goupin, also looking. "You'd think he'd be English."

"You don't seem to have read much, Captain," said Micheline.

"I've always been a slow reader, Mademoiselle, but I admire those who are well-read. People here seem to read a great deal."

Micheline lowered her eyes, first to his, and then beyond to the river, where it slid under mist toward the bridge. "We're not in Paris, Captain."

The melancholy of this produced a silence which Schreiber finally broke. "What sort of books do you prefer?"

"Would you guess philosophy?"

"No," he said, "Biography."

"I'm afraid that'll come before long," she said, looking away.

"There are only fifteen novels left, and then some poetry. Unless you have books I might read, Captain?"

"Micheline," said Goupin sharply. Schreiber was thinking of books that had been borrowed from him and never returned: his old Torts text by a southerner who lived down the hall in Langdell, *The Seven Pillars of Wisdom* by an absconding Phi Delt at Lehigh, and ten or twelve detective novels he'd lent Florence while she was at Radcliffe, and which, after the marriage, he'd searched for in vain one afternoon. To Micheline he said, "I should be delighted, Mademoiselle, but I have very few books in French, and I'm afraid they wouldn't suit your taste."

"Yes, one doesn't broaden one's taste in a tannery," said Micheline.

"Now that's a novelistic remark," said her father.

Micheline made no response. Her pullover was tight under her shoulders, and she could feel her bones bulging through the gray wool like rocks in a sack; she wondered if this was what caused Schreiber to stare at her, making sport at her expense.

At the sidepath, Goupin eased his eyes from Micheline's ill-kempt face to Schreiber's soft, blue-tinted one. "Will you come over this evening, Captain? We still have that Calvados in reserve for you. No better way to celebrate the arrival of spring."

"That's awfully kind, Goupin," said Schreiber warmly. "I'm afraid tonight's the night the Corporal drives me to Bourges."

"Good things can wait," said Goupin.

"Oh yes," said Micheline.

"I hope you'll feel free to bring the Corporal as well," he went on, carefully, because he knew that Americans, though often generous with enlisted men, were not always so with Negroes.

"I'm sure he'd be delighted," said Schreiber.

They parted with the usual ceremony of handshaking and small bows. Schreiber followed a beech-lined path to his billet while the Goupins went on up the Cher road. Micheline stared at Schreiber as he walked toward her aunt's house. His plump gracelessness seemed to her a burlesque of his position as the chief local representative of the liberating army. "It's that black corporal who has a soldier's posture," she said out loud, and then blushed, thinking that her father might be reminded of Willy. "German corporals are higher than American ones," she put in before she'd really thought about it.

"Perhaps," said her father with a small laugh, "but they don't have the staying power."

"To him, I'm everybody's fool," the girl thought. Her eyes bent to the mud road, the road she had walked so many times it seemed to her soaked in the life she'd spilled on it.

2

Schreiber's billet was a gray stone house which squatted in a small garden bordered by cobblestones. There, watering the radishes and scallions she'd raised there since 1940 instead of sweetpea and syringa, Madame Cassat, Goupin's older sister, waited for Schreiber's return. He often sat in the garden with her when he came home and they had pleasant talks which sometimes led to gifts from the PX in Bourges.

"Good evening, Captain Schreiber," she said when she heard him clacking on the cobblestones.

"Good evening, Madame," said Schreiber, and raised his cap as she turned around. Tonight, although Madame Cassat cleared her throat, arched her head toward the bench under the trellis, put down the hose, smoothed her apron, and widened her smile till she thought her cheeks would crack, Schreiber moved resolutely onto the entrance of his room.

"Have you seen my brother, Captain?" she asked desperately. There was supposed to be a thousand pounds of coffee rotting away in the Bourges PX.

"Just now," said Schreiber, halfway upstairs. "He sends you his best."

"He's got to pick the—," and she faded off as Schreiber did. "Be-

fore the war, we wouldn't have let him in the parlor," she growled
and picked up the hose, tightened the nozzle, and crashed the
stream against the radishes.

Her husband, thin and white as a celery stalk, moseyed outside,
and together they stared up at Schreiber's room where a typewriter
had begun to click. "Wonder what he types?" said Madame Cassat.
She'd looked at the cards and papers but couldn't read English. "I
think he takes inventory of the houses." Madame Cassat had night-
mares about invaders discovering her family treasures (a collection
of majolica cups and forty silver spoons).

Actually, Schreiber was working at something less useful: a study
of the villagers based in part on the letters he read as local Censor.
It had begun with his first administrative report, but he'd found
a peculiar charm in the refined snooping and decided to pursue it
on his own in scholarly fashion. He had never before done anything
so thorough, not even preparing for his bar exams. He felt he had
a natural bent for research; its techniques brought him more pleasure
than its potential results, or his Pisgah view of himself surrounded
by other amateur scholars, bearded, sherry-drinking, international,
the master of his fragment of the world. The books piled on his
desk, commandeered from Army Special Studies and the Biblio-
thèque de Bourges, were like fortress ramparts behind which he
scouted his empire. Even typing was a pleasure: the clicks were the
operations of his miniature factory.

In the evenings, he typed out the discoveries of the day, the rise
in complaints about poultry prices, the spread of grippe, jokes about
good Germans—Generals Eisenhower and Spaatz—and bad. Then
he read in the books, historical and topographical accounts of the
region, and made notes on memorandum cards. The thoughts came
dreamlike, and he typed as if the mechanics of wrist and fingers determined his conclusions. Part of his mind was free to wander, and
often it brought the long, rust-colored face of Micheline Goupin
under the silvery hammers of the machine. "Pitiful," Schreiber

would think, and he'd whack a semicolon into one of her muddy eyes.

When the dinner bell sounded, he stopped at the letter "c" in "specific," rinsed his hands in the basin, emptied the water into the slop jar, and went downstairs to the dining room.

This evening, as he debated the usual choice of *fromage à chèvre* or *port salut* at the end of the meal, Schreiber recognized the feeling which often came to him as he watched the Cassats waiting open-mouthed for his decision. It was the feeling that for the first time in his life he was really alive.

Before he'd come to France, five months before, in the fall of '44, he'd spent hours every week writing long letters to himself, or sometimes to Florence, about the bitterness of military life. Then, scarcely two weeks after his arrival in the village, he wrote Florence that his assignment gave him no time to write: she and Valerie and the corpulent, little white house in Rye were like blisters on his new feelings about life.

Schreiber had a notion that this life stood for more than itself. The choice of a cheese, a walk by the river, an exchange of greetings, all seemed oddly important, as if they were about something larger than themselves, never referred to, but always there, governing and checking.

"Do you think the *chèvre* too soft this evening, Captain?" asked old Cassat.

"Not particularly, Monsieur."

"It shouldn't be too soft, but when it's hard, it dribbles. Brittany's the place for it." This was said as a reproach to his wife for binding him to the goats of Cher. He sucked the curds resentfully from his gums, dentures rattling with the effort, and then took a knife to shave the skin from a fine Italian pear.

"I've been through Brittany," murmured Schreiber, staring at the yellow membrane spiraling from the white meat and thinking of Micheline Goupin.

3

Tiberius lived with Mme. Verna Zapenskaya just above her bakery
two blocks from the Hôtel de Ville on Rue Bulwer-Lytton. It was
not his official billet, but there were only seven enlisted men in the
village and Captain Schreiber did not worry them with regulations.
In return for her favors and domestic provisions, Tiberius gave Mme.
Zapenskaya the double distinction of living with a noncommissioned
officer and a Negro. In addition, her bakery was soon doing a lively
trade in American cigarettes, chocolate bars, razor blades, sugar,
soap, coffee, and other valuables from the Bourges PX.

Mme. Zapenskaya dreaded, and her female neighbors anticipated,
the release of her husband from the PW camp in Germany; as the
son of a White Russian officer's *valet de chambre* he was looked
upon as inordinately jealous and vindictive. Tiberius had numerous
offers to exchange the comforts of the Rue Bulwer-Lytton for similar
but less precarious ones. He had, however, a fondness for Mme.
Zapenskaya. Like him, she was an admirer of Franklin Roosevelt;
next to a huge picture of the President over his bed, Tiberius added
pictures of Colette and Alexander Dumas the elder, and under this
trinity, he lived happily.

Tiberius had studied French at Bucknell, and, within a month
of his arrival in the village, spoke it better than any of the other
Americans. He became one of the central forces of the village, a judge
of disputes and councilor of difficulties.

One night a week he drove Schreiber to headquarters at Bourges,
and on these drives he gave him reports on the village which
Schreiber then transmitted to the G-2 major. Tonight, the most
important news was Fougère's decision to close the tannery.

"What do you mean, 'close it'?" asked Schreiber. "It's been there
ninety years. What's the trouble? Have we been unfair?"

"He claims he's worn out, but he's got a *petite amie* waiting
for him in the Midi. He was down there visiting his grandchildren
last spring."

"God Almighty," said Schreiber.

Tiberius drove carefully over the bridge. "I guess you'll have to get that Goupin girl a job in the office."

"What about the other eight people?"

"They'll find something. Verna needs someone. Metayer too. They'll find something."

"I'd like to take the girl in. She's a little slow but quite nice. The old man invited me over tonight." He had meant to say "us," but didn't bother to retrieve the pronoun.

"She had a German boy last year. A corporal, except corporal's a little higher with them." He stretched his arm under Schreiber's jaw, so close to it that the stripes looked like scars on Schreiber's neck. "There's the cathedral."

"We've seen it," said Schreiber.

"They've got a lot of thirteenth century glass stored away. Maybe you can request it be put back in. It'd be kind of nice to see."

"I suppose it could still be shelled."

"Shelling's over around here, Max."

The major at headquarters worked at night and tried to keep his subordinates for drinks. As usual, Schreiber pleaded fatigue and managed to get away after an hour of fatuous questions. The sessions wore Schreiber out, and he and Tiberius usually went for some Pernod around the corner.

"Not tonight," said Schreiber. "He really wore me out."

"Just as well," said Tiberius, driving off. "They're letting the GIs swarm all over here now."

Ten minutes later, getting out of the jeep in front of his billet, Schreiber said, "She'll have to learn English, you know."

"She probably had it in school. Maybe you could teach her a little."

"We'll see," said Schreiber. "She's a pretty decent girl."

The Goupins were talking with the Cassats in the living room. Micheline was in the corner, head bent over a book. "Have you heard what's happened, Captain?" asked Mme. Cassat, calling out to him, as he walked past the door. "Fougère is closing the tannery in three

weeks, and Micheline is to be pushed into the gutter. Just like that,"
she cried, clapping her hands, as if Fougère's nose was between them.

"I've heard about it, Madame. I'm awfully sorry." Schreiber came
in. "One's big decisions always seem to involve displacing someone
else. But I've had a thought or two. I may be able to help. That is,
if Mademoiselle Micheline would consider working with us. We've
been needing assistance for some time. It's only a question of knowing a little English."

"English," cried Mme. Cassat. "Wonderful. She's studied it for
years, haven't you dear?"

"That's very kind indeed, Captain," said Goupin. "Very kind."

"I should never speak it," said Micheline.

"Nonsense," cried Mme. Cassat. "Why it's quite simple. I remember it myself, and it's forty years since I've said a word," and she
said quickly, in English, "Good morning, What hour is it? Jolly
good."

"I've never heard you speak English, Germaine," said old Cassat.
"It sounds elegant, doesn't it, Captain?"

"Yes it does," said Schreiber. "Mademoiselle shall learn it almost
as well if she wants to try. I should be happy to spend a few hours
helping her myself."

This statement produced a noticeable silence.

"That would be very generous, Captain," said Mme. Cassat softly.

"You will find me a difficult student, Captain," said Micheline,
looking up from the book.

"You learned German easily," said her father evenly, and there
was another wordless interval.

"We can begin tomorrow evening if you like," said Schreiber. "In
three weeks we should be able to do a good deal." He bowed and said,
in English, "Good evening."

"Ah, good evening," repeated Mme. Cassat, and looked at her
niece to see if she had caught on to the ease of English speech.

4

Schreiber told Micheline that the north side of the river lay in an exposed position within two kilometers of the freight yards and that they would do better to hold their lessons on the south side. "Of course, he doesn't consider our being blown up before and after the damn lessons," thought Micheline, but, nonetheless, twice a week she walked with him across the bridge below her house and a mile up the river to a clearing in a beech grove. Here they had the lesson.

Goupin went down to his sister's after they left, and he watched them cross the bridge, his daughter a few steps in back of Schreiber and stooping to his height.

"I hope he'll be as cautious as the German," he said to his sister.

"This type always is, Axel. Anyway, more can come from it. Willy was nice, but he took as much as he gave."

"Well, nothing much can happen to her. She'll have a job, some amusement, and she may even learn something."

Despite forebodings about her inadequacy, Micheline learned English rapidly. Schreiber was industrious and patient. After they left the house, he would ask her the vocabulary he'd assigned the preceding lesson. At the grove, he corrected, in the last of the daylight, sentences she'd written out. The last hour and a half was devoted to conversation. Here Micheline was brilliant. With a small vocabulary, she could say, after the first lessons, almost anything she wished. In one sense, she was more fluent in English than French: the feeling of exposure which hindered her in ordinary conversation disappeared in the foreign idiom. Although most of their talk concerned natural scenes or typical situations, Micheline managed to infuse her talk with more of her own feeling than she had ever before put into words.

"You amaze me, Mademoiselle," said Schreiber as they crossed back after the fourth lesson.

Micheline, to whom the word "amaze" was new, fathomed its

meaning and made it her own. "It's very nice to amaze someone, Captain. One thinks me amazing only for being not at all amazing. I am very *trompante* to Papa."

"We are nearly always disappointing to our parents," said Schreiber, hesitating over the participle to let her learn it. "And they to us." To himself he said proudly, "I'm beginning to sound like a Frenchman."

Goupin, walking up the road, noticed that they were almost flank to flank now. He waited for them at the bridge and called in English, "Have you learned much this evening?"

"It comes very slowly," answered Micheline in French.

"She's much too modest, Goupin," said Schreiber. "It's going amazingly well."

"Fine. Just fine," said Goupin. "Now come refresh yourself after your labors, Captain. We haven't opened the Calvados yet."

An hour later at Goupins, Schreiber mentioned that his work load was decreasing at the office, and, since the weather was so nice, that he would be willing to hold the lessons more frequently.

"You take too much trouble, Captain," she said.

"An extraordinary kindness, Captain," said Goupin.

"It is you who do me the kindness, Mademoiselle," said Schreiber. The Calvados had warmed and exalted him, and, after he'd said this, he wondered if it were not a careless product of the exaltation. He was afraid also that it might have sounded awkward, even compromising, but later, walking home, he decided that even if it had, Micheline Goupin would understand any meaning it could have, and would not disapprove.

5

"What was it like?" asked Schreiber when he met Micheline at the bridge the evening the tannery closed.

"Fougère called us in at four and told us we could go home an hour early. He said he supposed he would never see us again. Then we all cried."

"Europeans have such strong sentiments," said Schreiber. They walked across the bridge, and Schreiber touched her arm with his fingers.

"I've wondered sometimes if your wife is lonely in America," she said.

He dropped his hand and said, "I don't really know. I don't hear much. She's a very busy person. Though you never know. Maybe she is lonely." It was a condition he'd never associated with Florence, but, since loneliness did not depend on missing what was precious, or even useful—you could miss an old disease—maybe she did miss him and was lonely. To Micheline he said, "People around my part of the country restrain their feelings."

"We have our *tartufes* also," said Micheline. They walked to the grove and sat down. There were no longer any sentences to correct.

"The permission to hire you came through today. In a few days the money will be—we say 'allocated.' "

"I look forward to working in your office."

"You'll really be in Tiberius' office, but I come in there often. It's not bad work. You file—*classer*—letters. If you read them, it's interesting." They smiled at each other.

"I wonder how long it will last." They both understood the war for "it," and both thought of it being over and what would happen to them. "Maybe it'll go on for a time," she added. "The Germans are soft by themselves, but hard together. It could last for years."

Sadly, Schreiber said he was afraid that it couldn't last much longer.

6

Two days before the war actually ended, a report was broadcast that it had. Micheline was in the office at the Hôtel de Ville—she had worked there two weeks—when Tiberius came in with the news. She ran up to Schreiber's office, but he wasn't there. Then, like everyone else in the building, she ran outside. The streets were filled with people running in and out of each other's houses to announce that the war was over. Knots of celebrants worked the bars and cafés; a priest rang the bells, and farmers, hearing them in the fields, headed for town. Tiberius was at the wheel of a jeep packed with eight or nine people who passed around bottles of red wine and PX bourbon. There was a good deal of kissing, embracing, whooping.

Micheline ran home; nobody was there. She stood at the door looking down the road toward town. An hour later Schreiber lumbered up, sweating. "Come," he said. She took his hand and they walked quickly to the bridge, over it, and on down the other side to the clearing. There, they lay on the ground and held each other.

They were there about ten minutes when a blast of the jeep horn shook them up; they saw Tiberius drive over the bridge and turn up the path which led to the clearing. They jumped up, buttoning their clothes.

"Come on, Max," yelled Tiberius. "Climb aboard. Let the lesson go tonight."

For a moment Schreiber said nothing. Then he walked to the jeep and pointed toward town. An old woman in the jeep spilled wine on his jacket. "Get on back to town, Corporal," said Schreiber. "On the double."

Tiberius met his eyes. "Your vacation's over," he said quietly, and then he spun the jeep around, blowing the horn all the way to the bridge. Micheline touched Schreiber's arm; he shook his head, brushed himself off, and held out his hands to help her up. "Not now, dear. They might come back tonight."

7

Disappointment at the news of the false armistice was coupled with assurance that the real end was close at hand. Two days later, bells were heard from Bourges. In the village no one celebrated. People nodded to each other as if to say, "Well, there it is," and that was all. Those who had celebrated too wildly before kept inside as much as possible.

That night Schreiber met Micheline at the bridge as usual, but this time they walked beyond the beech clearing till they found a more secluded place off the path. When it got dark, they made love.

"Dear heart," said Schreiber. "My dear heart." The sweetness of love melted into his sense of belonging and discovery; it seemed to him almost historic, the real subject of the celebrations which drifted over the river from Bourges.

They met every night for almost two weeks, staying out till three or four in the morning. On the twelfth night, Micheline was at the bridge listening for Schreiber. When she heard steps which weren't his, she knew it was all over.

It was Madame Cassat. "He said you'd be here." She took an envelope from her sleeve and handed it to Micheline. It bore the legend "Passed by Censor." "He came back for an hour to pack his clothes and papers, and told me to give this to you." As Micheline read the letter, Madame Cassat rehearsed what she would say.

The note was in English.

They called me today, and I have to leave right now for Germany. I'll be on my way as you read this. I'll get leave (*permission*) before long. You know what I think about everything. We shall arrange things.

It was initialled "M," although she had never called him Max. Madame Cassat held out her arms. "These things happen, my dear."

8

Schreiber was assigned to Mainz. He drove there in the front seat of a three-ton truck; twenty enlisted men were in the back. They arrived at night and cruised around the city looking for quarters to requisition. There was almost nothing standing. Here and there smoke rose from a pile of bricks; sewer water gashed the streets. Nobody seemed to be alive. Down by the river banks, they saw a few hundred people curled up asleep on the grass. Women, children,

old men, and cripples. Two bridges stretched halfway across the
Rhine like broken fingers.

The disorder upset Schreiber. Lying on the bank, he tried to think
of Micheline, hoping that her image would calm him down. Instead,
he had visions of Florence, Valerie, Tiberius, and then himself,
nightmarishly spread out like a town through which a huge loco-
motive steamed. It made him nauseous, and he went down to the
river to throw up. A skinny old woman under a ragged blanket was
watching him. "I was sick," he said to her in French.

"Unflätiger Totschläger."

"Yes, sick. I don't speak *Deutsch.* No *Deutsch.* It's good to have
peace." He felt this answered whatever she could have said to him.

The next day, the soldiers set up headquarters, and started regis-
tering the populace, organizing supply and market lines, patroling
the area. Schreiber worked harder than he ever had in his life. He
went to bed every night as soon as he was off duty, the rasp of cranes
picking up rubble being the first and last noises of his day. The
cranes and the soldiers seemed to be the only moving things in the
city.

When the French took over the town, he had a little leisure, and
then he began thinking of Micheline. He wrote to her, putting the
letter into an envelope addressed to Tiberius. A week later it came
back stamped, to his amazement, "Absent Without Leave. Returned
By Censor." Then he wrote directly to her and, after a week without
an answer, he wrote again saying that he was going to be shipped
back to the States in less than six months.

It was nearly two months now since he had seen her. Absence and
mystery revived and sharpened his passion. He began to dream of
her all day long, the fine, rust-colored face on which he'd typed
semicolons. One day, standing before the wreck of the Gutenberg
Museum, he said to himself, "I'll stay in Europe. I'll take my dis-
charge here." He would never go back to the States, or at least not
until the affair had run the course he knew such affairs ran.

Then he requested and got a week's leave. He got a ride in a jeep to Strasbourg, and then waited two days for one to Bourges. There, for a Lucky Strike, he hired a taxi to drive him out to the village. When he saw the Hôtel de Ville, he told the driver to wait, and in an hour to drive up the road to Goupin's.

Hot with expectation, he jogged up the path. When he saw the bridge, he was so excited, he had to stop. He sat down under a beech tree and held it tight until he was composed. Then he got up and ran to Goupin's. There were no lights in the house. He opened the door and shouted, "Hey." No one was there. A five-foot stack of her books stood in the corner. He went over and looked at them, and then let out a kick. Off-balance, he missed; he picked up the top book, kissed it longingly and then ran down the road to the Cassats.

They were sitting with Goupin in the garden. "Who's there?" called Mme. Cassat.

"Schreiber," he called, running across the cobblestones, puffing and hot. "Goupin, where's Micheline?"

"Come in, come in, Captain," called Mme. Cassat, and she took him by the sleeve to the bench under the trellis.

He started to ask what was wrong, but couldn't think how it went in French.

Old Cassat said, "Micheline is gone, Captain, gone off."

"With your Corporal," said his wife. "No one knows where."

"Two months ago," said Goupin.

Schreiber touched his eyes, and turned away. At the gate, he said in English, "A taxi is waiting for me."

He walked down the side path to the river. He didn't dare look at the bridge. The taxi would be along soon, and he wondered if he should wait for it in the bushes and then roll under the tires. "I'm thinking of suicide," he told himself. "Over love." In his pain, he was almost proud. *"Un peu ridicule,"* he said aloud.

At the road he sat under a tree to wait for the taxi. The ground was wet and numbed his legs. It seemed incredible to him that he was here. When the taxi drove up, he said, "Back to Bourges," and climbed in. Halfway there, he started to cry. He wiped his eyes and nose on his sleeve, then blubbered again. The taxi driver handed him a red handkerchief, and at Bourges, he patted him on the shoulder and told him not to worry. Schreiber thanked him and gave him the two packs of cigarettes he had in his pocket.

CHAPTER THREE

I

The morning after the dinner at Mrs. Carroway's, Schreiber got a call from Bucceroni who asked him if he'd drive his car out to the house he was putting up in Norwalk.

"Joanna's car's in the garage, and she took mine into town. Could you pick it up for me at the beauty parlor on Pine? I'll drive you right back. I want to be in Hartford by three."

"I'll be right out."

Schreiber drove to the beauty parlor and got the keys from Mrs. Bucceroni's bag as she sat in the chugging core of the drier. She yelled something at him, but he didn't try to catch it. "There's a limit," he told himself in the Cadillac going out.

"Thanks, Max," roared Bucceroni from the roof, where he was standing with the carpenters. "Be right down."

Schreiber waited in the car, and Bucceroni came up slapping the wood dust from his blue suit. "I'll drive," he said, and Schreiber moved over.

"It's coming up pretty well," said Schreiber.

Bucceroni removed his fedora and wiped his pale head with a fiery silk handkerchief. "Forty-seven thousand already. Should be 'pretty well.' I don't know, Max. I may've bitten off too much."

"When?" asked Schreiber.

Bucceroni looked inquiringly at him. "What's the matter? Florence been fiddling with the nerves again?" The car leaped off and they drove to Stamford thirty miles over the speed limit.

"What's this Gabrielson business, Louie?" asked Schreiber after a minute.

"Gabrielson? A crackpot," said Bucceroni. "You know him?"

"I know the Chadwicks, or at least Florence's mother does."

"Christ, that woman's officious. She'd better leave you a pile."

"I'm not without hope."

Bucceroni laughed. "You're getting more worldly, Maxie."

Schreiber considered this, and then said, "We must have a bigger percentage of crackpots than Bellevue."

"We're riding in that percentage, Max," said Bucceroni, who liked remarks of this sort. "The bigger the percentage, the better off we'll be. Litigants are crackpots per se. If they're outright fanatics, they sue for therapy, and you can charge them for it. When they come in the office, eyes bugged, I light up."

"The law's beginning to bore me, Louie."

"It's always bored me. The better you are, the more bored you get, and we're pretty good lawyers, Max." Schreiber had heard this before.

When he got back to the office, he asked his ugly little secretary, Miss Bow, if she would like to get a cup of coffee with him. Her eyes widened with fright, and she said that she had better type the Morrison letters.

Schreiber walked over to the Roger Smith and had two martinis at the bar. He called Miss Bow to say he wouldn't be back, drove down to the shore, and looked at the boats of the Stamford Yacht Club. A blue yawl was moving out of the harbor, and Schreiber watched it fading into the Sound. Then he drove to his mother-in-law's house.

Mrs. Carroway, in dungarees and mink-edged sweater, was trimming the shrubbery around the paddle tennis court, her face blank with fatigue.

"What a nice surprise, Max-lamb." She clicked the shears at him, and he jumped back. "You're a good excuse to stop. I mailed the check to you this morning." She kissed him on the cheek. "No bad news, is there?"

"No. I just thought I'd drop around. I'm tired and felt like one of Joseph's martinis."

"Sit down and I'll tell him."

They sat on the davenport and smoked. "You tried Parliaments, Max? They're very good. Dr. Haneford recommends them."

"I spoke to Bucceroni about the Gabrielsons," said Schreiber, looking up at Joseph who'd come in with the tray.

"I knew you would, Max. I worried about interfering, but I thought something would be wrong if one couldn't ask one's own son a favor." She spat the olive on the floor as Joseph was leaving. He turned, and picked it up with his handkerchief.

"It didn't have any effect, of course. Bucceroni says the fellow's a crackpot, and that he'll be bottled up, but there's no reason why we shouldn't have a fee from him."

"Of course, Max. My only point was that the association damaged your reputation. Bucceroni might not understand something like that. In fact, you know, I've been wondering if Norris Williams might not be needing someone of your ability in his office. He's not a fledgling anymore."

Schreiber smiled at this late thought and said, "I've really come to tell you something very different from that, Mother. I've decided to leave here for a time, and to leave Florence for good. Nothing has worked out since I've come back from the army, and I'm tired of it all." He paused and saw that she had stopped drinking and was waiting for more. "I'm particularly sorry when I think how much you've helped us."

Mrs. Carroway's eyes were even wider and brighter than Miss

Bow's had been when he'd asked her out for coffee, but she did more than look at him; she threw the rest of the martini into his face and ran inside. He sat still for a while, and then wiped his face off with his sleeve.

2

When he got home, he saw the truck with the Vermont license plates and two men unloading the last of the hemlock for screening off the Peniman house. Valerie was standing by the truck watching them. She called "Hi" to Schreiber without looking at him.

"Hello, Vallie," he called back, and he went into the house, smoked a cigarette in the living room and then went upstairs.

"He's early," thought Florence, listening for the noise of the ice trays. When she heard him coming upstairs, she put on her pumps and lay back on the bed propping herself up with the pillow.

"I want to talk with you about something important, Florence," he said, hesitating for a moment as if he were in the office of a superior. He sat down on the rocker next to her bed. She looked into his eyes, and he lowered them.

"Yes, Max," she said gently, almost in the tones of years before.

"Florence, what would you say if I thought it would be best if I left?"

"Left?" she repeated, and caught her breath as if her body automatically sought to retain what was beyond retention.

"We shouldn't live together. I should go away," he went on. "Separation, divorce, whatever you want. I haven't thought of details. Only that together we're worse than animals."

"Yes," she said, and she squeezed the pillow to control herself. "Better than now," and this oddly abbreviated response led to tears, and she waved him out of the room. He went down and smoked on the porch, watched the men unload the trees, and studied Valerie, whose brown plaits were flung back across her shoulders like whips. Under his chair, Bucceroni lapped up cat meat.

PART TWO

C H A P T E R   O N E

I

When Theodore Baggish heard someone call to him while he was waiting at the Gare des Batignolles for his trunk to be inspected by the Paris customs and turned around to see Robert Ward, he could hardly control his voice to reply. The difficulty was that he had stolen Ward's toilet kit on the boat in the expectation that he would never see him again. Yet here, ten days later, he stood.

"How did you come?" he finally managed.

"The *Elizabeth*. Three days after you," said Ward.

Ward had been intended for one of Baggish's cabin mates on the *Queen Mary*. He'd come down an hour before sailing time with a sporty retinue to drink champagne in the cabin, but apparently none of the group had either remembered or known how small tourist cabins were, so they'd adjourned to a bar across the street from the pier. At five o'clock, while Baggish's two other cabin mates were arranging sittings with the purser, the steward had come in and asked Baggish which were Ward's bags.

"What's the matter?" asked Baggish. "Did he switch to Second Class?"

"He missed the boat, sir. These three, sir?" He pointed to three pieces of matched tan luggage on the bunk above Baggish's own.

35

"That's right," said Baggish.

"Four pieces with the trunk in the hold," said the steward. "Second time it's happened to me in three hundred crossings. The other was before the war, a Mexican who thought he was on the *Staatendam*. Sailed all the way to Cherbourg and probably thought he was in Rotterdam when he got off."

Ward had also left a leather toilet kit on the ledge above the wash basin. Baggish had been standing between it and the steward, and when the latter left, he turned the kit around to see if Ward's initials were on it. They were, stamped in gold, RWW, under the snap. Baggish tucked the kit into the bottom of his large suitcase and slid this under the bunk. His own toilet things were in a cellophane sack.

Now he thanked God that Ward hadn't hung any of his suits in the closet.

Ward was telling him about hiding out at home so that he wouldn't see people to whom he'd already said good-by. "Not even Mother came down to the *Elizabeth*."

The customs man said that the trunks hadn't come in yet. "That's fine," said Ward. "Took me two hours to find this place."

"Should be nothing at all for you next time, Monsieur," said the custom's man in quite good English.

"Insolent bastard," remarked Ward to Baggish as they left. "Let me buy you a drink."

"Fine," said Baggish. Ward was the first person he had sat down with since he'd left the boat.

They had dinner together, went to a movie in Montmartre and afterwards to a *café chantant*. They arranged to meet the next morning at the American Embassy. Ward said it would be wise to register there in case there was any trouble with the French.

When Baggish returned to his hotel, he removed the toothpaste, hairbrushes, and soap container, from Ward's kit and dropped it into the wastebasket. "No chance of turning it back to a French store with the initials. Besides my French isn't good enough yet." Looking at the kit in the basket, he shuddered a little.

2

Baggish's shudder was not one of relief at his escape from possible discovery, but one of revulsion at the waste of the kit. The years of his life which he wished to remember were memorable to him largely because they had been brilliantly waged campaigns against waste, years of accumulation and preparation.

Baggish's father and mother owned a tiny grocery in Providence, Rhode Island. Baggish went through the Providence public schools and had a year at Rhode Island State in Kingston as a scholarship and self-help student. When it looked as if he were going to be drafted, he went to work in the mailroom of the Boston Department Store. The war ended before he was called up, and he stayed at the store. After ten months, he was made a junior salesman in the men's shoe department. He lived at home and saved all of his money but the fifteen dollars a month which he gave his parents for room and board, and another hundred dollars a year for bus fare, movies, razor blades, and socks. He smoked cigarettes from the grocery store and wore as many of his father's clothes as he could. As his father kept no liquor in the house, he didn't drink, although for New Year's Eve he bought a bottle of vodka which he drank up with grocery store tonic during the succeeding week. He passed most of his spare time in the Providence Public Library or up at Brown. Occasionally, he sat in the rear of evening and Saturday classes at the University.

He had no friends, although he nodded to people with whom he had gone to high school and with whom he worked. On weekends he often walked down to the wharves and watched the boats going out, or he took a bus to the airport and looked at the planes zooming in over the ocean. During the four and a half years he worked for the Boston he took but one vacation, and then, as a kind of joke,

went up to Boston for three days, spending most of one day looking
through the open shelves of the new Lamont Library in Harvard
Yard.

By August, 1949 he had saved $3,850.00. The week he reached this
sum he pushed over a counter of hats and accused the saleswoman
of insulting him. He was fired immediately and received two weeks
severance pay. A month before, he had finished buying, on the
Boston's Employee Discount Plan, an Oxford-gray flannel suit, a
tweed sport coat, and some Cheltenham trousers, a pair of white
buckskin shoes, two nylon shirts, nylon underwear, two suitcases,
a small Emerson radio, and the *Concise Oxford French Dictionary*.
Two months before he'd applied for a passport and bought a one-
way ticket to France on the *Queen Mary*. For two years he had
been studying a French grammar.

He'd introduced his intention of working in Europe to his parents
the previous spring, but they were not really aware of it until they
saw the first sign of its realization, the heavy envelope from the
State Department containing his passport. They had always been
more proud of their son than not, and they were now proud of the
intrepidity which, joined to his usual taciturnity, gave him the air
of someone with important business at hand, an air they valued
above all other immaterial things and the lack of which in him had
been their sole worry about, and hence, their chief notice of him.

His leaving relieved them in some ways: his fifteen dollars a month
did not make up what he cost them, even taking into consideration
the wholesale price of the grocery items. On the other hand, he was
a familiar presence, and losing him meant the loss of a possession,
one they had watched change for a quarter of a century and upon
which, in recent years, they relied in small ways and hoped to rely in
larger. They both worked very hard in the store and consequently
lacked the time and energy for leisurely friendships; their son formed
a kind of interlude in their schedules, an outlet for whatever conversa-
tional needs their weariness left them. In the three weeks between
the arrival of his passport and his sailing, his mother said three or

four times that it was hard when boys grew up and left their parents to age by themselves, but after the first utterance, it was said without particular feeling or meaning and was accepted as another of the formulas which protected them from life.

As for Europe, it was so reduced in their notion of it to a newspaper word that the reduction made it manageable, domesticated it. They even began to create associations with it: Mr. Baggish claimed that he'd come within an ace of being shipped there in the First World War, and Mrs. Baggish recalled that her maternal grandfather, a Presbyterian minister and the noblest entry in her family history, had either visited or known someone from there. (The fact that the minister's own father had been born in Scotland was nowhere at all in her shabby awareness.)

At parting, his father said good-by to him with a shaky voice before he went around the corner to open the store, and an hour later his mother went down to the station and kissed him as he boarded the New York train. "Write now, Theodore," she said, and he said politely that he would.

The third morning of the voyage, he sat near an attractive girl in the writing salon and decided that he would write home an account of the voyage. When he went to post the letter and saw the stamps with the picture of George the Sixth on them, the blissful fact of his departure really came to him. He never again wrote to his parents.

In Paris, he stayed at the Hôtel de France on Rue Budapest. It had been the nearest hotel to the Gare St. Lazare which charged under three hundred and fifty francs a night and turned out to be the only respectable hotel on the street; the five or six others were inhabited by prostitutes. It was three or four nights before Baggish could walk to his hotel without hearing a barrage of, "Come on, Joe" or "Wassa matter, Joe? You seeck?" from the eight or ten girls on duty in the doorways. A couple of times he went down to the café at the end of the street, a rendezvous for the girls and their trade, the produce men and porters who worked around the station. The second night he went there, he heard a "Hello, Pal," and as it was one of the few recognizable sounds he'd heard all day, he turned to see a Negro prostitute whom he had watched undress from his window across the street. Her call seemed to be an acknowledgement of his unremunerative patronage. He asked her if she were American. *"Moi?"* she said. *"Suis putasse."* The answer pleased Baggish enormously: he too was beginning to feel international.

3

In Ward, Baggish discerned what he liked to call—adapting a business term of his father's—a specimen of the "prime cut of America." He had first seen the species on the Brown campus, and when he saw it, he studied it. He was conscious of being able to pass as a member of it in the standardized vision of foreigners, but he was more aware of the key distinctions in Ward's make-up which were not in his. The distinctions included ways of talking and gesturing, confidence in certain matters, naïveté and lack of interest in others, a psychological obtuseness which, Baggish knew, could be taken advantage of, and, pervading all, a whitewash of youthfulness.

Ward was open-faced, squarish, blue-eyed, and fair. His speech was the casually precise, vaguely confident one of the ten or twelve leading Eastern preparatory schools. Though somewhat clumsy, he seemed graceful, or at least athletic. Baggish studied his walk and his talk with the absorption of paranoia.

The morning after their night in Montmartre, they met at the Embassy, and then went to a café on Rue Royale where they exchanged histories over *croissants* and hot chocolate. Baggish told Ward that he was from Omaha (his parents had been visiting Providence when he was born, he added, thinking that Ward might see his passport), his father owned a machine implements plant, he'd attended the University of Nebraska for three years after a year in the army at Fort Bragg, and his father had allowed him a year in Europe before he finished college and started work in the plant.

Ward's history was equally uninvolved, but it was related with less serenity and coherence. He was from Montclair, New Jersey, had gone to Hotchkiss and Yale, been drafted for three years after his first year in college and come to Europe after graduation in June so that he could make up his mind what to do. These facts were mingled with Ward's doubts and troubles. These consisted of his shame at not having been an officer in the army, a love affair with a Bennington girl which ended by her marrying his roommate, and a general conviction that everything that happened to him was "second-rate"; as examples of the second-rate, he cited going to Hotchkiss and Yale instead of St. Mark's and Harvard, and the fact that his father was only vice-president of the firm for which he'd worked for thirty years. To Baggish, it was a book of Revelations.

Ward had decided to enroll in a Paris school to give his year in Europe a serious cast. His father had suggested a technical or commercial school, but he'd decided upon the École des Hautes Études de Science Politique. Every morning he attended André Siegfried's lectures from ten to twelve, and then met Baggish for lunch at the Café de Royale St. Germain. At twelve-thirty he descended from the Number 16 bus at St. Germain and waved to Baggish sitting at one of the tables with an *apéritif*. It was a nice moment for both of them. Together they planned the rest of their day with the help of *This Week in Paris* (after a few days they switched to *Cette Semaine à Paris*) and a *Plan de Paris*. They walked over the city, went into hundreds of shops, museums, cemeteries, and churches, attended the Opéra and Opéra Comique, the Comédie Française and the Gauguin exhibition at the Orangerie; each day they crossed off another section of the *Plan* and another few entries in their Guide.

Baggish enjoyed his solitary mornings even more. On rainy ones, he stayed in his room and studied French, reading books he bought at the *bouquinistes* along the Seine, *Cousin Pons, La Peste*, Brantôme's *Les Dames Galantes,* and Funke-Brentano's history of the Middle Ages. Otherwise he walked down through the Tuileries along the right bank of the river and had beer at a café flanked by two pet shops. He'd stay an hour watching the birds and fish, crocodiles, turtles, frogs, and monkeys, contemplating in them much that he'd discerned elsewhere. Then he proceeded to the Île de la Cité and sat in the little park behind Notre Dame reading a newspaper—he bought a different one each day—looking up new words in a pocket dictionary. At quarter of twelve, he made his way to the Café Royale to wait for Ward.

Always Baggish was aware that these days were an interlude, a reservoir of accumulation for what he regarded, in his almost muscular apprehension of the future, as his enormous prospects.

CHAPTER TWO

I

A few months before he'd sailed to Europe, Baggish looked up the origin of the continent's name in the Brown library. He discovered that it had first been used as a place name in one of the four Greek poems known as the Homeric Hymns. The name apparently stood for the outline of the northern lands as they appeared to Greek sailors. Its etymology related it to the phrase, "wide prospect," which pleased Baggish, for he *knew* that the coastline of his own future was congruent with Europe's, and he scouted both like a bird of prey.

Baggish also *knew* that there were certain preliminary steps to be taken before his real career could start, certain experiences and knowledge that he had to have. One reason for coming to France first was that he shared the American folklore view that one sort of experience was most readily acquired there. This was experience of women, one which Baggish lacked almost entirely. That knowledge of women could be the pursuit of a whole life, a whole race of lives, seemed an absurdity to him. In his view, women were functions rather than ends, objects instead of subjects, essential to his own prospects but potential compromises of them. Yet he knew that he must have experience with them. Firstly, his desires were often unmanageable: that is, they took up time which he needed to invest elsewhere. Secondly, he believed that experience with women put a mark on one's face and gestures which was perceivable and respected by men of like experience. Therefore, he decided to give much of his first two months in Europe to the temporary exhaustion and thus, he hoped, to the permanent mastery of the secondary passion.

In his twenty-four years, Baggish had never kissed a girl, never touched or been touched by one in meaningful fashion. His mother and his mother's sister were the only women with whom he had any sense of familiarity, and this was that of a palm to the coin it holds and proffers. Twice in his life, once in the service elevator of the Boston Store, and once after midnight on the tourist deck of the *Queen Mary* he had so come into contact with the arm and shoulder of a girl that any motion forward on his part would have led to something more. But there had been no motion, and not because there had been no desire; it had been merely want of motion, a suspension protracted by embarrassment and ignorance. Since his fifteenth year, Baggish's desires had been roused and fed by seeing women in the street, movie stars on the screen, cheesecake pictures in magazines, heroines of comic strips. He would ride in crowded elevators in order to brush against women, and then try to retain in contracted muscles and magnifying nerves the warm solids of their flesh. A year before he left for Europe he spent a month working up to ask a cashier in the store to go to the movies with him, but this too led to nothing: the fear of spending money collaborated with that of being refused, and he satisfied himself on his sheets. This failure reinforced an old feeling that he was unattractive to women, but here he was wrong.

Baggish was one of the many people whose faces do not register the force and passion behind them. At first glance, his features seemed airless: his eyes didn't shine, his lips weren't moist, and his nose didn't seem to inhale. He had straight brown hair, was slightly under middle height, and stocky without being especially strong. His chief distinction was that his impassivity was, at least partially, the effect of his will, and there were certain women, women for whom the observation of men was a serious study, who sensed the play behind the impassivity, deduced the passion behind the play, and sometimes plotted to make themselves its object.

2

Birgitta Fröng was such a woman, and she foresaw an involvement with Baggish in her first glimpse of him. She met him the day after her Italian friend, Giro Uras, told her that he had to return to Perugia with his dance band. She did not imagine that Baggish, or anyone else for that matter, would be able to sustain Giro's pace, but there was no one else around at the moment, and Birgitta was bored to death. She had spent too many of the hours between eight and five-thirty—when her permanent boy friend, Dr. Charley Hams, worked at the American Public Health Service—in anticipatory yawns, posing on her bed and regarding the customers of the *pâtisserie* down the street.

Birgitta had learned few French words in the eight months she'd been in Paris, but *ennui* was one of them, and, though it could hardly be said that Birgitta ever spent time really thinking, she'd considered *ennui* as well as suffered it, considered it an almost living enemy. In the short interval between her last permanent boy friend and Hams, she had tried to escape it by going places with Maria, the girl with whom she had left Upsala for what had been intended as a six weeks vacation from the Brio toy factory.

Maria had taken her to a museum, a tennis match, an auction, a movie, and twice to the races, once at Auteuil and once at Longchamps. None of these was a match for *ennui*. Then one day she saw Maria walking arm-in-arm with Remy Moustingue who, only three days before, had informed Birgitta that he was on his way back to Dijon to be a pharmacist. "I don't care," Birgitta had told herself. "He's only a cast-off," but she would not go to the races or anywhere else with Maria after that. Instead she took to window-shopping on the Faubourg St. Honoré. For a few days, this kept her interest. Very few, because walking wearied her and because she disliked the women who passed so elegantly in and so much more elegantly out of the shops.

Her encounter with Baggish had begun in the Club St. Germain, a *cave* she and Hams went to almost every night.

At eight-thirty, Hams had asked, "Wonder where Baggish is?"

"Whose baggage?" she'd asked.

"Some geek."

"Maybe it's up in the bar," said Birgitta.

"Wait here," said Hams. "I'll be back in thirty seconds." He knew this was Birgitta's maximum span of fidelity.

He was away nearly a minute, long enough for Baggish to come in the back way and approach her. He was primed for his debut. "Bryn Mawr or Holyoke?" he asked.

"Sorry," said Birgitta. "No French. Only Swedish and English."

"Oh," said Baggish. "You look like an American I know."

Birgitta saw Hams jumping down the stairs and charging across the dark floor, but before she could raise a finger, his red head had butted Baggish back against the wall. "I'm going to scatter your gut over the boulevard," he said. The spectators turned toward Hams' weekly engagement, but, to their disappointment, Hams pulled Baggish up and shook his hand. "Sorry," he said. "I took you for one of these frogs," and he drew a chair up from the next table. "Have a seat."

Hams' sociability worried rather than relieved Birgitta; his belligerence was for her a sign of security, and, even seeing in Baggish a temporary counter to *ennui,* she resented Hams' uncritical welcome of him. "I guess he gets tired of checking lungs and talking to me, so he's softening." This insight was only partially relieved by her recollection of his last examination of her—he had examined her twice a week since their second meeting—when he'd poked her in the stomach and kidneys and warned her that she wouldn't last twenty more years unless she took off some weight.

If Hams had softened, he was still Hams. He spent the evening assaulting French wine, French food, and France itself—he had seen Cherbourg and Paris, and from the train, Rouen. "It's the pothole of the universe," he asserted, "and the receptacle for every bum on earth."

"I've just come," said Baggish.

"Watch out," Hams warned, grateful, however, that Baggish was no intellectual, tourist, or GI bum.

They'd barged into each other at the American Embassy Annex that morning—Baggish had gone to read in the library—and just as Hams had been about to shove him out of the way, Baggish had said, "Excuse me," at which Hams had stuck out his arm, and said, somewhat tensely, "Hams, Charley, Princeton '42. I took you for a frog."

"Baggish, Theodore, Yale '49," said Baggish.

"Quite a knock," said Hams. "Ever do any fighting?"

"Not since the war," said Baggish, and he massaged the small of his back.

"I was a medic," said Hams.

"Useful," said Baggish.

Now Hams elbowed Birgitta's ribs and said, "We'll have to get Maria for him," and he added to Baggish, "Not as pretty as this one, but better built." Seeing Baggish frown, he flipped his thumb toward Birgitta and said, "Don't worry. She doesn't know English."

"She looks so American," said Baggish.

At midnight, Hams rose and pulled Birgitta with him. "Come around again, Baggish. It's not bad meeting a non-bum for a change."

To Birgitta's dismay, Hams didn't even frown when she shook hands with Baggish, and said she hoped he'd come the next evening.

The card Baggish found in his palm suggested an even earlier meeting, eleven o'clock the next morning at the Café à la Corne d'Abondance just off Place Luxembourg.

When he got back to the room he shared now with Ward at the

Hôtel Vidame de Chartres, the latter asked him if he were ill. "Not yet," said Baggish and added that he wouldn't be meeting him the next day at the Royale.

"Well, well, you connect pretty quickly."

"It may not work out. There's a possibility for you too. Name of Maria."

"Good man," said Ward. "I've been horny for three weeks."

Baggish noted the prime-cut word and slid off to sleep. The next morning he arrived early at the café, deliberating strategy. Only when Birgitta came up to the table and took his hand did deliberation cease. As they sat outside drinking *fines,* the sweet autumn air sank in him like music. He had never known anything like it. In fact, he was so discomposed, he suggested they take a taxi to the Bois de Boulogne.

They got out near the Longchamps track and walked around for nearly an hour trying to find a quiet place on the grass to sit, but people were coming to the track from every direction. "The horses is going today," explained Birgitta.

Baggish, oblivious to prodigality, suggested they go also.

"Naturally," said Birgitta.

They bought tickets in the enclosure, and, for Baggish, this was the end of oblivion. Now that they were surrounded by people who were obviously "prime cut," he noticed that Birgitta's manner was out of place. When he went down to the betting windows, she called, "By-by Baggish. By-by baby," till he disappeared under the stands, and she greeted his return by pressing his hand to her stomach and circulating it. Once she stepped—not accidently—on the foot of someone whom she had pointed out to Baggish as Cary Grant, and in response to his "Pardon," had said, *"Un grand plaisir,* M. Cary." In addition to embarrassment, Baggish lost six Show bets.

Birgitta was soon even more unhappy than Baggish. She realized that she had overestimated his capacity to amuse her, and foresaw the painful business of finding a new companion for her daytime hours. Secondly, she had picked three winners, and the success led her to form a dismal equation in her head, "Lucky with horses, unlucky with love." In disgust she heaved her winnings, four thousand francs, into a bush. (Baggish retrieved and pocketed them.) All this, however, was nothing to her strong suspicion that she had seen Maria and Giro Uras leaving the track together.

Shoulder to shoulder with Baggish in the autobus going back, she mapped out regimes of exercise and diet, scarcely aware of his suggestion that they meet the next day in the same place.

During the night, Baggish recovered much of what he had felt about Birgitta earlier in the day. Her beauty was such that he regarded her foolishness as a kind of charm contrived to set it off. He waited for her at the café the next morning with far less nervousness than he had the day before. When she didn't come, he was puzzled. "Hard to follow," he told himself. "Politically, they're very reliable people."

He went home with a bad headache which lasted off and on for two days and brought with it a fog of pessimism such as he had never known before. "Maybe Europe was a mistake," he thought. This was to be one of the last wasteful thoughts of his life.

The third day Ward announced that he was going to head down to the Midi in a BMW motorcycle he'd bought. "Want to come along?" he asked Baggish. Baggish said he'd think it over.

By the next morning he'd decided against going with Ward, but decided also that he would leave Paris. "I want to see another aspect of France," he told Ward. "I'm thinking of Versailles. I can get into Paris when I like, but I won't have the strain of living here. It's a terrible strain."

Ward said he thought that leaving the city was a good idea. "Moving from Omaha to Paris is no joke, Ted. Taking it in stages is the ticket."

"I need quiet," Baggish said.

To himself it came out, "I've got to regroup my forces. Anyway, girls in the provinces are less finicky." That afternoon he took the train out to Versailles, left his bag in the station, and made inquiries about places to stay.

CHAPTER THREE

I

Baggish took the only available accommodation at the Pension Louis Quatorze on the Rue Maréchal Joffre in Versailles. M. Merbihon, the *patron,* told him that it wasn't one of the regular rooms, and that he wouldn't be charged a cent for it. "Just for board, laundry, and maid service, M. Théodore." (He had given up with "Baggish" after one attempt.) "Altogether, without wine or extras, eleven thousand, five hundred francs per month. You'd not find the like in Paris. And the first regular room we have, you shall have."

"I may not be around longer than a couple of months, M. Merbihon," said Baggish. "Almost anything will do for that length of time."

M. Merbihon snuffled ambiguously. "You have the spirit of the bivouac, M. Théodore. I admire Americans. Shall you see it now?"

"Please." Things had begun well. He had understood every word of M. Merbihon's discourse, he liked the pension, liked being called M. Théodore, and more than anything else, liked living in a house with servants. He followed the *patron* up two flights of stairs and down a small passageway into the room.

"All right?" asked M. Merbihon.

"It will do," said Baggish, after a moment.

The room had the intimacy of a cave. It was split by a dipping ceiling so that one could only stand in the half which held the bed. There was a sink in the other half where the ceiling jutted lowest. A single window above the bed gave on a yellow wall across the street, and from the bed one could see a dirty rag of sky. A straight-backed chair and a bedside table completed the furnishings. Baggish put his books on the table next to his Emerson radio (M. Merbihon put on a French plug for him), his two bags in a corner, asked for and got a reading lamp, and considered himself established.

After a week in Versailles, he settled into a routine as pleasantly simple as his Parisian one had been. At seven-thirty, one of the maids opened his door and put a soup plate of chicory and half a *baguette* by his bed on a tray; he dipped the bread into the chicory, ate half of it and went back to sleep till ten. Then he dressed, walked down the Rue Maréchal Joffre, bought a newspaper, climbed the grand staircase of the Orangerie, and sat at the top of it by one of the great stone vases. Then he walked among the women, children, and the occasional December tourists, feeling after a few days, especially when the sun replaced the chill, moist loneliness of the chateau with a warmth that glittered in the hundreds of aligned windows, a withdrawn, heady possessiveness, regal and benevolent. At twelve-thirty he walked back to the pension for lunch. In the afternoon, he went to the Municipal Library (M. Merbihon was his sponsor) and read till closing time at five. Then he rested before dinner, and afterwards, either read, went to a movie, or played ping-pong with M. Chad, one of his tablemates. He was in bed by eleven, and then came the happiest hour of his day. In the dark, he turned on the radio and listened to the programs and station breaks from Madrid, Amsterdam, Frankfurt, London, Marseilles, Milan, Brussels, and Moscow. Europe was sealed up in the little box in the middle of his cave, available for his manipulation of it.

2

There were eight or nine families living at the pension, the most prominent of which—by virtue of noise and number—was the Del Prados, who included Mme. Del Prado's parents, the Le Tourneaus. M. Del Prado was a handsome Spaniard who recruited talent for cafés in Burgos, Santander—and San Sebastian, his wife—a voluptuous blond Frenchwoman, and there were two daughters, Maria, sixteen, and Josephine, nine, who were supervised by Mme. Le Tourneau. M. Le Tourneau was a retired Assistant Supervisor of the *Chemin de Fer du Nord-Ouest,* and the most distinguished guest of the pension. Occasionally, he bowed to Baggish in the garden and asked him if he would kindly explain the meaning of this or that term in the English or American book he was reading. He read the novels of Sinclair Lewis and works on the development of heavy industries.

M. Le Tourneau was seventy-five, but he was not the senior member of the pension. That was M. Placide Prud'homme, a retired naval officer, who was eighty-three. He was one of Baggish's table-mates at supper, and for their nightly encounters he would dredge his memory for vanished English, with no success but the single phrase, "How are you today?" which became his evening greeting. M. Prud'homme was an expert crossword puzzler, and he would often show Baggish a particularly amusing or difficult answer.

"Here is one, M. Théodore," and he'd point with trembling finger to an item in the puzzle. " 'They love their fellow men.' Can you guess the answer? Nine letters? No? Cannibals. Ha, ha, ha." The puzzle would frequently launch M. Prud'homme into a fragment of autobiography. "You know, I was once the only white man in the village of a cannibal tribe, the Akuseis in Mogandi-bel-Akrima. I was sent down there in 1892, stayed two years, and never saw another white man. I was judge, priest, and doctor. I married them by saying, 'You're married,' and often cured them by saying, 'You're cured.' "

"That's what I'd like to do in Paris," said Baggish.

M. Prud'homme spat a phlegm pearl into his handkerchief.

"I had a tent, a wife or two, and some books. I taught myself calculus and Portuguese. Time passed very quickly. When I came home, I got married and settled down for good. I'd had my share of the bizarre."

"I never cared much for bizarre things," said Baggish. M. Prud'homme nodded sadly, as if aware that the night could well bring him a final share of the bizarre, then rose to take the pitcher of steaming water the maid brought him for his evening toddy and hot water bottle, made his farewell with a quivering, *"Messieurs, dames,"* and was off up the stairs. Baggish watched his question mark of a back affectionately. He liked Prud'homme, and indeed, most other old people: they were *hors de combat.*

"If there's a cold wind tonight, we may be seeing our last of old Prud'homme," said M. Chad.

"He's an intelligent old man," said Baggish.

"He knows only facts," said Chad, who was an extracurricular student of the French existentialists and who brought with him to the table the tomes of Sartre, Marcel, and Merleau-Ponty which he read between courses and sometimes during them.

"Do you play ping-pong?" he asked Baggish one evening.

"A little," said Baggish, who had played in high school as an escape from rope-climbing and the parallel bars.

"They have two tables at the Bar Foch. Want to play?" The first evening, Baggish declined, but when Chad asked him again the next, he decided he'd better accept. "He'll dog me, if I don't. I'll play badly and he won't bother me again."

It turned out, however, that the ping-pong engrossed him almost as much as it did Chad. Though not in the same way. Chad played with ferocity and accelerating excitement. When he won, his five feet four inches swelled until he looked almost square, and his eyes dilated madly under the thick horn frames. To calm down, he had to see himself as conqueror, and he would comb his hair in front of a little pocket mirror. For Baggish, the interest stemmed from his ability to control Chad's mood, almost from shot to shot, as he either stroked toward his weak forehand or his smashing backhand. When he wanted to win, which wasn't often, he hit consistently down the forehand and plopped the weak returns out of Chad's reach just over the net. Defeat and despair went hand in hand for Chad, but instead of exhausting him, they engendered fantasies of triumph which had to be at least partially fulfilled before he would consent to return to the pension. His return, as he told Baggish one night, was featured by frightening dreams of ping-pong matches, the paddles and balls of which were existentialist arguments. "The dialectic is sometimes so severe I have headaches for days."

"Something like that happens to me when I think of women," said Baggish, partially to afford Chad some fellowship in sufferance.

"I've had almost nothing to do with women."

"Just as well," said Baggish benignly, and then added, as if sequentially, "What do you know of the elder Del Prado girl?"

"You're joking," shouted Chad, this under the darkened windows of the pension. Baggish said, "Sh." "She's a grotesque," continued Chad with no decrease in power. "Something off a cathedral," and he altered his voice to imitate the commanding summons of Mme. Le Tourneau which resounded through the pension ten times an hour, "Ma-ree-ya. Mah-ree-ya. Anyway," he said in his normal blast, "the grandfather is not poor."

"Why don't they have a house of their own?"

"They're not millionaires. And the Spaniard has no money, or what he has, he spends on his neckties." Chad caressed the filthy rope which constituted his own single piece of neckwear.

Despite Chad's monumental disdain, Baggish thought not a little about Maria. The galling encounter with Birgitta had been, he realized, a serious miscalculation. He had to begin with someone as simple and untried as himself. Maria was at least that. For Baggish there was an additional attraction, and this was the nobility which, in his view, the Spanish "Del" emblazoned. Maria's stiff angularity, flat chest, hairy legs and large black eyes all supervised by an ugly, laconic gracelessness seemed to him the proper semblance of nobility.

Although Maria was only sixteen, Mme. Del Prado, sensing Baggish's interest, relieved the tedium of her days by working out a strategy of alliance. Her daughter's physical poverty seemed, beside her own blond affluence, a footnote of rebuke; to repair the error of the genes was one of her central concerns. In Baggish she saw an American who had the means to travel without the visible prop of employment, and one whose restraint and dignity seemed almost spirituality compared to the Americans she had seen in the cafés of Spain and France.

One morning she delayed her shopping until she saw Baggish going downstairs. She waited until he'd finished exchanging a few words with Mme. Merbihon, and then caught up with him as he passed the woodcutter's stall down the street.

"M. Théodore," she called.

He heard her, but as he had the excuse of the woodcutter's saw, he didn't turn around until she called a second time. "Ah, good morning, Madame," he said.

"Are you going downtown, M. Théodore?"

"In that direction, Madame. May I accompany you?"

"I was hoping you would. A dirty little shed, that, isn't it?" she said, aiming her blond head at the woodcutter.

"For me it's picturesque, Madame. I wish we had more evidence of such traditional occupations in America."

"Can America really be so different?" asked Mme. Del Prado. "Certainly our European traditions must be very strong there." She quivered suddenly at a vision of Maria walking, thin and abused, in the midst of a cloud-rimmed steel jungle.

"Of course, Madame. It is partially nostalgia for the traditional individualism central to our country when, for instance, my ancestors first came there, that prompts so many Americans to admire as picturesque what you in France regard as merely dirty."

"You know, M. Théodore," said Mme. Del Prado, fearing as

she said it that she might have interrupted him, "you speak French now almost like a Frenchman. It was difficult to understand you the first two weeks you were with us. I hope you'll forgive my saying it, but in less than a month—isn't it?—"

"Six weeks, Madame."

"—you have mastered our language. There are very few mistakes, and the little accent you have is an added charm in your speech." After a pause, Mme. Del Prado veered to illuminate another subject. "I saw you having a session with our *patronne.*" She smiled coyly at an elderly priest pedaling by on a bicycle.

"Yes," said Baggish. "I was wondering if she could send up a little butter with my bread in the morning. An American habit which she appeared to excuse on that ground."

"I'm afraid that I don't have that excuse for my own indulgence," said Mme. Del Prado. "We are fellow sybarites." She was beginning to enjoy the conversation on its own merits when Baggish announced that, as they were at the Rue d'Orangerie, he had to be leaving her. "Thank you," he said, "for letting me accompany you."

"I enjoyed our little talk, M. Théodore. May I ask if you are going to visit the chateau?"

"I am, Madame. I study there frequently, or, as today, I may only walk through the woods."

"It is absolutely ravishing there. Unique in the world. We often come over," she said, hinting at the flexible promise of the pronoun by drawing it out.

"Good day, Madame."

For a moment the luxurious possibility of exchanging the daughter for the mother filled Baggish with excitement. He bought *Figaro* at the newsstand as if he were assuming a sceptre and mounted the famous stone steps in the manner of their former masters. Moving over to the view of the Grand Canal, he sat in front of the Fountain of Latona, where he readjusted his passions to the course he had set for them. "Maybe later," he thought. "I can't risk another *gaffe.*" He took out his pocket dictionary and with its aid read the account of the newly installed Bidault ministry.

Baggish was up to the review of *The Third Man* when someone croaked, "M. Théodore" at his elbow. It was Mme. Le Tourneau with Maria and Jacqueline in tow. Baggish turned his head in surprise; he had not expected the conversation with Mme. Del Prado to have such immediate consequences. "Jesus," he muttered. "The woman's got the push of a Talleyrand."

Mme. Le Tourneau, plopped down in one of the folding chairs, was swooped upon by the hag guardian of the state's property, handed her two francs as if she were endowing an institute, and summoned her grandchildren to shake M. Théodore's "amicable hand."

"Mama said that you might be here," Maria said so rapidly that Baggish was only sure of the first word and unsure whether he was hearing French or Spanish. Mme. Le Tourneau thrust two fingers into Maria's spine, the girl straightened, and then sat at her grandmother's knee, suffering her braids to be twirled on the bumpy digits.

"It is a lovely place to be," said the old woman before Baggish had finished deciphering the girl's remark. "Are you enjoying Versailles, M. Théodore?"

"Very much, Madame. It is a beautiful town and ideally located with respect to Paris."

"It is not so pretty as it used to be, as one can see," she said, tossing her white head toward the pools and fountains as if she were remembering contemporaries at the Sun King's court. "Like everything else it has lapsed into a vile desuetude. You follow me, M. Théodore?"

"The words are almost the same in English, Madame," said Baggish, not quite sure of "desuetude" in either language.

"To be sure," said the old lady. "The gardens are like all of us, most beautiful in the spring. On Sundays then the fountains play. I hope that you will be here to see them."

"I hope so also."

"In summer we have the fireworks, a sight unique in the world."

"I hope that I shall have the pleasure of seeing them, Madame."

"I haven't seen them since my husband and I visited here before the war, little thinking we would one day settle here." The thought of her present establishment summoned her from recollection to business. "Have you seen the Trianon, M. Théodore?"

"Only from a distance, Madame," said Baggish, who had taken a tour through it his second day in Versailles.

"Well, then, perhaps you will let Maria show it to you one afternoon. She will be able to supplement the guide's remarks."

"Oh, Grandmama," said Maria.

"That would be delightful," said Baggish.

Business terminated, Mme. Le Tourneau rose to go. Baggish accompanied them on the slow return to the pension. When they entered the dining room together, he felt himself the cynosure of titillating suspicions.

"Ah-ha," said Chad, as Baggish sat down across from him. "Our gallant American seems to have had an arduous morning."

After lunch, in the garden, Maria nodded to him and held up two fingers. Failing to understand whether this meant two o'clock or in two hours, and not knowing where they were to meet, Baggish went up to her, smiled in the face of her terrible blushes and asked for information. "Two o'clock by the statue of Louis Quatorze," she whispered. "Mama says it's all right, but we mustn't let my grandparents know," and she passed on like the third sister in the fairy tales. The ungainliness of it all depressed Baggish, and he shook his head back and forth while the pensioners watched him and smiled. In the face of this, he almost decided to go into Paris and see *The Third Man*. "Who knows, though," he thought. "Away from the mob, that girl might turn into a human being."

The optimism proved to be unwarranted. The promenade with Maria was, for Baggish, boring beyond belief. Maria never began a subject of her own accord, and her responses were not meant to

communicate anything but respectful attention. Only pity kept
Baggish with her. He saw in the rapturous dilation of her black
eyes that the afternoon in the familiar maze of Versailles wonders
was the most exciting of her life. At the Hameau, she answered his
questioning of the cottage's function by saying that Marie Antoinette
must have grown weary of frivolity; at the Grand Trianon, she ignored Baggish's question about Mme. de Pompadour and informed
him that Napoleon ate dinner under the black marble columns.

"Have you studied French history, M. Théodore?" she asked,
looking away from a guide who was lifting the seat of Marie Antoinette's privy to the delight of seven tourists behind them.

"Very little," said Baggish. "It is nice hearing an informed person
talk about it."

They parted two hours after their meeting at the statue. "I shall
see you tomorrow, Mademoiselle. Thank you very much for per-
mitting me to accompany you and for your interesting lecture." As
she looked questioningly at him, he added, "I must catch the four-
thirty train to Paris."

Maria stared after him as he walked toward the station in his
strange American topcoat; the contrast of his unfettered movements
to her own constrained ones made her wonder how it was that men
and women ever came together.

3

"Well," reflected Baggish, as the train pulled into the Gare des
Invalides. "I might as well be hanged for a wolf as a sheep."

He'd been coming into Paris twice a week since he'd gone to Versailles, and it never failed to excite him. He walked past the Quai
d'Orsay and the Chambre des Deputés, swelling in the presence
of great events in the making. The notice on the parliamentary
walls enjoining urination there made sense to him today. "They
take nothing on trust. And for good reason." It was here that he
had to decide whether to cross over the Concorde Bridge and walk

down the Right Bank—which would probably lead to an evening at the Comédie Française—or down the Left which would make his day more indeterminate. Tonight, while he stood debating, the lights came up like a tiara on the bridge. "That's a good sign," he thought, though he did not go in much for signs. A taxi discharged a passenger and a flood of carbon monoxide into his face. Coughing and raging, he staggered back against the monitory placard, suppressed an impulse to take the taxi and beat the driver out of the fare, then walked down the Left Bank, stopped for a Pernod at a café, and went on until he came to a restaurant across the street from the École des Beaux Arts. It was a noisy student place with better food than most; Baggish remembered Charley Hams saying you could find comparatively "clean meat" there, a phrase which Baggish was willing to explore.

He sat alone in a corner eating a cutlet, overwhelmingly *garni,* when a feathery-looking girl at the next table asked him if he could spare her the salt. "And other things as well," ventured Baggish, handing it over, and looking from the girl to her friend, a dramatic blond who smiled at Baggish and said, "Zank-oo." The girls broke up at this witty rejoinder; Baggish was pleased to see that the blond looked even better when she laughed.

"We've been noticing you," said the feathery one. "You don't seem a student type. Are you Marshall Plan?"

"Not exactly," said Baggish, and flicked the smile that said my-work-is-secret-but-if-you-knew across his face. "Are you students?"

No, they both worked in the Lido, the feathery girl, Pauli, as a cigarette girl, the blond, Monique, in the chorus. "She has nice legs," said Pauli. "What I have nice, I don't show. At the Lido, anyway."

They left together, Baggish having asked if he could walk them to work. Or walk Pauli to work, at any rate, for Monique was under suspension for missing a performance, and was debating a return to her home in the Midi.

"I hope that you'll stay here with us," he said.

"Ah, she'll stay," said Pauli, taking his hand as they walked in the dark toward the river. "What's your name, darling?" She said the last word in English.

"My name is Teddy," said Baggish, for the first time in his life.

They crossed the river at Concorde, the wind whacking their bodies. Baggish put his arms around the girls, and on his thumbs felt the warm poise of their breasts; he could barely talk for the joy of it.

Pauli pointed to a huge willow tree at the edge of the Champs Elysées across from the statue of Clemenceau. "That's our tree," she said. "We sit under there sometimes, just for nothing. You can share it with us."

"Now?" asked Baggish.

"It might be nice," said Pauli, "but it's too late and too cold. Sometimes the cold doesn't matter."

At the Lido, Pauli gave Baggish her telephone number and blew him a kiss. "Let's go, Teddy," said Monique. "I better not hang around here."

"Shall we go back to the tree?" asked Baggish, thinking boldness the proper counter to inexperience. Monique's presence seemed to call for something more specific than Maria's in the garden of Versailles. Here he was with a genuine French chorus girl, and though Baggish placed little faith in classic situations, his senses urged him now toward the simplest version of the one he was in.

Monique said that the willow tree was "a stupidity of Pauli's. Let's walk a little, and then I'll go home."

Baggish was a rapid adjuster. He calmed himself, took her arm and walked up the avenue. They had walked a block and a half when they heard the whine of cramped brakes and the ugly noises of a minor collision; a small Peugeot had backed into a Renault. Out of the Peugeot lunged a huge man with a gray pompadour; a lithe little fellow came more slowly from the injured Renault. There was an exchange of accusations which drew in the evening crowd. The little man was taking off his topcoat when the big one unfurled a kick at his head which, had it landed, would have torn it off the neck; the crowd expressed approval of this natural development. The little man was ready for the second kick; he grabbed the foot and tried to spill its proprietor, but couldn't hold on, and the other hit him with a right cross to the jaw that knocked him on the pavement, then aimed a kick at his head. At this, a little fat man with glasses threw a coat in the big man's face. The latter's fist thumped the fat man into a wall where the eyeglasses disintegrated. Another man now leaped on his back, pinned his arms and kneed him in the kidneys. This struggle spread over the sidewalk and then into the lobby of a movie theater, the crowd like a protective membrane around it. Two *gendarmes* moved through, swinging clubs. They jabbed both men hard in the ribs, and started taking testimony. The crowd resolved into human beings, and Baggish walked on with Monique. They were sweating and trembling with excitement. Breathing hard, feeling something unleashed by the scene, they looked at each other. "Tigers," said Monique. She drew Baggish off the Champs down a side street. The exchange of silent dark for the agitated flare of the avenue excited Baggish still more.

Opposite a small hotel on Rue Georges Mandel, Monique said, "That's where I live." She held out a hand, and he pressed it as she started to shake. They were the same height and their faces were within inches of each other.

"When will I see you?" he asked, thinking that it was now he had to do something.

"Call me at the hotel. If I've decided to go back home, I'll leave a message with the concierge. Good night."

"Good night, Monique," moaned Baggish, as he watched her cross over to the hotel. Then he ran after her, caught her two steps from the hotel, pulled her away from the entrance lights, and pushed himself against her. They kissed. Inside his body he felt a glacier thaw. "Ahhhh," he moaned.

"Good night, Teddy," Monique said, and walked around him into the hotel.

He hardly noticed her, but leaned against a wall, a secular saint in a secular niche. The years of privation, the suffering over Birgitta

were part now of the orchard of pleasure. Hardly conscious of anything but his discovery and triumph, he walked to the Gare des Invalides, entered the train to Versailles, walked home to the pension
and put himself to bed. It was only the next day, as he woke up
to his buttered breakfast bread and plate of chicory that he realized
that what had happened to him the night before might be little
more than a prologue to the liberation of his need.

En route to the station to take the early morning train to Paris,
Baggish stopped off at a pharmacy on the Place de l'Eglise. He had
looked up the word for "prophylactic" in the *Concise Oxford Dictionary,* and its similarity to the English word was his insurance
against forgetting it in the moment of purchase. An old saleslady
bid him an enthusiastic "Good morning" and asked what she could
do for him. Baggish, head down, and red with tension, demanded
the article. The woman did not understand the request, and he
repeated it, head up. Her eyes glazed, she walked to the back, returned with a packet, said "Sixty francs," and did not nod to him
when he left.

It was a marvelously warm day. He took off his topcoat; holding
it in his arms as the train went through the suburbs gave him the
sense of a mission, something on his hands and mind which di-
rected the energies piling in him.

He called Monique's hotel from the station. The concierge would
not disturb her. "A good sign," thought Baggish. "She's still here."

"Tell her to meet M. Teddy, T-e-d-d-y, at the Madeleine, at three
o'clock this afternoon."

"Charting the route for them is the only way," he told himself;
confidence and foresight steadied each other like a good tandem.

4

In front of the Marshall Plan offices in the Hôtel de Talleyrand
Baggish pretended to official status and was taxied over to the Personnel Offices in the Hôtel Wagram on Rue de Rivoli. There he filled

out an eleven page form only to be told as he signed the last that
there were no civilian jobs in France and none envisaged. "If I were
you," said the Personnel woman, "I'd head for Heidelberg."

"How so?"

"It's the Army's headquarters in Europe. State Department's
in Frankfurt, but you have less chance there. I could put you on
a Cable of Availability, but you can't even get thrown into the wastebasket unless you're in front of their noses."

"Heidelberg sounds like the place to be then," said Baggish, and
went down to the taxi stand to get ferried back to the Talleyrand.
He went into an OFFICIALS ONLY door and called the Paris offices of
Standard Oil of New Jersey, Coca-Cola, Paramount International
Films, General Motors, and five or six other American firms. Meanwhile, he stared coldly at anyone who passed through the office.
The calls, however, came to nothing. Except for specialist jobs,
only French help was hired. Baggish briefly considered passing
himself off as an engineer. "If I'd only had a year of physics," he
lamented. For his last call, he asked the operator to put him through
to Mr. Attlee at Downing Street, Number 10, London.

"May I ask who's calling, sir?"

"You may not," said Baggish, and slammed down the receiver.

He walked down Rue Royale, bought a seventy franc edition of
Stendhal's *Napoleon,* went to a bar and spent two hours over a
sandwich jambon and two glasses of beer reading it. The reading
restored him, confirmed his habitual self-appraisal and retendered
the promise he had held out to himself so many years. One brief
passage he learned by heart:

Il pensait avec force, il avait la logique la plus serrée. Il avait immense-
ment lu. . . . Son esprit était vif et prompt, sa parole énergique. . . . il
plût aux femmes par des ideés neuves et fiéres, par des raisonnments
audacieux.

He bought a small bouquet of violets from a peddler, walked to
the Madeleine, and waited at the top step, feeling in the swish of

wind a promise of sensuality which only Napoleonic discipline enabled him to control.

At ten to three Monique arrived. "But I'm early," she said. "How nice that you're here."

"I thought you'd be early," he said, taking her hand. He was half-sick with relief.

"Pauli would have wanted to come too. Are you unhappy that I didn't think to ask her?"

"Only that you think about her now."

"If I had gone back home, I was going to send her to you."

"Is the Lido taking you back?"

"Yes, but I might have stayed anyway. Paris is beginning to seem nicer."

With the confidence of a somnambulist, Baggish took her down the steps and to the theater where they queued up for *Le Troisième Homme*.

"I'm mad for Orson," said Monique. "He's so funny in this. Cynical, you know. Very cynical."

"You've seen it?"

"Four times."

"Perhaps they'll let us return the tickets."

"Nonsense. I could see it a hundred."

The picture was not that exciting for Baggish. He hardly followed the story. His excitement centered in the arm which lay on his and the body which his elbow and forearm occasionally touched. By the time they came out of the theater into the Paris dusk, he was sweating with desire.

"It is unseasonably warm, isn't it, Teddy?" said Monique, wiping his brow with a dirty handkerchief. "Or was it the agitation of the picture?"

Baggish passionately groaned.

"That's sweet, Teddy. Shall we have dinner?" They walked down the Right Bank, past the pet shops, then across the Île St. Louis into a restaurant with sawdust on the floor where they ate pork

chops marinated in wine. They ate so hugely that Baggish's other
appetite was somewhat blunted.

"Shall we go to the Club St. Germain for a while?" he asked her.

"For what it is, it's so expensive," said Monique.

"Not always," said Baggish, praying now that he would get what
he was paying for.

At the Club staircase, he saw that he was going to have a dividend:
Birgitta and Charley Hams were at their usual table. Baggish paraded
Monique by them, nodded to Birgitta and greeted Charley. He refused the latter's invitation to join them—not that there was room
—and went to the darkest of the room's dark corners, his desire
complicated now by reprisal and nostalgia.

For the first time in his life, he wanted to drink, and did, a great
deal more than he ever had before. The liquor resolved the balance
of his needs. Hours later, under the long, secret branches of the
great willow tree, with the cafés of the Champs closed and the
streets empty, he put his lips on Monique's and murmured drunk-
enly, "Birgitta darling."

"What does that mean, Teddy?"

After a moment, Baggish said, "It means 'I love you' in Swedish."
A moment after this, Baggish gained the experience he had so long
sought.

5

At the Pension Louis Quatorze, Baggish sensed something uncomfortable in the atmosphere. His fellow pensioners knew of his promenade with Maria in the Chateau grounds, and this led them to
induce a relationship which Maria's shyness and youth precluded
her from soliciting and encouraging, although not enduring and
even enjoying. The expressions of Maria and Baggish were the
pianoforte upon which the leisurely pensioners played, and they all
played in the same key. Observance had become expectation, although of what—considering the girl's age—they could not be sure.

Mme. Del Prado and her mother, however, had begun to feel that they had exaggerated the advantage, and certainly the possibility of a useful relationship. When the pensioners questioned them, however indirectly, about the matter, they answered with a special coldness which made the former think that something unpleasant had occurred, something of which Baggish was of course culpable. Baggish, absorbed by thoughts of Monique, seemed to them absorbed by guilt, and the case seemed clear. One day he was summoned by M. Merbihon.

"M. Bageesh," he said, trying the name he had abandoned at his first attempt eight weeks before. "May I speak to you a moment in the office?"

"Certainly," said Baggish sternly, piqued at the form of address.

"I do not know how to begin, Monsieur—Monsieur Théodore," said Merbihon, relaxed now away from the brutal regard of his wife, "but let me be direct. I do not think that you have acted quite properly. We are all men and understand the conditions of being men, of life, but Monsieur Théodore, were you tactful? No. Your choice was bad. Better the mother than the daughter." He picked up a pencil, wrote figures on a pad, and then worked it through his ice-gray hair. "Anyway, you said that you did not intend to stay here long." He scratched in his nostrils with the pencil point. "I like Americans. I like you, but what I must say is that *la patronne* has informed me that you have been making advances to the young Del Prado, who is, under the law, too young for such business. Her grandfather was a *Sous-directeur* of the *Chemin de Fer du Nord-Ouest*. After all. May I, Monsieur Théodore, counsel you—if you remain here—to be particularly cautious, that you refrain from seeking your pleasures on the Rue Maréchal Joffre, *numéro Trente-Cinq*." He put a large hand on Baggish's shoulder. "Men are alike all over," and then, shaking his head, "but such a choice."

Baggish smiled at Merbihon and said that he had to leave within the next forty-eight hours as he had been offered a job by the American State Department in Germany. His letters—he had never received any at the pension—should be forwarded to the American Express in Heidelberg. "I understand the way you feel, my friend," he concluded. "I understand, and I sympathize," and he took Merbihon's hand in his, held it a moment, then shook it affectionately.

That afternoon he bought a single violet and sent it to Monique in an envelope with a note which read, "I'll return soon. Birgitta, birgitta, Teddy."

PART THREE

CHAPTER ONE

I

Gladys Culley's nose flared out of her face like Florida off the Atlantic Seaboard. She had early learned that it could not be disguised and would not be ignored; the difficulty was resolved by converting all stares into ones of admiration. When Herman Culley, who owned the bowling alley in Elkins, proposed to her on her thirty-first birthday, Gladys' self-confidence was fortified to the extent of laughing at Herman's pleasantry that he was the only man in Elkins lucky enough to have his business advertised on his wife's face. Despite this advantage, the Culley marriage lasted less than four years, ending one evening when Herman's punch drew blood from the facial plug. The punch and his declaration that he wouldn't live another day with a woman who looked as if she were toppling over when she was sitting down sent Gladys into her room to pack. That night she took the train for Chicago, and within the week she became a Civil Servant. She was in Personnel and made great strides; by the time she was forty-three, her rating was GS-11, and she was given the opportunity to go to Germany with an overseas allowance. It was the climax of her career.

Gladys had another physical peculiarity: the upper part of her body was disproportionately long, so that when she rose, it looked as if she had a kink in her leg which prevented her straightening to full height. Sitting, she looked formidable; Schreiber, whom she 'processed in' the day after he arrived in Heidelberg, felt quite subdued by her.

"You know you don't get your thirteen until you have done nine weeks of satisfactory work?"

"Yes."

"Sign here," and she indicated the square on the forms.

"You receive free billets, but they are subject to inspection at any time. You are not allowed to have visitors in your room after ten-thirty. If you have a guest coming to town who wishes to use your quarters, you must make suitable application thirty days in advance."

"Any chances of getting billeted with a German family?" asked Schreiber.

"What do you mean?"

Schreiber explained that he had been at great disadvantage in Germany during the war because he hadn't known the language; now he wished to learn German well and to acquire a more intimate knowledge of German life.

"You'll get all you want of that in the streets," said Gladys. "Anyway, it's strictly forbidden."

She waited until he said, "I understand."

"Your Washington papers list you as married, yet you're applying for bachelor quarters."

"My wife's final decree comes through next month."

Her nose quivered a little, and under its shadow, Schreiber saw a smile. "Then I'll just change this box here to 'divorced.' "

"That would be less confusing," said Schreiber.

"I'm divorced too," she said.

Schreiber began to say, "I'm sorry," and then realized that Mrs. Culley wanted him to say, "I'm glad."

"Oh," was what he said.

"It's a problem," she said.

"Yes. It isn't quite what you expect."

"Do you have time for a cup of coffee?" she asked, putting a bronze paperweight on his dossier. "There's a good snack bar just up the street a ways."

"That would be nice."

When she rose, he gasped a little, although he was glad to see that he was taller than she. Gladys' system had long since ceased to register gasps.

"The girls' bachelor quarters aren't as nice as the mens'," she said as they stepped out. He felt her fingers on his arm. "Watch out, Maxie." They waited five seconds for a truck to pass; the fingers remained around his arm. "I'd better keep hold of you. My name's Gladys."

The snack bar was very noisy. "These dependent kids are the limit," said Gladys. "Last March, one of them nearly beaned me with a firecracker he flung out of a bus. That's all they do all day long, ride the Army buses back and forth flinging their darn crackers. I'd like to shovel a few of them into their throats."

"They're very noisy," said Schreiber.

The kids were playing "I've Got a Lovely Bunch of Coconuts" over and over again on the jukebox, and the improvised lyrics alluded to Gladys' nose. Schreiber frowned once or twice at them, but as it was apparent that Gladys didn't hear them, he concentrated on following her discourse. It was not easy.

"Sometimes you wonder whether you weren't better off before."

"Sometimes," he said.

"You must have had a tough time. That the reason you came over?"

"Partially."

"I've had seven proposals since, but, you know, once burned, twice shy. You've got to find just the right one."

"I wonder why it's so hard," said Schreiber.

This pleased her. "Most people aren't sincere. They're always looking for the humorous side of things. I used to eat in a Doughnut Shop on Wabash, and I memorized their motto. It's all over the walls and on the menus, but most people only think it's humorous," and she quoted, " 'As you go through Life, Friend, Thinking of your Goal, Keep your eye upon the Doughnut, And not upon the Hole.' "

"I see," said Schreiber.

"I used to listen to a little station in Chicago that played nice music, and a girl friend of mine asked me, 'What do you listen to such a weak station for? All you can hear is static.' So I said to her, 'You listen to the static, Jer', but I listen to the music.' The next time I saw her she said she'd turned that remark over in her head the whole night. 'Talk about sermons in a nutshell, Glad.' That's what she said." Gladys looked at her watch. "Uh-oh. Fifteen minutes. We got to get back."

An hour later they completed the processing. "Now go over to the Housing Bureau in the Bristol and get yourself Quarters. I live in Dornröschenstrasse. I hope I'm going to hear from you, Max." She got up and held out her hand. "Welcome to Heidelberg."

He went off to the Bristol feeling somewhat as he had two days before as he stepped off the boat in Bremerhaven. It had been a tedious, body-rattling trip, and he had been sick six of the eleven days. "A penance," he had told himself, thinking that Florence was probably laid up with the flu back in Noroton.

Divorce had been harder than he'd imagined; each paper they'd signed in the lawyer's office had hacked at the splitting wood, the final cut leaving them free but gashed, lighter but deformed. Years before, Schreiber had had a talk with his father about a girl whom he had wanted to marry when he was a sophomore at Lehigh. He had gone to his father's optometrist's shop, and they had sat at opposite sides of the counter as if for a fitting. "Marry in haste, repent at leisure," his father had said, and he remembered studying his face in the three-sectioned counter mirror trying to make his expression serious and mature. "You can rectify mistakes," he'd answered, and his father had shaken his long, hairless head back and forth in an ethereal semaphore, and said that divorce was a wound which could never heal.

Schreiber chose a room in the Hotel Ritter; he took the blue trolley car down the cluttered Hauptstrasse into the heart of the *Alt Stadt.*

"The finest baroque survival of the Thirty Years War in Heidelberg," said the desk clerk as he handed Schreiber the key.

The room was on the third floor. It was large and had a private bath. Looking out, Schreiber saw that the windows were flanked with stone knights of the Palatine, and below, he made out the tarnished gold letters of the word *Invicta.* The Heiliggeist Church was directly across the street.

"Very nice," he said to the clerk, returning the key.

"For the money," mumbled the clerk.

2

His first weeks in Heidelberg were lonely ones, and Schreiber felt that living in the Ritter was part of the loneliness. It was not so much that most of the people in his office lived in the hills or in the army housing development near the command post caserne, for Schreiber did not want to spend his leisure time with them, and they accepted his reason for declining their invitations, a "study" he was doing, by interpreting "study" as "German mistress." (The excuse was unreal except as a nostalgic recall of the unfinished study of his French days. The only writing he did now was in a notebook he'd started keeping on the boat coming over.) The chief disadvantage of the Ritter had at first seemed to him its chief virtue, namely its location in the *Alt Stadt* where there were almost no other American billets. It proved to be, however, an American island near which all Germans spoke or tried to speak English and to and from which army buses carried passengers to other American islands. Schreiber felt that his national identity was isolated and exaggerated, and that he was thus precluded from entering into that European life of the spirit for which he had come.

One day in August he decided he would move, and opportunity

almost immediately followed. The proprietor of the fruit store next to the hotel brought him over one evening to a young man in *lederhosen* and introduced him with, "Here is another American, Herr Harden, and a lonely one, I think."

Schreiber, who'd caught only the first part, said, "Of course that's not a rarity here."

"Well, I should say that it was," said Harden, who knew German perfectly, was very gregarious and never lonely. "Shall we have dinner together?" and he offered Schreiber a pear.

The initial misunderstanding perplexed but charmed Schreiber, and so did Harden. First of all, he was not American but South African. Secondly, he brought Schreiber to the loveliest restaurant he had seen in Heidelberg. It was in the courtyard of the Palatinate Museum, and the tables were occupied by the most distinguished looking natives Schreiber had seen in Germany.

"It's too expensive for the students," said Harden, sipping at a fine Moselle, "so it's a relief to come here occasionally."

"I've wondered where the famous German blonds had been hiding," said Schreiber. "At least one sees vestiges of them here."

"The blond beauties are all Scandinavian," said Harden. "It's the source of German belligerence: the men invade places to get cracks at decent-looking women." He pointed past the tables and sarcophagi in the courtyard toward the dark museum. "Ever seen the jaw? It's kind of an inn-keeper's sign for the restaurant."

"I'd forgotten the Heidelberg man," said Schreiber. "It's rather comforting that the area has been habitable so long."

"I'll take you to see it before I leave," said Harden.

"Leave?" asked Schreiber with great disappointment.

"I'm just here for the summer session," he said, somewhat embarrassed at Schreiber's disappointment. "Why don't you take my place? I think you'll like it. Get away from the army atmosphere, learn German, and enjoy a good view of the river. It'll cost you next to nothing."

"Why not?" said Schreiber, happy after all at the result of the meeting, and he pictured himself for a moment sitting like Harden in *lederhosen* talking with airy authority over a fine Moselle. "And you know," he added to Harden as if communicating a rare formula, "I wouldn't mind paying quite a little for something like that."

3

"Mr. Harden said that you wish to take his rooms, Mr. Schreiber." The old lady sat with him on a yellow lounge at the lighted end of the huge dark room behind the larger of the two grand pianos. She spoke excellent English into which she introduced a rather charming lisp.

"Yes, Frau von Stempel, I would like to very much."

"Frau von Gode. Stempel von Gode," she said softly without the lisp. Then resuming with it, "May I ask Mr. Schreiber, why, since you already receive free rooms from the Army, you are moving where you must pay something?"

"I prefer to live in the atmosphere of the country I'm living in, Frau von Gode. You see, I work in an American environment. After hours, my hope...."

"Mr. Schreiber. I understand. You're not married, I believe?"

"I am no longer married."

Frau von Gode considered this and repeated it in interrogative form.

"That is correct. I am divorced."

She touched his hand with a long, sharp finger. "No girls up here, Mr. Schreiber, *nicht*? My father's house, you see. We have had experience. My son...." An explosion of coughing sent her scurrying behind the second piano where Schreiber heard phlegm drummed against a waste basket. The percussion lasted nearly two minutes. Then Frau von Gode returned, breathing heavily, her body caved in and disheveled by the attack.

"A little cold," she said hoarsely. "Pardon. My son takes care of the arrangements. He is upstairs." She pointed to the door and fell back against the couch.

Schreiber closed the door, went upstairs and knocked at the first door he saw.

"*Bitte, herein,*" said a harsh voice.

He opened the door and saw a girl in a slip sitting on the bed, reading. "Thought you were someone else," she said in German, and then added in English, "Understands German?"

"*Entschuldigung,*" he said, and continued in German, "I understand most things."

She stood up; her shoulders were beautiful, and she blushed as he stared at them. "American?"

"Yes."

She looked at her bathrobe on a hook by her bed and then back to him. She put out her hand. "Traudis Bretzka."

"Max Schreiber." He pronounced the name with German intonations.

"Ah, so. Poppa German?"

"Excuse me?"

"Your father was a citizen of Germany?"

"No. Five or six generations ago."

Her eyes were black and very bright, and she had short black hair. Her only noticeable defect was that she was gap-toothed. "Were you looking for me?" she asked.

"Dr. Stempel," he said.

"Three doors down on the right. Are you taking Harden's room?"

"I hope so. Do you know him?" He wondered at Harden's not mentioning her.

"Not well. He was only here this summer."

"I hope to see you again," said Schreiber. He bowed slightly, walked down the hall and knocked on the third door.

"Who's knocking?" came back in German, not loudly but with great distinctness.

Schreiber gave his name. A large shiny head which in the odd hall light seemed to slide off into two gray bunches of hair at the back appeared above a latch. "You wish to see me?"

"If I may."

The door opened all the way, and Schreiber saw that the head had only been inclined over the latch the better to peer into the hall, and that straightened up, it was six feet in the air.

"Please come in. So you are Herr Schreiber?"

"I am."

"You speak German, Herr Schreiber. Good. I read English, French, Swedish, and Latin, but I speak only German. I lack the mimic sense."

The room was much newer and brighter-looking than the rest of the house. A picture window at the far end looked over the river at the castle and the *Alt Stadt.* "Lovely, isn't it?" asked Dr. Stempel, pointing with one hand and drawing up a chair for Schreiber with the other.

Schreiber said that it was.

"You'll have some wine, Herr Schreiber?"

"Thank you very much." He stiffened as Stempel roared, "Lilli. *Zwei Gulmbacher.*"

A side door opened and a young blond woman came out with a silver tray and two glasses of wine. Schreiber stood up, and Stempel introduced them, "Frau Stempel, Herr Schreiber." Smiles and handshakes were exchanged, and Frau Stempel left.

"Second wife," said Stempel. "Swedish. Was in my office during the war. What do you think of her?"

Schreiber frowned at the question, and Stempel nodded approvingly. "That's good. Harden spoke to me. I have the agreements drawn up." He went to a desk, took four typewritten sheets from a drawer and handed two of them to Schreiber who read the terms of which he understood less than half. The figures were clear, however, one hundred marks a month exclusive of heating and maid service.

"Very reasonable," said Stempel, and he handed Schreiber the other sheets. "A small matter. You must register at the Heidelberg Housing Office tomorrow and show them this agreement." The rent on the new sheets was noted as sixty marks a month, all-inclusive. "They want us to live on our fingernails, ox-heads. You're very lucky to get in the house. If you don't like the arrangement, you are free to go elsewhere."

Schreiber signed both sets of forms, finished the wine and said he would move in the next day. Dr. Stempel patted him on the back as he left. "Hold on to the railing, Herr Schreiber. Oh yes, thirty pfennigs for each telephone call, forty pfennigs for a bath, and the tub must be spotless. Good evening."

The door was shut, and Schreiber went down the lightless stair well a step at a time. As he came to the second story, Dr. Stempel's door opened, and the great head moved down the hall. There was a knock on Traudis Bretzka's door. *"Bitte, herein,"* he heard again.

4

A week later Schreiber was well-established in Haus Stempel von Gode, so well in fact that he received an invitation from Dr. Stempel to witness the Castle Illuminations from the third floor balcony. At eight-thirty he went upstairs and found Stempel in an armchair, his wife on a stool, their two blond daughters on the stone floor, Traudis and two young men in *lederhosen* on a sofa, and behind them, in straight chairs, two older men in dark suits, one long, the other short. Below, on the second floor balcony, was Frau Stempel von Gode, whom they could see spitting now and then into a waste basket.

"Drs. Fläche and Pilzmauer," said Stempel introducing Schreiber to the older men, and then leading him over his children's knees to the couch. "Fräulein Bretzka, Herren Schmigl and Franck. *Meine Damen und Herren,* Herr Schreiber, an American of German blood." The students leaped to their feet, clicked their heels and repeated their last names. Schreiber shook their hands and sat down beside Traudis.

"A pleasure to see you again," he said.

"Good," said Traudis in English.

Fireworks began exploding out of the castle and streaming over the river. Everyone looked respectfully upwards. Each white flare dissolved into colored components which drifted into the dark. Frau Stempel sighed, *"Wie schön, wie wunderschön."* Schreiber and Traudis pressed closer to each other, and Stempel began talking into Schreiber's ear. "Fläche is a Latinist. Disgraced. Edited for years what turned out to be a very late forgery of Dion Cassius. The exposure killed his mother." Schreiber shifted nearer Traudis; the voice got louder. "Pilzmauer's a chemist. Discovered a substance which induces paranoiac states in normal people. Took it himself before he learned it was habit-forming. Half the year he's completely mad. Don't worry though. He's in a transitional stage now. See the notebook? He takes soundings on his lapsed condition." Against his inclination, Schreiber looked up and saw that Pilzmauer was writing furiously in a large notebook. Stempel had begun a sketch of Herr Schmigl when the fireworks ceased. He sat up, cuffed the children on the head, sent them to bed, and called for wine. "What an expensive, tedious display," he said.

"Horrifyingly beautiful," said Pilzmauer.

The Latinist intoned ten or twelve mournful lines to which everyone on the porch gave rigid attention.

"He has made Ovid's exile his own," said Herr Franck.

"Ovid," said Pilzmauer, "a man of moods."

"Ach," groaned Stempel, and he waved at the lighted castle and at the kayaks with Japanese lanterns in their prows down below in the Neckar. "This is not Germany, Herr Schreiber. Lights without purpose. That is French."

The two students excused themselves to walk along the river. "That is more German," cried Stempel to their backs, "the river watchers, the source seekers. Of course, the real Germany is finished."

He put his arm across Schreiber's knees and his palm on Traudis's. "*Nicht*, Fräulein? *Finito*, Benito, *nicht?*"

"Let us go down to the river, Herr Schreiber," said Traudis. "Everybody goes down after the Illuminations."

They bade a general "Good night" to the balcony and left, Stempel bombarding their backs with, "Even the exiled Germans feel the call of the source, *nicht*, Fläche?"

Hundreds of people walked along the river banks or sat on the grass. Every fifty or sixty yards stood a vendor of ice cream or sausages. "Germans at play," said Traudis, waving to the scene as they came to it from the hill.

"Quite pleasant," said Schreiber.

They bought chocolate ice bars and sat down in a small clearing on the banks across the river from the Old Armory. "And what do you think of this Stempel *Schwein?*" asked Traudis.

"I've known worse."

"Worse *Schwein?*"

"I don't know him well."

"Where did you live?" she asked.

"Connecticut."

"In Heidelberg, I mean."

"The Ritterhof."

"If you have kept the room, I should like to take baths there."

"Is that permitted?"

"Permitted? Whose water is it?" and she swept her arm from where the river came around at Neckargemünd all the way past the two bridges to the plain where the Neckar went out to meet the Rhine. The sweep finished with her hand on Schreiber's shoulder.

"You may certainly use the bath," he said. "I'll tell the clerk. Stempel told me there was a tub in the house."

"It is in his apartment," she said, "and the price is more than pfennigs, the *Schwein.*"

They got up and walked through the crowds. "People, people,

people," she complained. "How are you for a climb?" and she threw
her head back at the hill which rose way beyond Haus Stempel
von Gode.

"I'm quite short-winded," said Schreiber.

"It's an easy slope. The Philosophenweg. Very famous. Come on.
There's a classical amphitheater up there."

Schreiber looked at the hill which, in the dark did not seem high.
"All right," he said.

It proved, however, to be the longest climb he had ever taken,
one which, though never difficult from yard to yard, exhausted him
when they finally reached the amphitheater. He lay down on the top-
most of the fifty stone rows, his chest so constricted that he feared
an attack. None came, and with his breath he not only recovered
buoyancy, he felt actually heady and confident.

"Can you hear me?" came Traudis' whisper from what he thought
was next to him.

"Of course."

"Look. Down here," she called, and he looked. "On the stage."

"It's too dark," he said. "I'll come down."

For the next half hour they sported with the acoustics, sang,
yodeled, and growled. Schreiber recited the opening sentence of the
Declaration of Independence and Traudis did an imitation of Hitler.

"At Harvard," he said, "there is a sound-proof room."

"Not without interest," said Traudis.

"You can scream as loudly as you want, and you can't even hear
your own voice."

"Sufficiently horrible. What is the association?"

"I don't know," said Schreiber. "This reminded me of it. Both
make you feel shut off."

"Where?"

"Nowhere."

"Do you feel shut off?"

"Naturally not," he said. "It's the sensation."

She rolled her skirt up high and put her legs over his. They were
unshaven but well-shaped. "Explain this Germanic theorizing. I
shouldn't have brought you by the Philosophenweg."

Stroking her legs, he said, "Well, here you tend to exaggerate yourself, so you become conscious of yourself, so conscious that you think
of little else. That's like being shut off. In the other place, you cannot
reach anyone at all, not even yourself. After that, you asked me where
I was shut off, and, as I said, I meant it was only psychologically.
I'm too tired to talk any more German."

"Not too bad," said Traudis. "I can't even lie in English." She
bent over him. They began to make love, but were interrupted by
bursts of whooping and laughter which thundered around the dark
amphitheater. Schreiber put his hand to his heart.

"So my Fäustchen and Gretchen," came Stempel's voice, and by
a cut of moonlight they saw him walking over the stone rows followed by Pilzmauer and Fläche. "Pardon our manifestation, but
we had come to enjoy a more mysterious view and thought it was
best to warn you before it was too late to prevent your sharing it
with us. Come, let us look at the castle."

Behind him, Fläche muttered enviously, *"Dulce est dissipere in
loco."*

"Let's get out quickly, Herr Schreiber," whispered Traudis, the
sounds echoing in the hills.

"I have my little car, Fräulein," said Stempel trying to find them
as they moved away. "Let me save you a few steps."

Traudis strode off with Schreiber. At the top of the theater, she
turned and, with all her power, shrieked, *"Schwein."* Schreiber put
his fingers in his ears, but Traudis pulled them out and took him
off down the hill.

5

They went to Das Schwarze Loch, an ill-lit, tiny tavern on the
Unterestrasse. It was arranged like an angular pretzel` so that the

tables were hidden from each other and from the entrance. A weary-looking dwarf played the violin, and now and then the hidden patrons sang along. Traudis led Schreiber to a table where Schmigl and Franck sat drinking beer. They rose and shook hands.

"Glad you came, Herr Schreiber," said Schmigl.

"You're somewhat friendlier than your predecessor, Mr. Harden," said Franck. "Some beer?"

"Please," said Schreiber.

Franck rapped his glass with a spoon, and a waiter appeared. "Four beers," he said. "That is unless you prefer some wine, Herr Schreiber. The few occasions when Mr. Harden did join us, he was kind enough to order wine. They have an excellent *Schäumenden Assmanshausen* in the cellar."

"A bottle then please," said Schreiber.

The three Germans beamed, and so did Schreiber who enjoyed the ease with which he had brought such pleasure.

"You work for the army here?" asked Schmigl.

"He has consented to let us use his bath in the Ritterhof," said Traudis.

"Very kind, Herr Schreiber," said Franck. "Dr. Stempel offers less than ten centimeters of hot water in the tub, and then orders you out so that he can use the water himself while it retains some heat."

"A *Schwein*," said Schreiber.

"One learns quickly," said Schmigl.

The wine came and was drunk with remarkable rapidity. Schreiber tapped his glass with a spoon. "Perhaps we could order two more now," he put to them, and, as there was no demurrer, he nodded confirmation to the waiter.

"Are you a bachelor, Herr Schreiber?" asked Schmigl.

"I'm recently divorced," said Schreiber.

"Children?" continued Schmigl.

"Child."

"Of what sex may I ask?"

"Female," said Schreiber.

"Ah, I'm so sorry," said Schmigl.

This response disturbed Schreiber enough so that for a moment he conjured up a tender thought of Valerie, and remembering the pigtails, which had usually struck him as the affectation of an innocence she did not possess, he thought of them now as pitiable reminders of the fatherless state to which he had abandoned her. A rich sense of guilt, soaked in the wine and joined with the other sensations of the evening, made him almost dissolve with melancholy pleasure.

"Girls are fine," he said.

"Of course," said Traudis. "Let us stop examining Herr Schreiber."

"I must apologize for my rudeness, Herr Schreiber," said Schmigl.

"Not at all, Herr Schmigl. I was a student not so long ago myself, and I still possess a remnant of the spirit of inquiry."

The three Germans seemed astonished by this, and Schreiber was equally so that they should be. "Yes," he continued, "less than fifteen years ago, no, seventeen, I was in law school and, though much has passed since that time, I feel very close to those years."

"Have you been a soldier in the interim, Herr Schreiber?" asked Franck respectfully.

"A captain in the Army," said Schreiber. "I spent a short time in Mainz. After the war," he put in apologetically.

"Oh so," said Schmigl. "An occupier."

"There is something military in your bearing," said Traudis, rubbing her leg against his.

"Have you read *Servitude et Grandeur Militaires?*" asked Schmigl.

"No," said Schreiber, smiling at Traudis's compliment and further acknowledging it by putting his hand on her knee.

"Have you read Friedrich Meinecke on Moltke?" pursued Schmigl.

"My college speciality was economics," said Schreiber in explanation.

"Meinecke," said Traudis, as if crushing a roach. The name un-

locked a torrent of discourse which was so bulky with endless forma-
tions and diverse allusions that Schreiber could not follow it. He
concentrated on the music. The dwarf was playing *"Ich Hab' Mein
Herz in Heidelberg Verloren"* for the third time and a rapturously
melancholic voice contributed lyrics from one of the hidden booths.
The song seemed to liberate Schreiber from the constriction which,
in the amphitheater, had appeared to him an incipient heart attack.
Now, assimilating the forces released in his body by the climb,
mingling them with the deft misery of the violin and the aggravated
disputing at the table, Schreiber felt a strength surging into his blood
which he realized was the rejuvenation he'd hoped would come
from his return to Europe.

When the dwarf came up to the table with a cigar box, Schreiber
dropped five one mark coins into it one after the other, his own
smile matching the increasing breadth of the dwarf's. From then
on, the music came from their table, and Schreiber continued to
make the dwarf and himself happy with his largesse. At two o'clock,
when they finally left, he acknowledged the dwarf's bow with an
even more profound one of his own.

6

When Schreiber awoke the next morning, the sense of heightened
pleasure was still with him, and he endeavored to prolong it as he
dressed for work by imagining the other nights he would have in
which to continue his absorption in the good, new life.

He was, however, to be disappointed. What the night of the Illuminations provided, it also exhausted.

The next evening he rushed home from work to knock at Traudis'
door. "But what do you want?" she asked, peering into the hall.

"Dinner, I thought. With you, I hope."

"But I'm working," she said. "Look," and she opened the door
so that he could see a pile of books and manuscripts on the desk. "I
can't celebrate every evening of my life."

"I'm sorry," said Schreiber. "Forgive me for disturbing you. Perhaps I can try tomorrow."

But it was the same then. He spent the evening writing an account of the night of the Illuminations in his notebook and listing the books Schmigl and Franck had mentioned in the *Stube*.

The night after that, he didn't even try knocking at Traudis's door, yet when he returned to his room after dinner, there she was. "Surprise," she said. "Shall we go to dinner?"

"Of course," said Schreiber without hesitation, and he took her to the restaurant in the Palatinate Museum courtyard. Traudis was too absorbed in her steak to notice his lack of appetite. When they got back to Haus Stempel von Gode, she stayed in his room till dawn. Before she went upstairs, she said, "May I borrow forty marks from you? I'd almost forgotten that the rent was due today."

"Of course," he said, but he was depressed about it all day, and he did not go home after work. "I understand," he told himself, but he understood also that the understanding was insufficient to account for his pain.

The next day he thought that it was just as well. "I've got to learn to keep a perspective on these things. It's the second time women have tripped me up. The third if I count Florence."

Such resolve comforted him for a time, but, over the months, as Traudis' eccentric behavior assumed a pattern—for each month she stayed with him twice and borrowed the rent money once—he came to be less and less attached to her and to the life with which he had so happily associated her.

Stempel's increasingly arrogant intimacy disturbed him also. As they passed each other in the hall, Stempel would remark, "Still reaping the benefits of German life, Herr Schreiber?" and chuckling, he would leap up the stairs.

The old Frau Stempel von Gode was even worse. She usually averted her head when he passed near her; once, as he ascended the hill toward the house, he saw her watching him from the second floor balcony and then, as he rounded the final turn, she released a bloody spume into the weeds under her window and inclined her white head to him as he passed.

As for Schmigl and Franck, they continued to be friendly. One evening he went to Das Schwarze Loch with them, but, although he ordered quantities of sparkling *Assmanshausen,* and although they included him in nearly all their talk, he found that without Traudis to give point to them, they seemed dull and crude.

That they used the bath he knew. The clerk at the Ritter threw up his hands every time Schreiber went in for his mail. "What have you up there, Herr Schreiber? A seminar or a house of pleasure? The red-headed boy is up there for the third time this month."

Schreiber knew no red-headed boy, and the presence of one in his bathtub determined him to speak to Traudis about the whole arrangement. When he did, however, she countered fiercely, "What do you want us to do, Caesar? Stink?" He was obliged to apologize.

All in all, it was unsatisfactory, and when in March Frau Stempel went off with her children to visit her parents in Sweden and Traudis moved into Stempel's apartment as housekeeper, he decided to move back to the Ritter.

When he queried Traudis about her move, she replied, "It's cheaper. Did you think I liked borrowing the rent from you?"

"I understand," he said. "One cannot always afford to be what one is."

Traudis interpreted this remark in harder fashion than it was intended. "All occupation costs will be met," she replied. "You will have your money this week."

Schreiber did not wait to get it, but moved back to the Ritter the next day and joined the circle which his work opened to him. His office friends were pleased at his comfortable if peripheral presence at their parties and expeditions, and except for occasional playful allusions to his "completed study," they were so pleasant to him that he did not regret his decision to return.

About two months after his return though, the loneliness which he had not felt for a long time came upon him. He felt an enormous desire to see Traudis. He dialed the house number and waited breathlessly until he heard Stempel's distinct voice on the other end. He dropped the receiver back on the hook.

As he stood there thinking, he found himself humming a tune. It was "I've Got a Lovely Bunch of Coconuts."

"My God," he said, 'No," but before he knew it, he was looking up and then dialing Gladys Culley's number.

"Schreiber?" came her voice. "Max? GS-13? Intelligence?"

"That's right," he said. "Divorced."

"What do you know. I was afraid you'd been transferred over my head, Maxie."

"After all," laughed Schreiber uneasily as the taxi brought him over to Dornröschenstrasse. "Where there's static, there might be music."

CHAPTER TWO

I

Baggish went to Germany via Basel so that he could exchange his money at the favorable rates of the Swiss money market. There was, as well, a casualness about his itinerary which he considered in terms of the triangle the trip covered—Paris to Basel to Heidelberg—and enjoyed as a painter enjoys his insights into facial geometry. For Baggish, indirection was direction, *reculer pour mieux sauter;* not only the four cents profit on the dollar (via French francs to Swiss francs to German marks) but the no less realizable "money in the pockets" of seeing two more countries.

The trip began badly. At a *brasserie* opposite the Gare de l'Est, he had an altercation with a waiter about the number of *croissants* he'd eaten. The waiter numbered the saucers piled in front of Baggish who countered by slamming his fist on the table and bouncing three of them to the ground where they smashed into bits. Satanic with joy, the waiter demanded reparation. Baggish tossed the price of a Metro ticket into his coffee cup, took up his suitcases and crossed the street. The waiter followed, grinding out a crescendo of demands which did not cease until Baggish disappeared around a luggage dolly. "Lousy American pig," he heard, and muttered, "A race of petty thieves."

Half an hour early, he went from compartment to compartment
looking in vain for a seat that had no Reserve placard on it. In a
third class compartment he unpinned six of the eight placards from
the seats, tore them up and flushed them down the toilet at the end
of the car. The five other unreserved seats were taken almost immediately.

Baggish was the first to be displaced. An officious-looking young
man asked to see his tickets, and then showed him his reservation
stub. Baggish stuttered that he parleyed no français. The young man
gritted his teeth and said in English, "I look the agent to displace
you, mister."

"Goddam legalistic swine," said Baggish and moved into the
corridor.

For two hours he stood jammed up against a door which every
ten minutes opened to unleash a draught of icy air into his sinuses.
Phlegm dripped into the back of his throat; he swallowed fire. Only
a superstitious fear of interrupting his triumphant journey stopped
him from getting off the train at the first stop.

Outside Chaumont he got a seat. A man who looked like a seven-
foot corkscrew with a black beard unwound himself from a compartment and bumped against Baggish as he opened the door. "I
hope you will forgive my jolting you," he said very loudly, in French,
"but you were obstructing the proper egress."

"Excuse me," said Baggish.

"Very well," said the man, after weighing the request. "You may
use my seat while I nourish myself. Try not to soil it."

"Thank you very much," said Baggish, too dazed with relief to
bother about the form of the invitation. He sank back into a window-
seat opposite a gray-haired woman and a boy of fifteen. There were
five other people in the compartment, a corpulent man in dirty
tweeds, three young women in kerchiefs who chewed chunks of
bread ripped from *batârd* loaves and drank almost black wine from
an unlabeled bottle they passed each other, and an old woman knit-
ting at what looked like a lapdog's mitten.

Just before they reached Langres, the bearded twister stepped back into the compartment, on and over people's feet. Baggish rose to leave, but the lady with the canine garment put it into a paper sack and said, "I descend here, Monsieur." Baggish took her place next to the gray-haired woman just as she asked the tall man—using the familiar pronoun—if he had eaten well. "Fish-turds," was the response to this. The three young women collapsed in laughter, discharging particles of winey bread into the compartment. The twister stretched his legs across so that the woman and boy had to cramp theirs. The three eaters got off at the stop after Langres, and the twister hoisted his legs up on the seat and rested his head against the window sill. Now and then he screwed around, looked out the window, and jabbed the boy in the ribs with a forefinger, *"Regarde la jolie vue,* Blaise." The boy would nod coldly and turn to look.

The man in tweeds took a book from his pocket. Baggish peered at it, and saw, with surprise, that it was in Greek. The man read for a few minutes, and then further surprised Baggish by looking into his face as if he were catching a pickpocket. "Don't stare so rudely," he said. He was English.

"What?" exclaimed Baggish.

"Don't you know Greek?" the man continued.

"Only the alphabet," said Baggish.

"That's something. American?"

"Yes," said Baggish, "and you?"

"Not that it's your business," said the man, "but I have two passports, British and Swiss. One, a nation of arrogant spivs and puling Teddy boys, the other a tribe of muffin-headed money-changers." Baggish wondered if the man's violence camouflaged importance or flight.

"People don't know Greek, and they don't know war, and they don't know love," the man said slowly, as if he were translating from the book.

"I'm afraid that goes for me," said Baggish. "Or most of it," he added, with some pride in his recent accomplishment.

Here the twister put in with, *"Menin aide thea, Pelayadiu Akileus.
Oulomenon, e myri Achaios alge etheken, Pollas—"*

"The pedagogue's accent," said the tweed man in French.

"You may speak English," said the other.

"My husband is an American," said the gray-haired woman with
a French accent. "We have spent the war and its aftermath in
America."

"Cowards," muttered the Swiss Briton, but the twister's voice
overrode him. "You have intuited correctly about the profession I
follow. I am an instructor in the old tongues of France, Spain, and
the Lowlands. Allow me," he said, and drew from the pocket of his
flannel shirt a card which he flashed first before the man and then
before Baggish. It read "Artulphe Pierre Jean-Baptiste de Faillance."
"Virginia Huguenot," he explained.

"My name is Thompson," said the other. "Malcolm Thompson."
This was said to the descendent of the Huguenots as if the contrast
between the simplicity of the name and its true greatness would over-
whelm him.

"A plain, but not necessarily ignoble name," said Faillance.

A short silence followed which was broken by the gray-haired
woman. "This is the first time that I can remember being in a
European compartment in which everyone spoke English."

"Of a sort," added Thompson. "The boy knows the language?"

"English, French, Spanish, Italian, Dutch, and, I hope, German.
Kannst du noch Deutsch sprechen, Blaise?" asked Faillance, placing
his head so close to his son's that the latter's face was sprayed by
beard.

"No," said Blaise.

"And who are you?" asked Thompson of Baggish.

"My name is Theodore Baggish. I've been a student until recently
at Yale University, a school in the state of Connecticut."

"I am aware of the location," said Thompson.

"American universities," said the Huguenot with a grimace so profound it seemed part of his ruined back. "Indistinguishable traps for
the spirit and intellect."

"I am more loyal than perhaps I should be," conceded Baggish. "My husband too has the trait of loyalty," said the woman. "Do you see his poor back?" and she ran a hand across the twisting length. "From the war. It was one of three such wounds in the United States Armed Forces. My husband was studied at Walter Reed Hospital for nineteen months."

"Maman, je t'en prie," said Blaise.

"I agree, *Maman,"* said the injured one.

"I too, Madame," said Thompson. "Here, however, your husband would have done better to have occupied one of the seats reserved for the *Mutilés de Guerre* at the end of the car. It would have helped relieve the congestion which troubles us all."

This brought an even longer silence which Baggish broke by asking Thompson what his profession was.

"The well-nurtured never pry," said Thompson. "Nor do the intelligent identify persons by their professions; or, if so, the persons are not worth identifying."

"You are a rude man, Mr. Thompson," said Faillance.

After another wordless interval, Thompson said, "We are strangely uncongenial. Why is it, I wonder? We are united by a common tongue, but divided by subcutaneous instincts. I have never in my life taken so immediate dislike to casual strangers." With this, he put his book into his pocket, rose, reached for his valise, and, stepping on and over feet, left the compartment.

"Extraordinaire," said Mme. Faillance.

A moment later, Faillance said, *"Regarde le beau fleuve,* Blaise."

"Laisse-moi, Papa," said Blaise and went into the corridor.

"A brutal world," said Faillance sadly. He removed his shoes and socks, put two monstrous feet on his wife's lap and went to sleep.

2

That evening, in Basel, Baggish followed the Faillances from the station to a hotel a block away. When Faillance noticed Baggish following them into the lobby, he said, "The hotel's getting lousy with Americans. Let's cross the street." He passed by Baggish without nodding.

Baggish registered, washed up, and then had dinner in the hotel restaurant. Afterwards he walked up to the cathedral and looked out over the river. The moon canted off the steeple and made silk of the Rhine. Alone on the parapets, Baggish let himself dissolve into the loveliness of the river and its historical effluvia. Then he threw in a rock and found himself wishing that it contained every man and woman he had seen that day with the exception of Blaise. "Lice," he said out loud. His dissolution had been temporary. He shook a fist at the river, and walked back toward the hotel. At a Bücherei, he bought a German-English dictionary and a German grammar, and before he went to sleep that night, he had spent three hours in tigerish study.

The next morning he left Basel with fifty-two hundred marks, thirteen of which he carried in his wallet and the rest in two envelopes fastened to the inside of his underpants with Scotch Tape. It was an unnecessary precaution. He wore a sweater, a dirty pair of khakis, and replied to the official question "How many marks are you carrying?" by saying, "Sixteen, I think," and then opened his wallet to count. He was waved through the barrier with a smile.

The only other person in his compartment was a young German salesman who talked with him in a difficult mixture of English and German and taught him the words for "train," "station," "seat," "sky," and the like. "A race of pedagogues," said Baggish as his instructor got out at Freiburg.

Baggish could not get to sleep because of the cold, the wooden seats, and his worry that he would miss the Heidelberg station. He went into the corridor three times to ask the conductor when Heidelberg came, and understood only the third time when the conductor raised three fingers which looked like stunted sweet potatoes, and said slowly, "Karlsruhe, Bruchsal, Heidelberg. *Eins, zwei, drei. Dritter Aufenthalt.* Karlsruhe, Bruchsal, Heidelberg," and the three potatoes waved back and forth under Baggish's nose. "*Dreisig*

Minuten." Baggish responded with, *"Danke schön,* craphead."
It was eleven-thirty when he got off at Heidelberg. He walked
down a long, open platform, and handed his ticket to the official.
"Da drüben," said the latter pointing to another exit five feet away.
"Dieser ist für Amis reserviert." Baggish handed his ticket at the
other exit and came out into a large semicircle made by trolley car
tracks which turned off a large avenue so filled with cars, buses, and
taxis that Baggish's cameo image of the old German university
town turned to dust on the spot.

In the station, a sign over an enclosure read U.S. TAXI SERVICE. Baggish walked up to it; a man came out of the enclosure, took his bags
and put them into a taxi. "Do you know a good rooming house
around?" asked Baggish, following him. The man said, *"Verstehe
nicht,"* and motioned him over to a young fellow behind a dispatcher's desk, who got up when Baggish approached. "What can I
do for you, sir?" he asked in a heavy accent.

"I'm looking for a room."

"The taxi will take you to the Billeting Office, sir, although if you
prefer to walk, it's only down the street a few blocks."

"Are all Americans entitled to the services of the Billeting Office?"
asked Baggish, foreseeing a useless trip.

"I see," said the young man, and he took off his dispatcher's cap.
"You have no AGO card?"

"I have a visa from the Tri-Partite Commission for the Western
Zone of Germany. Is that what you mean?"

"No," said the dispatcher. "If you have no AGO card, it means that
you're neither a Department of the Army nor HICOG civilian, nor
a soldier, and so not entitled to our taxis. Are you a student?"

"I hope to be," said Baggish, thinking that this was better than
nothing.

"But you don't speak German," said the dispatcher. "How will
you follow lectures if you don't know the language they're conducted
in? German still has its uses here, you know."

"Perhaps for a while," said Baggish coldly. "Kindly inform me what service I can employ to find myself a room in Heidelberg."

"Certainly, sir," said the dispatcher. "Try the *Auslandsabteilung* at the University."

"What's that?"

"The Foreigners' Section. I'll write it down for you," and he wrote on the back of a dispatch card. "Take one of the German taxis on the far row over there. Or you can take the trolley car. It's only twenty pfennigs, and it takes you right to the University."

"*Danke schön,*" said Baggish. "I'll taxi." The German bowed him out. "It's the knees or the throat for these gutter rats," adapted Baggish. He showed the dispatch card to the driver of the first German taxi, told him to fetch his bags from the pavement, and then settled back for the ride down a narrow street filled with blue trolley cars and army buses. At a fountain in a square, the driver took a right turn, parked in front of an old stone building, and said, "*Die Universität, Auslandsabteilung* up," and he pointed up. "One mark, sixty."

Baggish handed him one mark and sixty pfennigs and entered the building. It seemed incredible to him that the most famous of German universities should look like this, one old brownstone and one new white building across the way, surrounded by the standard stores of a European town. "Yale wouldn't use this place for garbage disposal," muttered Baggish.

Inside, Baggish inquired of a young man in the lobby the whereabouts of the Foreign Student's Office.

"Second story," said the young man, almost without accent. "That's three flights up for us, you know."

"Certainly," said Baggish, and he walked up a rather grand marble staircase. At the third story his arms were drenched with weary pain, and he felt the cold which had assaulted his sinuses in the Paris train move in again. He knocked at a door whose sign duplicated the letters on the dispatch card, and a woman's voice called, "*Herein.*"

It was a large office with two desks and a few chairs in it. A girl at one of the desks asked Baggish in English whether she could help him.

"In every way," he began to say, but said instead, "I'm new in Heidelberg." He put his bags down and sat in a chair in front of the desk. "May I?"

"Please," she said with a smile.

"I'm planning to enroll in the University, but first I need a room. Do you by any chance have a list I might consult?"

"We do," she said. "Have you been admitted to the University?"

"I haven't applied. I trust there won't be any difficulties."

"Undoubtedly not. Do you have your papers?"

"In America," said Baggish. "If you mean my diploma and papers of that sort."

"You can send for them," she said, "and meanwhile take some courses for foreigners. The next term doesn't begin till April, but you should get used to hearing German first anyway. Do you know some?"

"Almost none, but I learn quickly with sympathetic instruction."

"Good," she said abruptly. "Let's find you a room."

She began leafing through cards in a drawer on her desk. "There aren't a great many this time of year. The living situation in Heidelberg is very serious. The population has doubled since the war."

"I hate to add to the difficulty," said Baggish.

"That's all right," she said. "Here's a place. An American civilian worker just moved out a few days ago. It's in a nice house just across the river. Used to be the home of a Classics Professor Ordinarius. Von Gode. The mother and grandson run it now. I'll ring up."

"Fine," said Baggish. "I like living near rivers."

She telephoned, and spoke at length in German, her eyes running up and down Baggish as she talked. "Such questions they ask," she said, hanging up. " 'Are you respectable looking?' "

"What was your response to that?" asked Baggish amorously.

"I said they'd have to look you over themselves," and she wrote down the address and gave him directions. "You can come back if you need help." She stood up, held her arm straight out, and pumped his hand three times. *"Auf Wiedersehen."*

"Auf Wiedersehen," said Baggish.

"Ah, ha," she said. "You have a not unpleasant accent."

"Thank you," said Baggish, adding to himself as he opened the door, "Frosted old fish-turd."

3

In the huge room with the two grand pianos, Baggish and Frau Stempel von Gode regarded each other with uncamouflaged dislike. The interrogatory formalities had been completed. "I don't much like your sort, Mr. Baggish," the old woman said reflectively. She spoke without her lisp. "But it is the burden of our times that nothing can be done about such feelings, at least in Germany." She spat a gob of bloody phlegm into a large red handkerchief.

"I regret your feelings, Frau von Gode. I cannot hide my own that we are uncongenial, but I take it that we will have little to do with each other. Money will be our sole bond."

"My son takes care of those details, Mr. Baggish. German women don't discuss money, don't handle it, don't think of it."

"Admirable delicacy," said Baggish. He bowed and left the room, leaving Frau von Gode a bit dismayed for she was relishing the interchange. Baggish went upstairs to Dr. Stempel's door.

It took but five minutes to get to the agreements. No wine was served. When Dr. Stempel proffered Baggish the two rental contracts, he signed both of them, put sixty marks down "on account," and moved in that afternoon. Two days later, when Stempel demanded the other forty marks for the month's rent, Baggish said, "Since I've deposited our sixty mark contract with the *Wohnungsamt,* I feel that it would be an act of dishonesty to pay you more."

Dr. Stempel understood little English, but this was clear to him. The blood left his face, he slapped his great forehead, and collapsed into the room's easy chair. Baggish went for a glass of water and returned to find Stempel erect and furious.

"Baggish, you are no gentleman." He shook a forefinger, which, in the act of shaking, became a fist. "We have the second contract also *unterschrieben,*" and he made a writing motion, "Pay or out."

Baggish looked coldly into his eyes. "You're either a clown or an imbecile. You get out and get out quickly. We have a contract, approved by the law, American and German. If you violate it, I shall have you arrested. If you produce the other contract, I will plead ignorance of German. Do you understand?" and he pointed to the door.

Stempel caught little of this, but he took in what Baggish intended he should, the truculence and threat. He went to the door, turned around and shouted, "This brings trouble. That I certify you."

"Do not certify me, Stempel," said Baggish quietly, and he narrowed his eyes à la Needle-Nose Labriola. "I'll call the M.P.s and have them haul you in. You're a spider, a predatory worm. Out! Son of a bitch!" He went into the small bedroom, closed the door and listened for Stempel slamming the other one. Then he smiled happily. "I'll knee them," he said. "I'll bring 'em to heel."

4

"May I help you?" the girl at the Allied Personnel Office asked Baggish the next morning.

"I'd like to apply for a job," said Baggish. The girl handed him a pile of forms like the ones he'd filled out in Paris. "Fill these out, leave them here, and come back tomorrow at nine."

"What are the chances?"

"Things are pretty slow, but you'll get something. Unless you got blots on the record. You don't happen to be an engineer?"

Baggish hesitated and said, "I probably have enough physics to get the certificate, but, no, I'm not an engineer."

"You could name your spot, France, Germany, Africa."

"I'm finished with science," said Baggish quietly.

"Just get into town?" asked the girl.

"Yes," said Baggish. "You been here long?"

"Two years," she said. "I've been trying to get something better, but it's tough when you're in Personnel. They clamp all the transfer regulations on you so they don't have to train someone new. I'm only a Five."

"You look pretty important to me," said Baggish honestly. "What's a Five?"

"A bottleneck. GS-5. Government Service Five, I think it stands for. Want to get some coffee? My name's Joan Poster. Call me Joan."

"Mine's Theodore, gift of God, but call me Ted."

"That what Theodore means? You should have known my Uncle Teddy. He was a gift from a horse's twot. How about that coffee?"

She got her purse, handed him her overcoat, leaned back against him as she put her arms through it, and led him around the corner to a little *Stube*. She spoke German to the waiter who knew and apparently liked her. They laughed at something and she shook a pudgy finger back and forth at him. *"Böse, böse, böse,"* she said.

"You speak German?" she asked Baggish as the waiter went off for their coffee and crullers.

"I'm learning," he said. "What does *'böse, böse, böse'* mean?"

" 'Naughty, naughty, naughty,' " she said. "I taught it in high school in St. Cloud, Minn. That's about what I came with."

"Why did you come?"

She smiled in a way which lightened the heaviness of her face, brought out the features, made her almost pretty. "I'm an opera bug, and where in the States can you see opera for fifty cents a night, or for any amount, as far as that goes?"

"I don't know," said Baggish. "I've never seen opera." He relished the lack of the article. "Does Heidelberg have any decent opera?"

"No, or rather, it's decent enough, but that's all. I've got a boy friend here in town." The waiter brought the coffee, slopping some of it into the saucers. Baggish emptied the overflow onto the floor. "German?" he asked.

"In a way," she said. "He's a Croat, but he's got a German passport." She hesitated, and then added as if just discovering the fact herself, "And manner." She dipped a cruller into her coffee and took a gross bite which wasn't half out of her mouth when she said, "He's an engineer. If he were an Ami, he'd be in clover. He's going to try in Yugoslavia this summer, as a German. They're offering foreign engineers a lot of money."

"You going too?"

"No. He's not going to stay—that is, unless they find out he's a Croat and keep him. We got to take the risk 'cause we need the money to get married."

"Don't you make enough?"

"Sure, but you can't be married to a German and make a dollar salary. I'm saving a little, but I'm tired of not being married. Besides," she said, finishing the cruller in one great gulp, "Something's happened."

Baggish nearly asked "What?" but said "That's tough," and blushed.

"I don't know," she said. "It's a way to get you to make up your mind. That's the danger of coming to Europe. It's a way of postponing decisions."

"For some," said Baggish. "Emerson said Americans go to Europe to be Americanized."

"What's the point of getting Americanized?"

"You're a goodish girl, Joannie."

"That may be too," she said, and pushed his nose with hers. "But good or bad, I got to get back pronto. We got a bitch named Culley in the office that watches our coffee breaks like a hawk."

Back in the office, another girl at a desk smaller than Joan's was watching over a middle-aged woman typing at a still smaller one in the corner. *"Halten Sie an, bitte,"* said the supervisor looking up from her watch. She scanned the woman's paper, and said, *"Das geht. Fünf-und-vierzig Wörter."*

"See," Joan said to Baggish, "We give out jobs every hour. Do you type?" and she pointed to the chair vacated by the successful applicant. Over the desk on the wall was a small blackboard to which was fixed a yellow sheet with a passage from the Military Code on it.

"Not well enough," said Baggish, regarding the code with a small shudder.

"Annamarie," said Joan. "This is Ted Baggish." She looked at Baggish to see if the nickname was all right. "This is Annamarie Bosco," said Joan.

"Hello," said Annamarie with a German accent. "You looking for a job too?"

"Yes."

"Always jobs for Americans."

"Isn't her name Italian?" Baggish asked Joan when Annamarie turned back to the woman.

"Her husband," said Joan. "He's a genius."

"And a *Schwein*," put in Annamarie, shaking hands with the woman who thanked her and left.

"He's a protégé of the philosopher Heidegger," said Joan.

"I know the name," said Baggish, who had seen it in a copy of *Time*.

"He was at our wedding," said Annamarie. "The only thing I have against him. Would you like to read the speech he composed for us? It's unpublished."

"I'd like to," said Baggish, "but I don't read much German yet."

"Don't learn it for this," said Annamarie. "We translate him into Italian."

"Why are you working here then?" asked Baggish. He was taken with Annamarie.

"That's what I ask my husband, but I haven't heard the answer. He's so great in the head you see. Are you a student?"

"I hope to be."

"You'll never make a woman happy."

"I've got to go now and try just that," he said. "I'll bring the forms back tomorrow." He shook hands, thanked them, and went off in a trolley car to the University.

"Good morning," said the girl in the *Auslandsabteilung*. "Did you get your room?"

"I want to thank you for helping me. It's a very nice room."

"Good," she said. "Now let's see what we can do about your matriculation."

"Something has come up," said Baggish.

"Pardon me?"

"I've been approached about taking a position with the Army here, and I'm afraid that I'll be persuaded to take it."

"Sounds important."

"Not really," said Baggish. "I foresee though the possibility of losing contact with Germany—I mean the real Germany—and even before I've come to know it. This is really why I'm coming to you. Will you be my friend? Will you let me go with you now and then to places of local interest? Am I being too forward?"

"You are being direct," she said, "but style has changed here since the war. Directness is permitted. I'll try to be your friend, and if it turns out that we are sympathetic, well, we shall see. We can have dinner together tonight if you wish."

"I would like nothing more," said Baggish, "but for a few days I'm going to be tied up by the Army. I'll call you tomorrow, however, and we'll arrange something at your convenience."

He got up, shook hands with her and left the office. In a second he was back. "I don't know your name or your telephone number," he said with a smile.

She wrote on a piece of paper and handed it to him. "Marianne von Rückhaller. 26871." "That's after six o'clock. During the day you know where I'll be."

Baggish went back to the Personnel Office and asked Joan if she would have dinner with him. The good will of the Personnel Office was indispensable to his immediate prospects.

"We'll be glad to have you home," she said, "but the rule is that guests bring their own food and liquor."

"I'll bring for you too," said Baggish, who though bearish by nature knew when the market called for bulls.

"You'll be all the more welcome then," said Joan.

5

In a week Joan steered Baggish to a job in the Staff Message Control as a cable editor, a post which sounded nobler than it was rated. The grade was GS-4. The biggest advantage of the job in Joan's opinion was the schedule—six days one week, four nights the next. "Three-sevenths of every odd week is yours," she told him. "You can see all of Europe."

"I'm not much on seeing for seeing's sake," he replied. "I've got enough to look at right here," and he goggled at her. He didn't know when she would steer him to something better.

For the moment though, he was content. "At least I'm launched." He thought of money coming in, and that had not happened for months. His salary was $2,850.00 plus room and maid service. Every week he could buy two cartons of cigarettes at the PX for two dollars and sell them for thirty-four marks. This would not only take care of a good part of his weekly food bill, but the pleasure of a transaction which involved a four hundred per cent untaxed capital gain made him pucker up for the Future's kiss.

Meanwhile he saw about his room. He was given a list of five choices, and looked at two of them before he came upon one in the Goldene Traube, a weary-looking hotel in the middle of the Hauptstrasse. He went up to inspect the room the evening after his first day at work. He took the key from the clerk who told him that Mr. Parsons, a C.I.C. investigator who shared the room, was upstairs. "But you'd better take a key," said the clerk with an odd smile. "He may be taking a bath."

Baggish took the key, went upstairs, opened the door, and saw on the bed near the window two naked men in an awkward embrace. After a few seconds in which four rabbity eyes fell before his unrelenting ones, Baggish shut the door behind him and said, "My name is Baggish. I have been assigned to this room." The young man who turned out to be Parsons leaped from the bed into a pair of pants. The other buried himself in the blankets.

"You've got us cold," said Parsons, and then he introduced himself.

"I suppose I have," said Baggish. "If I were the type, I wouldn't object, but it makes me nervous."

"I understand," said Parsons. *"Chacun à son goût."* He put on shoes, shirt, and tie.

"In a manner of speaking," said Baggish. "Is this a center for those who have *le gout?"*

"It has been sort of," said Parsons, hopefully.

Baggish walked over to the *lit d'amour* and peeked under the covers. "What's your name? Mine's Baggish."

A giggle from the blankets.

"That's all you'll get out of him," said Parsons. "He's a shy one."

"You know," said Baggish, letting the covers fall, "I might be induced to let you keep the rendezvous to yourselves."

"What would induce you?"

"Money," said Baggish, "And I don't mean a lot. Just enough to let me keep a room on the German economy. I know one I can have for a hundred and fifty marks a month."

Parsons raised the covers and held a whispered conference with his friend. Then he straightened up, took three bills from his wallet, and said, "Here's the first two installments. You're an angel, Baggish. If there's ever anything I can do for you, come see me. I'm with C.I.C."

"Useful," said Baggish. "I'll be by here now and then, but in case I miss you, you can mail me the money. I'll be in the Directory in a couple of days. I've just come." He walked to the door, then turned around. "I might want to take baths here. However, I'll always give you fair warning."

"Swell," said Parsons. "You're a good boy. If you ever want a ride yourself, just drop up without warning."

Baggish nodded and left. He walked to the Bristol and told the desk sergeant that he'd chosen the room at the Goldene Traube.

"You must like the sound of trolley cars," said the sergeant.

"Makes me think of home," said Baggish, and he signed for the key.

"No bitches after ten-thirty, laddie."

"I turn into smoke at ten-thirty."

"You're a funny one."

"I'm not one at all," said Baggish.

He jogged down the Hauptstrasse swallowing the cold air with a Spartan's harsh pleasure, stopped in the middle of the old bridge, breathing hard, and leaned on the rail. Lights bubbled along both sides of the river. "Who knows?" he told himself. "Heidelberg, Rome, Punksburg. When the sap's rising, boom."

PART FOUR

CHAPTER ONE

I

Mr. Hoover came to work on the night shift carrying a large bag of groceries, potato chips, ham sandwiches, peanut butter crackers, Hostell Cup Cakes, Mounds Bars, and two quarts of milk. "I eats to ease the fatigue," he explained to Baggish. "That's why I likes this night work; no one mind whever you eating or not."

Baggish disliked the night shift, but disliked the day shift more, and he added his preference to Hoover's.

"I feel better anyway at night," said Hoover. "Less people snooping around." A savage grunt came from the machine and a tube popped into the basket. "I'll take it," said Hoover. He got up in sections, he was so lanky and awkwardly angled, and no matter how neatly he dressed—he always wore coat, tie, and fedora to work—he looked as if he'd just been assembled from an erector set. He walked past the rows of polygraphs and typists, picked up the tube, took out the message, stamped it in the clock, initialed it, and sent the tube back through the shaft.

Mr. Ferris, the senior editor, stuck his head out of the Coke Room where he was working out the results of the office baseball pool, and asked if they needed any help.

"No," said Hoover, but Ferris came out anyway because the Night

Captain asked if he'd bring him a Coke. Ferris took the nickel's worth of scrip from the railing in front of the Inspection Desk and came over with the Pool Sheet. "Korea in yet?" he asked. This was the daily twenty page account of the minutiae of the new war, and the editors worked at least an hour on it, writing out the abbreviations, correcting the transmission errors, and checking unlikely events against material in the files. The first thing the night editors did when they came at six was to check the logbook to see if it had come in on one of the other shifts, and, if not, they tried outguessing it by taking their coffee time when they thought it might come in. Ferris had considered making book on it.

"No," said Baggish to Ferris, "It hasn't."

"I don't see nuffin wrong wiv it except its being boring," said Hoover.

"That's it," said Baggish. He took some of Hoover's potato chips, held them in his mouth until the salt crispness dissolved, leaving lard like a legacy of disgust for his gums. He savored it a moment and then spat it into a basket full of exhausted carbon paper. "That's it on the nose."

Mr. Hoover went for his coffee break at ten-thirty. Ten minutes later the Korean cable shot into the basket. Ferris tossed it to Baggish and went back to finish up the pool.

Baggish was halfway through when Hoover returned and volunteered to take over. "No thanks," said Baggish. "Maybe if I suffer a little, I'll get lucky in the pool."

But he didn't have any luck with the pool, and the cable took an hour-and-a-half to do, with Hoover peering over to tell him that "AD" was "ammunition dump" and had to be spelled out: the tubes kept shooting down the shafts, the electric typewriters clicked away, the polygraphs groaned on their rounds, the soldiers griped, and Baggish stewed with the misery of marching in place. He looked up at Hoover's mahogany cheeks and saw in them the walls of his own servitude. "The cable's mine, Hoover," he said. "You go have you a Coca Cola."

2

Once or twice a week Schreiber would descend—and he always thought of it in this fashion—to Dornröschenstrasse for an evening with Gladys Culley. These evenings centered about food; the hesitations, jockeyings, and mindless springs reserved, and, perhaps, biologically developed for the generic passion, were employed here around cuisine. Conversation about any other matter was tributary, stuttering, suspenseful; fulfillment was the wordless—though not soundless—immolation in meat and vegetable, sauce, fish, fruit, and wine. Sometimes they went out; mostly they ate at Gladys's. They both cooked, hoarding their surprises, breaking silence only to ask for implements or spices. The meals themselves lasted a couple of hours, and when they were over, the evening was over, and Schreiber would walk home, the guilt of satiety oppressing him more than his swelling bulk. Back in the Ritter, he noted the menus in his journal, starring the successful dishes.

It continued this way for a couple of months. Then the strain of unverbalized *gourmandisme* began to tell on them both. They became irritable, carping, unhappy. Gladys decided to vary the program by inviting friends, or rather, people who would come, her subordinates in the Personnel Office. The first two such diversions were comparatively successful. Schreiber and Gladys lost themselves in the drama of cooking for others, for a deadline, and, above all, for critical comment, constrained as it was by hunger, courtesy, and fear. These dinners lasted for three hours, the waste spaces being filled by fulsome praise and modest disclaimers, distant, always favorable comparisons, and, occasionally, vulgar reminiscing or boasting, impurities which were soon filtered by the disapproving silence of the hostess and—for this was Schreiber's announced role —host.

The third occasion took place on a hot June night. The guests were Annamarie and Signor Bosco, Joan Poster and Baggish. Anna-

marie was the only German to whom Gladys did not privately refer
as "Krauthead"; such a Culleyism explained why Joan's friend (for
Yugoslavians, indeed, any non-Latin people between the Rhine and
Outer Mongolia were similarly classified) was not there, and why,
instead, she brought Baggish. Gladys insisted on escorts; it affirmed
her own possession of Schreiber.

For Baggish, the invitation meant not only a free meal but the possibility that Mrs. Culley, a "power in Personnel," according to Joan,
might help him latch onto something big. Joan had told him about
a number of jobs, but despite fierce sorties on his part, none had
worked out: first he had written trial radio scripts for PIO, then
publicity for the Quartermaster Corps and finally he revealed to
Personnel that he had run a large grocery store in Providence with
the hope of snaring the PX in Fulda. The best that happened was
that in each case he enjoyed a week or ten days of suspense in which
he made plans for exploiting each of these jobs by fantastic extrap-
olations of their functions, selling PX items to the Germans on a
massive scale, and converting the marks into goods which would be
sold in the PX to GIs; planting publicity items in Stateside newspapers for fees; making tie-ups with European food salesmen who
wanted to get army contracts. Along with daydreams, he learned
German from Marianne von Rückhaller and his neighbor, Traudis
Bretzka; got to know them and their friends; and, each month, collected his salary with a tender avidity which almost mollified his
disappointments.

At Gladys's the first hour passed pleasantly enough. Schreiber
and Gladys "prepared" in the kitchen, and the guests drank sherry
in the living room. "Highballs kill the taste buds," said Gladys, handing the unopened sherry bottle and a corkscrew to Joan. Signor
Bosco said that he found this a delightfully amusing notion, but
happily, he liked sherry.

"We won't be a minute," Gladys had said, and then had disappeared for fifty. For most of these, Signor Bosco discoursed in German, French, and English about one of his unpublished works, a

discussion of the symposium as a literary form and social occasion from Plato and the Last Supper to—with some barbed wit—the present occasion. Without dropping a beat he shifted to his as-yet-unpublished critique of Croce's critique of Hegel, and his reply to Croce's reply to the criticism delivered in "a personal encounter in Bari" before "the *derniers* hostilities." Baggish had heard some of this before, but he found Bosco a splendid talker, and he liked linguistic practice. Annamarie was less enchanted, but she and Joan were moving toward that decent portion of insensibility toward which sherry and their inclination conducted them. It served until Gladys summoned them to the dinette where the six of them huddled over a small oval table in the center of which was a huge leg of lamb.

"But how distressing," said Signor Bosco.

"Excuse me," said Gladys.

"Is something missing?" asked Schreiber.

"It's Friday, isn't it?" said Bosco. "Ah well, Annamarie and I will content ourselves with the greenery."

Annamarie started to inquire about the sudden change in their religious practices, but broke off with a gasp at a vicious kick in the shins.

"I didn't know—" Joan started, but retired under a frightened look from Annamarie.

"You Catholics?" asked Gladys.

"We are," said Signor Bosco. "I take it that you are not or have lapsed. Don't let our medievalism distress you. Eat away and rejoice yourselves."

"Well, I suppose that would be the thing to do," said Schreiber, and he began to fill his plate. It was every man for himself at Gladys's.

"You could have let me know about this, Annamarie," said Gladys, wheeling her head like a gun turret and pointing the cannon at her subordinate's forehead.

"Perhaps," said Signor Bosco, "but I assumed that my spouse thought that the knowledge that Italians and Catholics are one and the same was traditional, a matter of common knowledge to all the heirs of Western culture. You are a Westerner, are you not, Mrs. Culley?"

"I most certainly am not," said Gladys precisely. "I'm a Midwesterner, from Chicago."

"Ah so," said Signor Bosco. "I was not certain of your provenience. There are certain aspects of your physiognomy which might pass, I think, for—"

Here, while Gladys Culley gripped the table to brace for the rare insult direct, while Schreiber held up his knife and fork in horrific silence, and while Annamarie and Joan trembled on the edge of an awful scene, Baggish leaned across for the roast and spilled Signor Bosco's glass of wine into his lap.

"Ah, my dear Signor Bosco," he boomed. "Will you forgive me?" He sprang from his chair and rushed to Bosco, dipped his handkerchief into a tureen of gravy and began rubbing at the streaks in Bosco's trousers. "What am I doing to you now?" he cried. Bosco exploded. Baggish recoiled, hit the table and bounced back knocking Bosco against the wall.

In the subsequent fracas, Bosco abandoned the international approach for a series of unmusical imprecations in his native tongue. "*A casa*," he yelled to his wife, and gripping her wrist, he dragged her out of the apartment. "Chicago thugs," they heard him yelling from the street.

Joan Poster followed, and, as Baggish turned to follow her, Schreiber took his arm and said, "Thank you Mr. Baggish. You were admirable."

"I thought it best, Mr. Schreiber," said Baggish. "I'm sorry it broke up the lovely dinner, and I hope we'll see each other again."

"Yes," said Schreiber, "and don't worry about the dinner. Good night."

That evening Gladys and Schreiber ate no more. It was, in fact, the last of their dinners, and for Schreiber, walking home an hour later in the spring air unencumbered by pounds of food churning in his stomach, the fiasco seemed the best way out. He saw Gladys the next week for lunch, and she spent this in weepy recapitulation of the disaster. Then they went their separate ways by mutual, if unexpressed, agreement.

For Gladys, the break with Schreiber was the end of her romantic hopes; in the manner of a jilted Spanish woman, she gave herself over to an isolation which, though in the world of affairs, was as desolate as that of a Carmelite.

3

Baggish saved the surprise that he was Schreiber's successor at Haus Stempel von Gode for their second meeting which took place three days after Gladys's dinner. It was three days because Baggish did not want to seem to be pressing Schreiber, yet did want to be remembered as the savior of whatever was salvageable that night. With that pure instinct for opportunity which, in the eyes of those who lack it, is usually called luck, Baggish saw, or rather, at this stage, felt, that Schreiber was a strait through which he would pass to his wide prospect. The feeling was, of course, an educated one; there was evidence to support it, although the evidence was far less than that on which non-Baggishes would proceed. The evidence, most of which came from Joan Poster, consisted of Schreiber's position as Chief Analyst of an Intelligence Section, his apparent wealth (he had gone to Harvard Law School, traveled, had lived in Rye and Noroton, wore expensive-looking clothes, was divorced, and had a sort of relaxed quality which Baggish took as a sign of financial independence and probably ease), his place in what was generally regarded as the chic social group in Heidelberg civilian circles (Baggish had seen him at their desirable table in the Casino), and, most of all, an air about him, which, for Baggish, cried, "Use me. Dupe me." Without malice aforethought, though without charity, Baggish moved in.

Schreiber got the call at his office. "Do you remember?" it began after the announcement of the name.

"Of course," said Schreiber, gradually filling in the blank with a picture of a stocky young man whose physical distinction seemed the lack of one. "What can I do for you, Baggish?"

"I thought we might get together. I don't know many Americans in Heidelberg, and I was hoping I could get to know you."

Not thrilled, but remembering how he himself had felt a few months before, Schreiber said, "That would be nice. Can you come on over for lunch? I'll introduce you to some people. You work out here, don't you?"

"Yes."

"I'm in Building B, Second Floor, 208. Twelve-thirty all right?"

"I'll be there," said Baggish, and hung up. The first principle of all sorts of economy was to never give away more than necessary.

This particular economy somewhat disconcerted Schreiber: an unconventional conclusion seemed to point to something less conventional than the making of a lunch date. "Or perhaps he's just a fool," thought Schreiber. "It's better than being a snob, I suppose." Snobbery was the vice of Schreiber's office circle.

"Mind if I bring along someone to lunch?" he asked Sara and Charles, his office mates.

"Civilian?" asked Charles, thinking that only Schreiber would have to be asked such a question; anyone else automatically gave the rank of a military guest.

"Yes," said Schreiber.

"What's he about?" asked Sara.

It was customary to reply, "A fellow who went to Amherst with my cousin," or "A nice kid who's been on a Fulbright in Athens."

"About? Oh yes. I know very little about him. He doesn't know many people and seems lonely."

"I think the janitor's looking for friends too," said Charles, but under his breath. His promotions depended on the efficiency reports Schreiber filled out four times a year, and although he had seen Schreiber just check off "Excellent" without looking at the names at the top of the sheets, he did not feel quite as much at ease with Schreiber's stolidity as did the other members of the group.

Charles and Sara were its mainstays. He was a graduate of Wesleyan who had flunked out of the University of Chicago Law School and had gone to Europe to save enough money to buy a nonworking-but-good-living-share of a profitable business, preferably in Europe. Sara, a sporty, popeyed girl from Watertown, Connecticut had come to Europe because she hadn't gotten married off with the rest of her class at Connecticut College for Women. Charles was a GS-9, Sara a GS-7. "I'm bucking hard for the Nine," she told Schreiber the first day, although it was considered bad form to care about ratings, and also to talk either too much or too little about them.

None of the members of the group was a regular employee of the Civil Service. They'd latched onto jobs in Europe to coast for a year, to see the sights, or to save money. Most of them had been in Heidelberg for at least two years. Each summer they prepared to go back to graduate school, business, or to better jobs in Washington. When someone did go home, his departure was capped by a rage of speculation as to the accuracy of his declared prospects. The only member of the group who never wanted to return was Jerome Mortimer, the manager of the local Chase National Bank, a square, springy, faintly effeminate snob; the snobbery helped disguise the effeminacy. Sara was another part of the disguise, for although Mortimer liked her, he liked people to think he liked her more than he did. He realized that he was expected—generally and by Sara— to go to bed with her, and this annoyed him, because he needed a more striking-looking woman to stir his appetite.

His first question to Schreiber had been, "Where did you prepare?" Schreiber, flattered that he still looked young enough to be asked that question, answered, "Hazelton High School." The answer had supplied Mortimer with enough history to govern their relationship.

At lunch, in the Officer-Civilian Dining Room of the Casino, he asked Baggish the same question. "Hotchkiss," answered Baggish.

"A nice Connecticut School," said Mortimer, for whom such schools were of acceptable, if limited currency. "When were you there?"

Baggish supplied Ward's dates.

"Did you know Billy MacKenzie?" asked Mortimer. "He probably did time about then?"

"I think so," said Baggish. "Tall fellow, rather shy."

"That's right," said Mortimer. "Though I wouldn't call him shy. He was like his sister who used to call my brother up three times a week till he told her she was compromising him in Eliot House."

"Elizabeth?" asked Baggish.

"Jean, I think," said Mortimer. "I guess there was a younger sister too."

Joe McBain, the young Political Adviser to the Command, questioned him about his years at Yale. Baggish grimaced and said, "I hardly ever went out of my house. I finished the damn school under protest." McBain did not pursue the subject. As the leading representative of the State Department in the area, he disliked detail; he needed only to see that Baggish's attitude was decent enough to pass general inspection. With his fiancée, Anne Pendleton, Sara's roommate, he went off to a party in his hotel, the Schloss, a posh, glassy structure reserved for V.I.P.s which looked in judgment over the Neckar Valley, and whose guest book was laden with the great names of the last hundred years. Baggish followed the pair out with studious eyes; he had never before been so close to the inner springs of power.

The other State Department member of the group, Marsh Willey, was the director of the local Amerika Haus, and Baggish was less impressed by him. Willey had come over with his wife in 1946 with the intention of saving money and having children while the government paid the hospital expenses. They had managed to have three children in forty months, but, although Nina worked until a week before each delivery writing news copy for the Public Information Office, while the maid they were assigned took care of the children, they saved nothing. And this despite the fact that Nina was the most assiduous retailer of American goods in Heidelberg. Every week she loaded the State Department Volkswagen with sugar, gasoline, coal, tobacco, nylons, and ten or twelve other staples, and drove over half the valley peddling. Once a month she went to Switzerland to make elaborate monetary exchanges whose complexity brought them not so much profit as the satisfaction that they were neglecting nothing in their assault on prosperity. Their failure to save was due largely to their passion for collecting ugly furniture, flawed china, and bad paintings, none of which they enjoyed, but all of which they hunted down with a fury not unlike the fury with which they purveyed. "It's killing us," they told everyone, but one look at Nina's watercolor of an old Vermont barn, not unlike the sort of structure they dreamed of converting into Bliss with their European accumulations, revived them sufficiently for their next plunge into the marketplace.

Willey spent the luncheon grumbling about his inability to swing a deal which involved buying checkwriting machines from a German firm and reselling them to the Army Finance Corps. It was clear to everyone that he was inviting a loan or subsidy. Mortimer tried to avert the indelicacy by talking about the only trip he had made back home ("home" was always the States) since he'd been discharged in Germany in nineteen forty-five. It was for his father's funeral. "The only time in my life I've been wronged by Father. Hardly got off the boat when the Revenue people met me with a three year tax lien. The whole point of staying in Europe gone up the flue."

"Those tax-rats," hissed Willey, and fury at his employer finally led to an overt appeal for a Deutsch Mark loan.

"I didn't think the Army was allowed to buy on the German economy," said Baggish, deciding to strike in with the majority.

"Yes," said Willey, his square face creased with disgust at Baggish's intrusive naïveté, "It's a complicated business." But he decided to drop the matter.

It was a minor coup for Baggish, and along with his general comportment—modesty, reasonable alertness with an undercurrent of

digestible eccentricity—and apparent gentility, it helped establish
him as a fit addition to the group.

4

It was after lunch that Baggish told Schreiber about the coincidence which reinforced the tie against which age, experience, and
temperament worked. He walked him back to Building B after
Charles and Sara had gone off to do errands in town. "You know,"
he began. "I've been a kind of fill-in for you."

"Oh," said Schreiber, more wary than surprised. Baggish pleased
him more than he'd imagined he would, although there was in his
manner a kind of undertow which ruffled him.

"I told a neighbor of mine that I'd met you the other night, and
she said that you used to live in Haus Stempel von Gode. In fact,
you'd just moved out of the room I live in now."

"Well, well," said Schreiber. He passed a handkerchief over his
forehead and then blew his nose into it. "That's quite a coincidence.
They must save that room for Americans. I was only there a little
while until the Housing Bureau found me something."

Baggish let this pass. "Strange little set-up there," he said, making
his tones ambiguous enough for an innocuous interpretation. Schreiber tried it out three or four different ways before he said that the
house had been but a base for him, and that he knew almost nothing
about whatever went on there.

"Make an interesting study for a sociologist," said Baggish linger-
ingly, invitingly. They were at Building B.

Schreiber paused at the door. "Which neighbor did you talk with
about me?" the word "neighbor" sounding antique, even perilous to
him as he said it.

"A girl named Bretzka," said Baggish calmly. "Rather nice girl
with black hair. Claims she knows you."

"I remember her," said Schreiber. He paused to recover and recon-
noiter. "Give her my best, will you?"

"If I see her, I certainly will," said Baggish. "I seldom do. Though she seems a nice sort of girl. And not unattractive, for a German."

"The pretty German types are mostly Scandinavian," said Schreiber. "Perhaps that's the reason the Germans go to war, to get a look at pretty women. Or so," he added conscientiously, "a fellow who lived in the rooms before me suggested."

"Ha, ha, ha," roared Baggish. "Not a bad little theory. Well, Fräulein Bretzka is a decent-enough looking girl, but she's hard to understand."

"The way she talks?"

"No," said Baggish, a babe-in-the-woods. "It's her manner, her way of talking, I can follow what she says pretty well, the literal sense, anyway. I'm just not quite sure what her drift is."

Schreiber took his foot off the door sill and smiled at the young man about whom, a minute before, he could have made the same sort of remark. Though he himself had been a poor student, he might, he thought, be a better teacher. Baggish struck him as a fine repository for his accumulation of sad wisdom. "You know, Ted," he said. "I'm in no position to lecture you about anything. After all, we hardly know each other."

He paused until Baggish supplied the assurance which continuation required. "I'd greatly appreciate your telling me anything at all, Max. I really would."

"Thanks for saying that," said Schreiber solemnly. "I might be able to save you a few steps here and there, but I don't just want to dump my notions on you and have you take them for gospel."

"I'll make suitable deductions," said Baggish.

"That's right," said Schreiber, a bit disappointed.

There was a third pause which Baggish broke by asking what it was that Schreiber was going to tell him.

"Oh yes," said the professor, mopping up again with the handkerchief, "It was this," and he thought hard for a moment, trying to water his rancour with pedagogical wisdom. "This Bretzka girl is, I think, an opportunist. I'd be careful about getting involved with her."

"Involved?"

"In any way, I mean."

"Little chance of that."

Schreiber blushed. "There are lots of ways of getting involved, Ted. More than you'd ever imagine. Why two weeks ago some girl rushed up to me in the streets waving a piece of paper, asking me to sign it. Down on the Hauptstrasse. A petition to stop the British from using Heligoland as a bombing target. Said she could tell that I was well-disposed toward Germans. Never saw her before in my life, but I couldn't get rid of her. Finally left after I told her that no one in my position could get involved in foreign affairs; it was strictly a German matter. But she wanted to involve me. See what I mean?"

Baggish said that, yes, indeed he did, and that indeed he would be very careful in his dealings with all Germans until he "got to understand them." He hoped Schreiber would give him tips here and there.

"I'll be glad to, Ted," said Schreiber, not unhappy that the session was drawing to a close, since it had taken more out of him than he could understand. "I'm glad we've become friends." Like good Europeans, they shook hands and said good-by.

5

The next day Baggish called Schreiber and met him for dinner. They went to the restaurant in the Palatinate Museum. Schreiber ordered a good Moselle and explained to Baggish about the *homo Heidelbergensis*.

"An unexpected place to have a restaurant," said Baggish. "You'd think the presence of bones would hold people back from snuffling up steaks."

"Europeans aren't as squeamish about life as many of us are," said Schreiber, pleased to see that Baggish reacted to the remark as he had to most of what he'd said, with eye-opened gratification.

After dinner, they went to a German movie about a pastor who saved the marriage of a Bavarian schoolmaster and his peasant bride by a personal renunciation which would have strained the belief-capacity of a millenarian.

"I see what you mean by lack of squeamishness," said Baggish as they left the theater. Although the pertinence of this escaped Schreiber—he had enjoyed the movie—the fact that it sprang from his own remark did not, and he was again gratified. Before he could think of a buttress for the remark which would hold Baggish till they met again, they were in front of the Ritterhof and Baggish was saying, "I enjoyed the evening a great deal."

"Are you busy for dinner tomorrow?" asked Schreiber.

"I am, I'm afraid. How about Friday?"

"Fine," said Schreiber. "I enjoy your company, and that's a lot more than I can say of most young men."

"You flatter me, Max. May I say that you're the first older friend I've had who didn't try to either patronize or kid me. I like to learn from you and like to be with you. See you Friday," and he was off across the Domplatz leaving Schreiber beaming with the compliments, which despite their somewhat gauche directness, pleased him as much as any he'd ever received.

6

They began to eat dinner together two and three times a week, went on walks also, down the Neckar or up the Philosophenweg. One Sunday they took a Special Service Bus Tour to the palace at Schwetzingen. That afternoon, as they moved along with the crowd over this demure echo of Versailles, Baggish suggested that Schreiber buy a car.

"There's nothing like a car to give you freedom," he said. "It's an extension of the human capacity for movement and vision."

"Haven't you thought of getting one for yourself?"

"I can't drive," said Baggish, letting Schreiber in on a deficiency which was one of his minor plagues. "We always had a man to drive our cars. I never learned."

"Strange," said Schreiber, fingering the marble antlers of a buck on the palace grounds with a kind of abstract envy. "There can't be too many American males of your age in that position. If I get one, I'll teach you."

"That would be nice," said Baggish diffidently, and for the benefit of a wild-eyed little Wac beside him, he goosed the buck.

A week later Schreiber bought a car. Baggish had listened to the used car announcements on the Armed Forces Network and when he heard of a Fiat station wagon going for six hundred dollars up in Wiesbaden, he called Schreiber, and the next Saturday they went up together in the train. The owner was a young man named Milton from Burlington, North Carolina who was a payroll clerk at Air Force Headquarters. He was going home on leave and then planned to bring back a new Pontiac from the States. I've bought some good china, I think ought to make up the difference in price," he said. He talked quietly, his eyes bent over Schreiber's coffee cup. (He didn't drink coffee himself for he needed nine hours sleep a night; a cup of coffee threw him off for a week.) "I've been shipping it home piece by piece for a couple of years. I've made a study of it. I don't just mean the marks of the different makes, which is what these soldiers here mean when they think they know all about it. I get it up to the light and see how good the stuff is. I got a German book tells you the design and periods and what's best. Trouble when you know so much, you see a lot of bargains that if you could afford them, you'd make yourself a pile, but you know, it takes a pile to make another. I could have bought a twenty piece dinner service of these Rothschilds all out of gold for about a thousand marks. You know how much a man could get for that back home?"

"I don't know," said Baggish, "But I understand the market's not what it used to be."

Milton looked worried. "Really? That's bad news. Just as well maybe I didn't get stuck with it. I figured it'd go for two or three thousand. Dollars. God, maybe I ought to keep the old buggy."

They overcame these belated qualms, made the transfer in the

Judge Advocate's office an hour later, and drove back on the Autobahn to Heidelberg.

Schreiber was much taken by the car. It was small, neat, and had a cocky rather than casual look; the upholstery was red and the top slid open over the middle of the body. It could do about a hundred, Milton said, though Schreiber hadn't realized that he'd meant kilometers.

The next day, Schreiber gave Baggish his first driving lesson. After an hour of general instructions and practice with the gear shift, they drove into the Odenwald. Although it was a wonderful, warm day, there were almost no cars in the wood, and Schreiber let Baggish take the wheel. He drove for twenty minutes, excited as he hadn't been since his night with Monique in Paris. The inability to drive had fretted him for years, and once in Providence he had menaced his economic structure by thinking of taking a twenty dollar set of lessons. "But I don't have a car," he had told himself, "so there'd be no practical point unless I hired one, which would be stupid, as there's no place I want to go."

"It was like not being able to read," he said of the driving to Schreiber, as he wheeled round a limp curve. "Like being impotent."

"You're a quick learner," said Schreiber.

"You could teach the car to drive me," said Baggish. Schreiber blushed with pride.

At the first car that came toward them, however, he let up on the accelerator, and stalled. Blushing himself, he started up again, saying to himself, "It's will, only will. Control your nerves and the machine trots behind you." The maxim didn't help with the second car, a Chrysler which passed them going sixty; he stalled again. He held his own with the third, and drove back to Heidelberg.

"Next week we'll work in traffic," said Schreiber.

They went out every day for a week, and then Baggish took and passed his driver's test. "It's like being let out of the galleys,"

he said. "Let's celebrate. We can go over to the Wiesbaden Casino
with our mutual friend." He leered pleasantly, and Schreiber turned
away, blushing. What was Baggish trying to do, pimp for him, and
with someone whom he had gotten to know on his own?

"I think not, Ted," he said mildly, for he did not want to rebuke
what might be innocence or misjudgement. "Another night, perhaps, but it's a strain for me, talking German, and the driving's
tired me."

"Of course, Max. I'm afraid my driving exhausts the old Fiat
itself, let alone a human engine." He took the small loss against
the large gain of his new mastery. And the loss would be redeemed
before long; this he *knew*. It was a matter of character, of Schreiber's
and of Traudis's.

It was becoming important to Baggish to get Traudis off his neck;
if he could do this by gratifying Schreiber, he would not only be
performing a humane act, but would be strengthening a position
he wanted to strengthen.

It was becoming important for him, because he had not only
reached the point of going to bed with Traudis without paying her
rent money—he had never done that—but, since Frau Stempel had
returned from Sweden, Traudis spent much of her time in his
room, eyes, hands, lips, and legs open to him with a cavernous and
disabling rapacity. It was essential to divert her to someone, and
Schreiber seemed the most likely possibility: he should enjoy returning to well-cultivated soil. *"Nostalgie pour la boue,"* was Baggish's
summary appraisal.

Schreiber was a bridge to the fortress he had to take, and although
he did not plan to lose a battle for a skirmish, as a hater of waste,
he hated to lose anything, and he decided to give the reunion one
big push. He invited Schreiber to a party given by a friend of
Traudis', Frank Horstmann, the American *lektor* at the University,
at Horstmann's rooms on the Schlossweg. "I think you'll enjoy the
crowd, Max. They're intellectuals, and you'll have more in common
with them than you do with, well, many people."

"Why not?" thought Schreiber. "I'll try again. It's what I wanted," and he thought happily of being warmed by the fires of university intelligence. "I'd love to come. I've known intellectuals in my time, and made out pretty well with them."

7

Schreiber's Fiat did more than strengthen the bonds between himself and Baggish. He began to be invited on the group's expeditions, rides up the Rhine valley, weekends to Rothenberg-ob-der-Tauber, excursions to the Wiesbaden Casino, or up the hill to the Molkenkur Club for Baked Alaska and coffee. The Schreiber who had been for them but pleasant filler, someone whose marital status and Hazelton, Pa., flavor—as they referred to his variant of the Seaboard manner—helped them feel that their society included many Stateside types, became, with the Fiat, someone genuinely useful, someone to be relied upon for lifts, an instrument of small pleasures.

Schreiber declined most of the invitations. The few he accepted were accepted mostly to soothe feelings hurt by his refusals. The group was the only acceptable source of refusals.

Mortimer would ask him if he wanted to go down for a week of skiing at Zermatt.

"I'm not the type, I'm afraid."

Mortimer poured a cup of the Casino's coffee into the little electric coffee maker he carried around in his pocket. "What 'type' of people ski? Half the noncoms in there ski," and he flapped a hand toward the indiscriminate skiing world of the Casino.

"I mean physically," said Schreiber.

Sara, who disliked references to the body, said that it was a question of good air, good food, and mostly, good company. "Mountains make for companionship," and her eye slid to a corner of the socket to inspect Mortimer's reaction. He repoured his coffee from the little cooker.

"I'll have to wait for something less dangerous," said Schreiber, but knew he wouldn't.

The more his position in the group solidified, the less he enjoyed their company. And the pressure on him and his little Fiat aggravated his discomfort. He seldom drove unless it was with Baggish, who understood what real friendship was, a mixture of respect, mutual learning and general good will. Baggish was almost European in sensitivity.

The Sunday of Horstmann's party, Schreiber took the little Bergbahn up the castle hill and walked to the outdoor café above which Horstmann had rooms. The café was closed for repair but the shivering air seemed to be remembering the noise of a thousand party evenings. Under the eaves, Schreiber took it in reflectively. At last he was back in an atmosphere he could breathe in. Below him floated the towers of the Heilliggeist Church and the University, and across the river he spotted Haus Stempel von Gode, the mist making its cocoa-colored stone look like a great paw hanging over the Neckar.

Horstmann came to the door, a big young man with huge features stuck on a narrow head. Schreiber introduced himself, and they shook hands.

"You're early," said Horstmann, "but that's O.K. We can probe each other."

Upstairs, he introduced his wife, a pretty blond girl who, next to her husband, looked as if she were evaporating.

"Want some *Rhenischer* brew?" asked Horstmann, opening a bottle. "It's not quite the vinegar Balzac called it."

"Thank you," said Schreiber. He passed on the glass to Mrs. Horstmann who declined. "I've got to feed the baby," she said. It was the only time that Schreiber heard her talk.

"She's of a retiring nature," said Horstmann. "The most valuable sort of wife. Wish I had two of them. 'Wives are young men's mistresses, companions for middle age, and old men's nurses,' as the bad Viscount had it, but the crooked bachelor didn't realize that a man might want all three at once. *Sates magnum alter alten theatrum sumus.* I don't really know Latin, but I've worked up about fifty tags from schoolbook editions. What's your game?"

"Not much of anything," said Schreiber. "Just more or less serving out my time."

"Poignant," said Horstmann. He nodded his anomalously small, overfreighted head. "You're a good man."

Schreiber found this label peculiarly distasteful, even disregarding its condescension. He stared at a Biedermeier desk until its great mass had given him a sense of base for countering.

"Goodness," he said, "is the last resort of a scoundrel."

This was not, he realized, anything he either meant, understood, or approved of, but the rhythm took care of the sense. Whatever the cause, the effect on Horstmann was gratifying. Two large hands buried the little head and rocked it back and forth till the mouth emerged from under the palm to gulp wine. "We might get along," he said. "Yes sir. I'm a great believer in the upside-down remark myself. 'By indirection, find direction out.' Now where is that from?"

Schreiber did not know what the antecedent of "that" was, but he smiled benevolently and said how much he admired the portly Biedermeier. "Belongs to the apartment," said Horstmann, "as does every object here not born of woman." He looked at his watch. "We might as well have something to eat. No one will be here for half an hour."

Schreiber had come twenty minutes after the time Baggish had named. "Don't bother to feed me. I eat about four o'clock on Sundays."

"Bad habit," said Horstmann, "but you'll have a bite," and he called, "Bring some supper in here, will you, Sugar?"

"That's very kind of you."

"Wait till you taste it," said Horstmann. "She's not very good with food."

This was not an inaccuracy. Mrs. Horstmann brought in two

plates on each of which squatted a pile of gelatinous potato salad, three slices of bratwurst, and a lettuce leaf soaked in a vinegar which seeped into the other edibles and spread its odor over the room.

Horstmann ate without talking, if not in silence. He managed to agitate a battery of sound even from the potato salad, and Schreiber gathered from the pleasurable nature of the sounds that this repast was a comparatively excellent one. He himself made the gestures of hearty eating, and, by mumbling now and then, the gestures of sustaining a conversation, something which Horstmann apparently found an unnecessary gilding of the pleasures of the table. The meal was finished in fifteen minutes, as protracted a quarter-hour as Schreiber could remember. Its conclusion was marked by Horstmann's pronouncement, "She outdid herself," and his wiping vinegar from his lips and jowls onto his shirtsleeve. Since there were no napkins, Schreiber trusted that no objection would be raised if he employed a handkerchief for the same purpose. He could, he realized, have used a rug without it being remarked: Horstmann had begun to talk.

He addressed Schreiber as if he were speaking to a class of four hundred college sophomores; the room bowed with his eloquence. The topics ranged from the products associated with the names of Chateaubriand and Chesterfield to Professor Oken's theory of cranial structure. Horstmann was a polymath. Schreiber could barely keep afloat; occasionally he looked out the window where, over the Neckar, he could see Dr. Stempel's picture window eyeing the gloom. Suddenly, happily, Horstmann, in the midst of an anatomical comparison of the cranium and pelvis, was interrupted by a knock at the door. He leaped from his chair, disappeared down the stairs, and came up a minute later in the midst of a chattering group of men and women, one of whom Schreiber was astonished to see was Traudis Bretzka. She was followed by Baggish. Horstmann, forgetting how Schreiber had been invited—or not knowing

—introduced him to both, "Another sympathetic American, Max Schreiber. Theodore Baggish and Traudis Bretzka."

As Horstmann then showered him with a guttural orgy of ten German names, Schreiber recovered enough to shake hands. Baggish's arm went around his shoulder. "Glad to see you made it, Max."

Traudis smiled and said in German that it was always good to see old friends. "A real surprise," she said. "I thought you had said by-by to us all." Schreiber found himself trembling under Baggish's arm.

"You astonish me, Schreiber," said Horstmann in the act of distributing people around the inhospitable expanse of the room. "I had no idea that you had fraternized with our former foe."

"Speak German," said Traudis. She sat down in a dirty violet armchair, and Baggish, on the floor, translated Horstmann's remark for her.

"Ah yes," she said politely. "Mr. Schreiber and I are old fraternizers."

"Some time ago," said Schreiber, reassembling his scattered German. "Fräulein Bretzka introduced me to much in German life—in life itself—which was new to me." He sank back on the sofa exhausted by the comment. "She was a great help," he summoned again after a pause during which the company gauged the tension and tried to do the same with its source.

Another knock at the door brought a new thrust of people, all German but one, the British *lektor* at the University, a lean, young man who talked German with incredible speed. Indeed to Schreiber, everyone's talk seemed to cannonade into the room, and he shrank from the uproar into contemplation of the embarrassing encounter. Still he discerned that the intense conversation was centering into the opposition of two groups, as, in a great war, a hundred viewpoints converge into those of two main camps. The British *lektor* was the champion of the smaller group, Horstmann and Traudis

the major contenders of the other. The argument was apparently
neither new nor especially galling, and yet it seemed to Schreiber
that had it not been for the attention which everyone gave to the
rapid replenishment of his wine glass, they would have been at
each others' throats.

Horstmann's contention was that the true meaning of Germany
from the eighteenth century to the present could be understood
only through a study of its music, that each nation should be
examined in terms of its single most important contribution to
culture. He pointed out the window as if to assembled legions,
"This country did not even exist till Beethoven replaced Mozart,
till the ripped-up dedication of the Eroica, till the collapse of classical
form in the *opera post* 95. There's the impulse to national self-
realization that Hegel and Fichte only gabbled about, and when
Bismarck finally got around to it by beating down the Frankfurt
Congress and its degenerate heirs, he could be regarded not only
as an epigone, but as a lifeless afterbirth."

The British *lektor* talked as if each sentence were a blood trans-
fusion for the company. "Germany isn't Fichte, von Moltke, and a
crowd of musical gad-abouts. It's Goethe, Nietzsche, Burkhardt,
Freud, the masters of the concrete and antinational. We have had
an orgy of the abstract. It's time to revive the concrete, the cos-
mopolitanism which does not shield the power struggle with foul
abstraction. Germany's mission in Europe was not, as Hitler said,
to purify the true aristocratic stock and culture; it was and is to act
as the German Confederacy did, as a buffer zone between east and
west, papacy and national imperialism, French rationalization and
Slavic mystification. It had no will to power until the artificial personal success of the two Fredericks invited the oversimplified inter-
pretations of the mission by Bismarck, Treitschke, Willem the
Gimp, and Hitler the Pervert."

This oration nearly collapsed the house, until Traudis' voice, like
a Wagnerian soprano finally surmounting the enemies of orchestra
and fellow singers, wrested the analysis of her native land from the

assurances of the Englishman and American. As she raged, Schreiber swelled with pride. Her discourse, studded with great names, and worked up with a passion that was more like that of a starved man's quest for meat than the inquiring intellect's for truth, made him think, "And that I had." When she concluded, he breathed freely, as if he had been holding his breath under water. Traudis watched him gasping while the Briton sprang back into the field with tidings from Bonaventura's *Breviloquium;* she moved to his side and asked gently if he were all right.

"Of course," he said angrily, and turned from her quickly, as if not to miss a syllable of the great debate, but her hand was on his knee and the convolutions of Bonaventura as they issued in the elephantine Germanics of the *lektor* coiled and tightened about his senses. The phrase "the Incarnation as the response to the Temptation" finally downed him, and he turned back to Traudis as if for help in a hard world.

"Did you ever in your life hear such a *Schwein?"* she said.

"He's brilliant," said Schreiber plumping once again for independence. "I think he's very brilliant," and he dived back into the cauldron until his head burned with something about the thirteenth century *Schnapsteufel,* the importance of "Brandewyn" from the Lowlands, and the provocations to alcoholism in German history. "My God," he thought. "I must have had too much myself," and he rose, and headed for the door. Horstmann followed, though manifestly suffering the pain of abated argument. (No one else suffered, for no one else abated.) After Horstmann, came Traudis, and after her Baggish.

"You're not sick, Schreiber, are you?" whispered Horstmann.

"A little," said Schreiber. "I'd better go home. It's been marvelously stimulating."

"Good," said Horstmann.

"I'd better go home also," said Traudis. "Perhaps I could walk along with Mr. Schreiber."

"He'd be most gratified," assumed Horstmann.

"Or partially," muttered Baggish, with greater surety. "I won't bother then, Traudis, as long as you're in such good hands."

Schreiber glanced at his fat palms as if to substantiate this claim. "They'll see Fräulein Bretzka home, at any rate," he said, the intellectual vertigo clearing off now, though leaving him slightly dizzy at the immediate prospect.

In the road, Traudis took his arm. A stiff wind blew up from the river; the sky was fuzzy with stars. Schreiber's nostrils swelled with the backwash of garden smells from the castle and the special earthiness of Traudis' unwashed body. She was saying that he had been awful to her. "I've missed you not a little, Max."

"That surprises me, Traudis," he said. "I thought that you were happily occupied elsewhere."

"That *Schwein?* No more. I pay my rent."

"A bold one," thought Schreiber, but the garden redolence transformed the other into a perfume which stripped disgust from desire and led him to squeeze her arm in his.

"Are we going to see each other?" she asked.

It was a too rapid advance, and it scraped Schreiber's scar. He detached his arm and said nothing. They were coming down into the Kornmarktplatz, and the streets, full of urban memoranda, of possibility, duties, and courses, helped him detach more than his arm.

"You don't wish to see me?" she asked.

"Upon occasion, we might be of use to each other," he said. They walked by the Rathaus, Schreiber sensing in the official Baroque bulk an admonition to his own. He regretted what he'd just said.

"You've become hard, Max," said Traudis. She looked into his face for a moment, said "Good night," and then crossed the Domplatz.

Schreiber went up to his room. From his window he could see her moving down the Steingasse toward the Old Bridge. Remembering the look and feel of the body that was moving, he felt the congratulations he was offering himself on his self-control shatter themselves against nostalgia and desire.

8

During those weeks in which he worked the day shift, Baggish would often come up to Schreiber's office for the morning coffee breaks and lunch. If he were a few minutes early, he'd sit by Schreiber's desk and read the Paris edition of the *Herald Tribune* or the *Rhein-Neckar Zeitung*. Reading the German paper, he would often ask Schreiber, Charles, or Sara what words meant, those he thought they would know. They were used to him now, and if, on a Monday, one of them looked up at ten-thirty and asked "Where's Ted?" and was told "He works nights this week," he would feel real disappointment.

Baggish's role in the circle was a more innocent one than he usually liked to play. He would ask such questions as, "You don't have to declare money gifts on your income tax, do you?" and when Mortimer answered, "Not up to a couple of thousand," Baggish would register a vague distress. Once he asked Joe McBain if the parents of a GS-4 would be allowed to stay in the Schloss Hotel.

"I'm afraid not," said Joe. "Your people coming?"

"They were thinking of shooting up from Biarritz in September," said Baggish, "and God knows I can't put them up."

Ten minutes later he would complain about the price of the Casino coffee cake and wolf the piece which Sara offered him. His principle of action was based on a La Rochefoucauld maxim about people not forgiving you the favors you do them but being gratified by the ones they do you. This strategy went well with his natural inclinations.

One Monday he came up to Schreiber's office late and found that the three office mates had gone off. He picked up the *Tribune* to read Art Buchwald and Walter Lippmann. Underneath the newspaper was a sheaf of yellow paper which had Top Secret stamped in blue ink on each page.

It was a Logistics Report on Emergency evacuation proceedings for American personnel in the European Command. Baggish read it casually, his interest stemming from its rarified classification. (He was cleared only for Secret in the Message Control.) As he put it down, the imp of his prospects cavorted before him on the yellow sheets; he took them up again and read them carefully. When, out the window, he saw Schreiber, Charles, and Sara walking back from the Casino across the marching field, he went down by the back staircase.

That night he started working on an article about the inadequacy of the American evacuation plan, pointing out, as the report had, that the evacuation center was in a town whose waterfront was controlled by a Communist union. He cast a third of the sentences in the form of deductions from the other material, and even introduced a couple of minor suppositions which the report had contradicted. He worked on the article for three days, polishing it so that the tone sounded as much like a mixture of straight reporting and Lippmann as he could manage. He debated whether to send it to the *Saturday Evening Post, Life, Look,* or to a newspaper, deciding at last that the chances of publication would be best in a large Midwestern paper which covered foreign affairs but did not have its own correspondents. He looked through American newspapers at the Special Service Library and came up with a number of possibilities. He decided finally on the St. Louis *Times-Journal,* signed the article with the pseudonym, R. F. C. Whitney, and, under his own name, wrote the following note:

The Editor of the St. Louis *Times-Journal*
Dear Sir:

I have been in Europe for some time now after my army service studying languages, politics, and just plain people, in the streets, the hotels, the bars, and the stadiums. I did some newspaper work in college and for a small weekly in Providence, Rhode Island (the *Weekly Chronicle*), but the enclosed is my first piece of foreign commentary. I hope it shows what I feel, namely that I'm beginning to get the lay of things in this part of the world.

My hope is that you'll read the enclosed piece, and, if you like it, that you'll use it (publish it, I mean, of course) under the following conditions: one, that you'll put my name (or rather my *nom de plume,* something that I use because it makes getting information easier) on the article only if you will permit me to write at least one article a month for you, and that, two, you'll secure official accreditation for me after you've agreed to Condition One. In this way, I'll be able to give up the job with the Department of the Army which I now hold and will not be bound by the restrictions governing even this eye-opening (I trust) article.

I send this to your newspaper because it is one of the five or six most influential in America, and one of the three or four most respected by people who've made some study of newspapers for the breadth, accuracy, and general objectivity of its reporting.

Sincerely yours,

T. Whitney Baggish

He typed three copies of the article and sent one off with the note to St. Louis.

C H A P T E R   T W O

I

Robert Ward was faced with the problem of going back to America. His parents's letters were filled not only with anticipation of seeing him but of his beginning a career, "whatever it is you decide upon, son." It was a problem for Ward because he was beginning to come to roost in Europe. The sentimental nest was a Mlle. Juliette Destorches, a nineteen year old novelist who had been ranked by *France Litteraire* as one of the five best writers of her sex and age group. In addition to Juliette, Ward had learned to treasure being far away from the entanglements which supplied him with the means of being away.

Until late spring, his year had been unfruitful. His tour of the Midi had been dull and lonely. He'd stopped mostly in International Student Hostels, although occasionally, fed to the gills with swapping anecdotes with fellow transients, he put up in third or even second class hotels. This hadn't lessened his sense of isolation, but, rather, had refined it; he'd begun looking forward to the clean or nearly clean bed, coffee, and rolls in the morning, the security of a large building to which to return at night so that like a turtle, he was always at home if never in the same spot. He spent a lot of time oiling and adjusting the motorcycle. It was like rubbing a wife's back. More intimate; for Ward felt that he and the machine were a single centaurlike structure, and when he put on his goggles and white cap, he and the machine became each other's property. When he left it to go upstairs to his room, he sometimes had a feeling he should send a meal down to it, or one of the murder mysteries which were his nightly bed partners.

Sometimes he talked with people in bars. This tired him most of all: he felt he didn't know how to put interesting questions to people who were different, different not in an essential or even national sense, but in the fact of their being rooted to the towns in which he met them, while he was without rootage in place or schedule. It was not a question of being a tourist, for tourists were also rooted by having to "see things."

One night in a sailor's bar in Marseilles, he talked with two Canadian brothers, who were traveling around the world, mostly by jeep. They'd started in Denmark, were on their way through the continent, then heading down through Turkey to Jerusalem, then to Iraq, Afghanistan, India, then Java where they'd ship to Australia and then to Canada. He'd overheard them debating whether or not to circle the rim of Africa before heading for the Near East. They'd noticed him staring at them, and asked him to flip a coin to decide. He did, and on the toss they omitted Africa. The elder brother, who was twenty-six, invited Ward to join them, they had plenty of room in the jeep. "I nearly refused to flip your coin," he said. "I'm not much for excitement. I wouldn't last as far as Nice." They took this as a polite way of refusing, but Ward had been very serious. The idea of putting himself at the mercy of a tossed French franc sickened him. Leaving the brothers that night was the low moment of his year. Again and again, he asked himself what he lacked to make such a trip seem so impossible. He got to sleep only when he decided that it was not a defect in him, but the presence of something which the Canadians didn't have, a sense of proportion, a fund of common sense. "I'm willing to try new foods, new places, new jobs even, when the time comes, but you can't make a profession out of letting the wind carry you." The next week he went back to Paris and started in again on his courses at the *Science Po'*. He also began a course of "serious" reading launched by a Christmas gift from his mother, Henry Adams' *Mont St. Michel and Chartres*. He sometimes spent eight hours a day in the Bibliothêque Nationale and the Louvre Library soaking up the story of the growth of Europe. In spring, he set off on his second trip, one which was to follow the growth of the Gothic cathedrals out of the molds of the Norman fortress-churches. He worked it out with a map, Henry Adams, and a history of France.

The first two weeks were all that Ward could have wished them to be. Each time he recognized something he'd read about in Adams or Viollet-le-Duc, a principle of design, or a particular masterpiece, he felt the satisfaction of a shrewd, lucky gambler. He went along the roads analyzing his experience to the handlebars, and then at night, in the hostels where he stayed, he worked up the history of the next place from the notes in his journal. By the end of the fourth week, however, he was sick with fatigue, unable to distinguish a castle from a church, and so fearfully conscious of his motorcycle that his body seemed but an aching continuation of it.

One day, riding along the Sarthe near Sablé, he was about to give up, when he looked across at a large gray building, not more than a hundred years old. "What's that one?" he thought, somewhat annoyed at passing something of at least respectable bearing which he couldn't identify. The annoyance gave him enough energy to ride across a bridge and go up to it.

2

As the motorcycle drove up, the Père *Portier* of the monastery, more startled by a noise than he'd been since the war, climbed off his high stool and stood at the entrance. Ward asked him if it would be all right to look around. The Père said "of course" and went off to fetch the Père *Hotelier*. Ward, in the anteroom, examined the medallions and books. The Père *Portier* returned with a frail, young monk, as serious as a rodent, who inclined a spectacled head toward Ward, shook his hand and bid him welcome. Would he like to see the Abbey? Would he like some refreshment? Would he like to put his motorcycle inside? Would he like to have a monk who spoke English assigned to him? To all offers but the first, Ward answered, "No thank you, *mon* Père." "I would very much like to look around," he said, "but I'm not a Catholic. Does that matter?"

"Not at all," said the serious Père in a way that made Ward think he would have minded had he been Catholic. They walked through a door marked *"Cloître, Entrée Interdit au Publique,"* and into a large garden where in a wall niche a small Virgin held her child with one arm, and anticipated his fate in the cross she held in the other. Ward's eyes widened at the gray lift of the monastery stretching above them. The Père smiled at his response. "Is it old?" asked Ward.

"The site is very old," said the monk. ("Most are," thought Ward.) "The building is nineteenth century, yet quite lovely, I think. The tower stems from the fifteenth. Very handsome."

They walked through the arches and looked at the refectory and the rooms which gave on the Sarthe, dark shafts whose plainness was hidden by the glint of holy fixtures. Here and there they passed other monks who bent shaved skulls toward them. It struck Ward that the clasped hands of the monks, the arched beams of the rooms, and the apex of the bent heads passing each other were all the same arched form which stood for submission. This was the first Henry Adams–like notion he had ever had, and it pleased him more than the sights which aroused it.

The Père said that he now had to go to a service and asked Ward if he would care to listen to it in the church.

"Yes," said Ward, feeling that he ought to get on but that he owed more than polite attention to what was closer to the root of the whole establishment than its architecture and decoration. He refused an offering of a room for the night, thanked the Père, and then sat in the church where the Père left him.

He was alone in the white nave. Sunlight battered the high windows. Up in front, two black lines of monks filed in, moved into the choir and began singing responses. For Ward, the interior became a great ear of which he felt a sensing part. He sat in the church five or six minutes after the monks filed out, and it was not until half an hour later as he roared down the main road south that he disengaged himself from the spell. "They nearly had me," he told himself. "A week of that, and they'd have had me." He was quite proud of his susceptibility.

3

Two days later he was riding into Tours trying to remember the date of the great battle. "732? Charles Martel?" he asked the handlebars. It was foggy, and he squinted at the fields which had stretched out flatter than a tongue since Cher, and populated them with Saracen bodies piling up before the firm line of the Franks. Then he remembered that the battle had been fought to the south, closer to Poitiers than Tours. He'd read Gibbon on it at Yale, and he recalled something about the historian's speculation that if The Hammer had not crushed the Saracens, the language of England and America would probably have been Arabic. The notion that he might be thinking in Arabic now, though something more lush and southern, eased his fatigue, and he nearly managed to recall a handsome Gibbonian sentence about "Merovingian might" and "Southern Something-or-other." He was just getting it when he felt the road change to cobblestones, and he rode to the first *Bureau de Tabac* and asked where the International Student Hostel was.

He tried not to wonder about the hostels till the last moment. Sometimes they were caves, sometimes castles. Usually twenty-five people were packed into the caves, two or three in the castles.

The Tours hostel was of the cave species, a long, single-story affair which looked like the cellar of a home which had crumbled away from it. The stone floor was edged by plank walls, a roof had been more or less fitted to them, and that was that. The small room contained a chair and a table; it opened up to the latrine on one side and the dormitory on the other. In the latter, twenty beds were spaced along the two long walls. There was no one around.

Ward threw his rucksack on a bed in the middle of the room and went back to the Registration Book. No one had signed in for two days. He wrote in the date, May 5, 1950, his Time of Arrival, 11:35 A.M., his Destination, South, his Next Stop, Chinon, Place of Origin, Paris, Nationality, U.S.A. He started to leaf through the pages but decided against it: he'd find the same names he'd been reading for a month.

He went to sleep, and when he woke up, took an old Baedecker from his rucksack and looked through the pages on Tours. "Not a very inspiring place," he thought, but he took out his notebook and wrote: "Tours-Roman. St. Gregory of (*Historia Francorum*), Balzac, Battle of (732), see Poitiers, silk, printing, machinery, porcelain, wines."

The fog turned to drizzle as he rode back to town, and he decided this would relieve him of sight-seeing. Perhaps he'd try St. Gatien's—if it weren't destroyed—and see the tomb of Charles VIII's children, but that was all. If the pyramids had been piled on the ruins of Persepolis ten kilometers away, he wouldn't have gone to see them. "I've reached a plateau," he told the handlebars. Even the flatlands he'd been riding over had seemed to be telling him, "Rest."

He ate a huge, three hundred franc dinner, went down the street to the Hôtel de l'Univers to use the toilet, and then decided to go to a movie. Outside the theater, the stills showed the Cannes beach. "Something lush and southern," he told himself.

It was a *policier,* comic, as far as he could tell, although the heroine's half-brother made love to her after shooting their father. "The Hammer would have laid the lot of them low," he muttered, but he enjoyed the shots of the beach, and the heroine looked like what he liked girls to look like.

He rode back to the hostel after drinking a half quart of the *vin de pays*. Inside there was a light. "Nuts," he said to the handlebars.

The light came from the fireplace. A couple stood in front of a large fire roasting something on green sticks. When Ward came in, he blinked and nearly retreated: the couple seemed to have no clothes on, but when they called *"Salut"* to him he saw that he'd mistaken their Bikinis for strips of shadow.

The girl offered him some sausage. *"Merci, non,"* he said. She looked a little like the girl in the movie.

In the dormitory, he switched on the overhead bulb. "Nuts," he said again. Opposite his bed were two beds pulled together. "Can't they separate for one night?" He heard them talking and laughing in the other room, not noisily, but as if they were in their own home. *"Y-a-t'il des verres?"* asked the man, and then Ward heard glasses clinking.

He took off his boots and lay down, debating whether to move his bed to the other room or at least over to the far corner. "Why in hell should I?" he said, accent on the "I."

It was difficult getting to sleep. "Not even the Saracens were this overt," he thought. "Maybe the Hammer lost a battle to someone else."

It was even more difficult to sleep after the Bikinis came in, but he finally got off about midnight.

When he woke, it was ten o'clock. He laced up his boots and started to go out before he remembered the couple. Then he looked over and saw that the beds were properly spaced again, and the blankets folded. He folded his own, packed his toilet articles, and went into the other room to sign out. He put sixty francs in a table drawer on top of the other money, and then opened the Registration Book. He wondered what their name was.

Under his own name he found two others, and for a second, he wondered if someone else had come in after he'd gone to sleep and left before he'd waked up. No, there was the girl's name first, Marie-Juliette Destorches, Time of Arrival, 5:30, Destination, North, Next Stop, Amboise, Place of Origin, St. Savin de Blaye, Previous Stop, Azay, Nationality, French, Time of Departure, 9:00 A.M.

The other name was Philippe Maragon, Time of Arrival, 7:00 P.M., Destination, South, Next Stop, Azay, Place of Origin, Orléans, Previous Stop, Amboise, Nationality, French, Time of Departure, 9:00 A.M.

Ward felt derailed. He began to recall the evening to see if he could reinterpret it in the terms suggested by the entries. It was beyond him. Recalling, however, brought him to the girl and to a reconsideration of his own itinerary. After a while, he said, "Leonardo died in Amboise."

On his way back north, the flatlands reminded him of the desert. "An Arabian desert," he assured the handlebars. He wondered how long it would take to catch up with her.

4

It had taken half an hour to catch up, a day to persuade her to sell her bicycle and join him on the back seat of the motorcycle, and two more to persuade her to settle in with him in Paris. The rapidity, ease and harmony of it all constituted the triumph of Ward's international experience, one which spurred on his intellectual and spiritual triumphs as well. He returned to his studies with earnestness and vigor, coming home each evening with burgher-like regularity to Marie-Juliette.

Juliette was in the middle of the first draft (she usually needed a revision) of her third novel. It was an "American" novel, and as Ward was Juliette's first American, she relied on him for the occasional idiom or local detail that would mark the reality of the scenes. Juliette was now looking for a critical success: her first novel had been a *succès de jeunesse* (she had been sixteen), the second a *succès de conséquence*. Now it was the *succès critique* that she wanted, with one of the annual prizes as her certificate. Of money she had enough: after a spree of clothes—car—jewelry—and sports-equipment buying, she turned her money over to an investment banker and lived, frugally, on the income. Notoriety had also glutted her; she was now at the point where there were seldom party invitations to refuse, even fewer photos in *Paris Match,* and *"Saluts"* from passers-by. "I've been a fad," she told Ward, "and it's time now to build a solid foundation. I'll be twenty next month. The world of letters has a short memory for those who thumb their noses at her." With many of her other remarks, this one was entered in Ward's notebook. He regarded her less as a private delight than a public trust, and he guarded, observed, and even mounted her with the urgent respect of the engineer of a city reservoir.

It was in the bloom of this routine that Ward received an insistent letter from his father, hinting at a cessation of his allowance if he remained in Europe. In the same mail, he received a letter from Baggish saying that he was coming to Paris on an assignment. The conjunction seemed a happy omen. "He'll know what to do," he told Juliette of Baggish. "He's a man with a level head on his shoulders."

"Not without piquancy," said Juliette and noted the idiom in her *Journal du Roman.* "It'll do for Dr. Booze." (This was the American dermatologist who, in her novel, returns from six years' work on the lepers of the Belgian Congo with a formula for distilling uranium from human tissue.) Ward noted her pronouncement in his own notebook. Neither of them was long without pencil in hand.

5

Baggish drove to Paris in Schreiber's Fiat bearing with him the clipping of his first article in the *Times-Journal.* Ward produced Juliette as his own badge of honor. Baggish replied in kind with Monique, and the four of them spent most of a week in each other's company. In bars, cafés, restaurants, on benches, the Seine embankments, the Tuileries grass, in the intermissions of concerts, jazz sets and plays, their talk bound and thickened their relationship. It was not, however, until the day before Baggish was to return that Ward raised the difficulty posed by his father's insistence, and counterposed by his own contentment. They had gone to a movie at the most advanced Ciné Club in France. The film, *Le Nez du Caroline,* was the production of a group of artists called *les peintres cliniques,* the chief of whom had been Juliette's lover the year before. The leading, or, as it turned out, the only visible human role in the film was taken by the corpse of the Chief's last mistress; he was its director and only living actor. The full import of this information, which Juliette supplied on the way up to Montmartre, did not hit them until after.

The film consisted of the following simple action: the severed head of an ugly, middle-aged woman was fixed on a small pedestal. A hand thrust a scalpel into the right nostril of the head and emerged with a long jelly-like string on the hook. By this time, the theater was a riot of shouts, laughter, and groans (tape recordings were made at each showing). The scalpel plunged back and forth into the nose withdrawing more and more of the interior. By the time the brains had been picked out, the audience had disintegrated with shouts, curses, screams, ecstatic laughter, and sensual writhings.

At the exit, Juliette pronounced it "a noble experiment. If I weren't afraid that Jean-France would molest me in my seat, I'd see it again."

"Horrifying," said Monique. "This is not French culture."

"No," said Juliette, "not like the Lido."

"The human spirit isn't tortured in the Lido."

"Says who?" was the novelist's response. She raised her eyes to the black sky, and pointed. When the others looked also, she intoned, *"'La Curiosité nous tourmente et nous roule, Comme un Ange Cruel qui fouettes des soleils.'"* The hand lowered to a table in front of the Brasserie Hugo, and they all sat like marionettes.

"What was that?" asked Ward, pride in Juliette dousing his dis-

gust at the film; he jotted down the reference she supplied, followed
by a sentence about the way it was used.

Baggish shook his head, as if to break the puppet strings. Juliette
was stirring him to battle. "Curiosity is a coward's substitute for
accomplishment," he said quietly, as if he were reading the message
on a worn tablet.

Juliette moved from a survey of the stars to the lesser orbit of their
faces. She seemed to have difficulty locating the source of the remark. Her own face, pug and eager, seemed to be speaking before
she actually spoke. Baggish had gone on, "Like variety," he said.
"People who seek it out are incapable of doing any one thing."
Juliette's face took off like a mob for a palace. There was a
riot of *"Non, non, non"* and then, "Idiot, cretin, horsehead, mouse-
brain. First, you didn't get within two miles of the lines. Baudelaire
says it torments us; it's not we who seek it out. Two, curiosity gen-
erates everything that counts in the world and a lot, like your ugly
mug, which doesn't. Thirdly, your French is impossible. You have
no right to speak it. Fourth, what do you know about art or anything else?"

Point Four seemed the place to move from. "I know what I like,"
said Baggish. He summoned a waiter and ordered four Pernods.

"A whiskey for me," said Juliette. To Baggish she said, "What
you know is what you know. Zero equals zero. You should try to
extend yourself. You're still young. Try to find some new experiences, look for something different. Life will mean more to you."

"Difference," said Baggish solemnly, "is not the criterion of anything but itself. Watch out for the man who sells you a pair of shoes,
a new form of government, or a novel"—this with a polite nod to
his opponent—"by telling you that you'll be reconciled to its ab-
surdities when it becomes familiar to you."

The word "novel" affected Juliette the way an insult does a pro-
fessional duelist. "Don't even think the word 'novel' in my presence,
Bageesh. When you've served one up, then talk about it. In your
own stupid language, the word itself means difference, newness.

What do I think when I face the page? I say to myself, 'A novel traditionally develops a single situation, identifies you with a single person, and that one more or less sympathetic at the start. One either follows his chase of a girl, or his gradual enlightenment, or his rising fortunes.' I say, 'Juliette, sweetheart, write me something new, something different, something which displaces this single-situation tyranny'—I'm speaking of the small novel now, you understand, not this monster English-Russian-Scandinavian hodgepodge—'something which knocks the reader on the head by bringing in characters who don't recur, situations which work only in the roundabout ways of contrast and comparison.' I never let the reader take hold. When he thinks he has me, I'm not there. Ha, ha, ha, ha, ha," and she slapped her forehead.

Baggish, warming to Juliette's excitement, felt like kissing the slapped head. But he went on, "That's a third-rate excuse for incompetence." Her dark blue eyes bulged in disbelief. He went on further, "A novel is a roller coaster of distress and sympathy, love and desire. Everything must count in it, or the car shoots off the coaster. Nothing is worse than commentary. Novels which talk about novels are worse than violinists who discuss the piece while they're playing it. Such talk breaks the artistic rhythm, the world of the art form. It gives the viewer an in to the real world which shatters the other. I know. I'm a real novel reader, and I know how to separate my two worlds."

"I could vomit," said Juliette, "throw up, disgorge my gut and gall in your ugly puss. Your traditionalism enervates me, kills me. You are trying to strangle the very scene I'm writing now, one in which a character talks against the form of the book in which he plays a leading role, while another character, an obnoxious one, imported clearly for the purpose, defends its technique. All this in a brief, classical study of a zoology student's seduction, corruption, and annihilation of an old roué introduced to her for sheer *frisson* by his third wife who detests her because she designs her own clothes with more brilliance than the wife's own Paquins and Balenciagas.

This is the function of art, to commingle the inversion of the tradition with both celebration and violation of it. I could scream with the pleasure of it." This is what she proceeded to do. They were forced to leave the café.

"She isn't usually like this," said Ward to Baggish, as they walked along. "You seem to bring out something bestial in her. For me, she's a wonderful new experience."

Baggish could not shake his pontifical tone. "Experience is never its own good. People who say it is are disguising their lack of philosophy with a hand-me-down slogan."

"I disagree," said Ward, his own argumentativeness ripening, now that Juliette was out of earshot. "Look at us now. Here we are, walking along with two lovely girls—" the girls were twenty feet in front of them—"having drunk Pernod in Paris, seen a movie, watched people, talked with friends. Isn't this fulfillment? Do we have to justify it? Is this only prelude to something else?"

"No," said Baggish. "It's intermission time. We're buying orange drinks at five times their value and overhearing complaints about the narrowness of the seats."

"I don't get it, and I disagree. I think it's good in itself."

"All right, Robert. I'll cede it, but for me, it's at best charging batteries. If I manufactured shoes, I'd be noticing people abuse their heels. If I were a dentist, I'd be taking in decay spots in molars. If I were a composer, I'd be picking up the rhythm of the cars. Since I'm nothing, I'm just taking in flavors. If you want to call it pleasure, fine with me."

"What about love?" asked Ward studying Juliette's rocking butt as they caught up to it.

"A career in itself, when all others have failed," said Baggish.

"I forgive you, Baggish," said Juliette. "What are you insulting the airwaves with now?"

Ward told her.

The blue eyes darkened, and the body seemed to coalesce for a leap. Then it relaxed. "You're a very nice American boy," she said, "and maybe someday I can show you that variety may have something."

"My curiosity torments me," said Baggish, with a low bow.

"Not tonight," said Monique, and in Baggish's ear she whispered, "A little birgitta, Teddy?"

"Later," he said out loud. "Robert wants to ask me something."

6

It was after a midnight meal in Ward's apartment that he put his problem to Baggish. Monique had gone home with a headache and a curse on Discussion. Juliette cleared the remains and washed dishes while Baggish and Ward sat cross-legged on the double bed drinking Calvados.

"What do you think I ought to do, Ted?" Ward asked.

Baggish leaned back against the bolster, thought a minute, and said, "Robert, you'll have to think a little beyond your immediate pleasures. If you think your father'll support you another year, put the importance of your staying to him. If you feel ashamed to do this, then how much of his displeasure are you willing to incur? If little, then you'd better go back now."

"I've thought of it," said Ward. "Or maybe I could get a job in Paris?"

It was Baggish's debut as a sage, and he was making much of it. "There's every difference on earth between working eight hours a day at something you dislike—and that's what your feelings will be at the only jobs you'll be able to get over here—and having those eight hours and every other hour to yourself."

"I suspect you're right," said Ward, "but I'm not afraid to go to work."

Absolutely serious, because he was tired, Baggish said, "It's the joy of life." It was too much. He had to wipe this up. "Look, why don't you write the old man that you want to get this stuff out of your system once and for all so that you'll have no regrets when you go back to work? Ask him to carry you for six months, three in Paris, with the *fille* there—that ought to take care of that—and the rest for a big trip through Europe, the Near East, Africa, wherever you want. How does that sound?"

Juliette came in, and Ward leaned back against her hip. "Maybe. Let me think. I'll go take a walk. I'll make up my mind in half an hour. Can you wait, Ted?"

Baggish was about to refuse, but seeing Juliette looking studiously at him, he said, "Sure. What do you have to read?"

CHAPTER THREE

I

When Baggish borrowed his Fiat and went off to Paris, Schreiber felt lonelier than he had since his first days in Heidelberg. He hardly ever saw the office crowd now, and he did not feel like seeing Traudis. In the office, there was some unpleasantness in the air which Schreiber could not define, but which he felt had to do with the rumor that someone had a connection with a stateside newspaper to which he fed classified information. A number of articles had appeared in the St. Louis *Times-Journal* which concerned matters which only certain people in the Command knew about. People spoke about it in joking fashion, but the jokes were edged with suspicion and discomfort. A C.I.C. investigation was rumored to be underway.

One day Schreiber came back from lunch to find a man going through the papers on his desk. "What's going on here?" he demanded.

The man looked up calmly and said, "C.I.C. Parsons. Just checking on some stuff. You Max Schreiber?"

"That's right. Have a seat, Mr. Parsons."

Parsons sat in Schreiber's chair, Schreiber in the visitor's chair in front of the desk. "You don't lock the office when you go out,

Schreiber. The Security Code is specific and unambiguous about
locking offices in which classified material is kept. Even if you're
only going to the can." Here, to Schreiber's surprise, Parsons giggled;
it was like seeing shaving soap on the nose of an after-dinner speaker.
Parsons continued in the original tone. "This goes even if you put
your materials in locked drawers. If that was the case." He fixed
Schreiber with a dirk of suspicion. "Now I'm going to come clean
with you. Stuff which you've been handling has been leaked to un-
authorized persons, in fact, to the newspapers. We don't think it's
a matter of espionage, because we've checked your record pretty
thoroughly."

"*My* record?" put in Schreiber.

This was ignored. "You did live on the Germany economy when
you had rooms at the Hotel Ritter, but that, we gather, was an affair
of the, uh, heart?" Another giggle rippled the investigative front.
"But you've been careless, Schreiber, either in the office or with your
mouth outside, and you're liable to find yourself in a mess of trouble.
That's all for now, just a little warning."

Parsons left, and Schreiber put his head back on the chair rest. By
the time Charles and Sara came back he was in a cloud of sweat.
"Hold the fort for me this afternoon, will you?" he asked them.
"I'm feeling punk."

He took a bus back to the hotel. Just outside the fruit store, two
German schoolboys in *lederhosen* were squared off against each
other, arms folded across their chests. As Schreiber approached,
one of them jumped against the other, knocking him off balance. A
swift recovery was followed by a reprisal in kind. "*Schwein,*" called
the first. "*Hund,*" responded the other, and their eyes resumed war-
fare. Schreiber walked between them and said they mustn't fight.
They put their eyes and arms down, and did not square off again
until he turned into the hotel. The proprietor of the fruit store came
out then, cracked their heads together, and spun them off in opposite directions, kicking one of them as an instructional dividend.
Schreiber went upstairs, lay down on his bed, and almost imme-

diately dreamed of a large field of cabbages, which, as he passed, were transformed into the heads of Micheline, Gladys Culley, Florence, Traudis, Sara, a girl at Hazelton High School who had refused his month-long-prepared invitation to the movies, and Mrs. Carroway. As he ran terror-stricken through the fields, the cabbage heads launched themselves at his head. He heard the cracking of his bones as the vegetable women hit them, and he woke up sweating to hear the cracking outside his window.

Across the Domplatz, the driver of a beer wagon was lashing the drayhorse attached to it. *"Halt an,"* yelled Schreiber out the window. The driver, a limbed version of the barrels, jumped off the seat and socked the horse in the ribs. The animal fell over, the wagon tottered, and the beer barrels rolled off into the square. One split against the curb in front of the church, and beer stormed into the street. Schreiber ran downstairs. Thirty or forty people surrounded the driver whose head lay on his horse's fractured side, weeping. The sun burned in the dark pools of beer, some of which was being scooped up by people with glasses, cups, steins, even cardboard boxes.

For Schreiber, the scene extended his dream; it smelled of a brutal finality like the vicious climax of an international struggle, bloody, occult, mysterious in origin and meaning, but clear in its vileness. He stood by the bookstalls under the church while a jeepful of M.P.s and two German policemen dispersed the crowd, reassembled the beer barrels, and carted off the driver.

The snort of a horn shook him, and he saw the tipped white glove of Nina Willey scooting up the Hauptstrasse in her Volkswagon. Schreiber waved to the four cartons of Chesterfields sticking out of the large wooden crate in the back seat. Then he went down Altstadtgasse to the Neckar and walked slowly up the river toward Neckargemünd. The river was filled with kayaks paddled by tandem teams of young men and women. On the single track up the river, the blue trolley with the gold eaglet insignia crackled past. The sun tumbled gold into the hills. Schreiber walked between the tracks and the embankment, letting the warmth loosen the hard clots in his stomach.

At Neckargemünd, he drank a half bottle of Niersteiner on a terrace restaurant overlooking the bend of the river. He felt adrift, relaxed, available, and lonely, sweetly lonely. After two hours, he took the trolley back to Heidelberg, bought a bag of nectarines at the fruit store, and an Everyman's Library book called *The Natural History of Selborne* at a bookstall. He went upstairs to eat and read. He read himself into a half-trance, stopping after he found himself rereading for the fourth time a passage about a tortoise named Timothy, the former property of a Mrs. Snooke:

When one reflects on the state of this strange being, it is a matter of wonder to find that Providence should bestow such a profusion of days, such a seeming waste of longevity on a reptile that appears to relish it so little as to squander more than two-thirds of its existence in a joyless stupor, and be lost to all sensation for months together in the profoundest of slumbers.

"Old Timothy," said Schreiber. "You weren't so dumb." He copied the passage in his notebook and went off to sleep.

2

The first letter he opened at work the next morning contained an envelope within an envelope. In the second, an engraved card informed him that Mrs. Sylvia Hampton Carroway announced the marriage of her daughter Florence to Mr. Peyton Achille Chadwick, Your Presence Requested at the Reception, Carroway House, Friday, April 25. Schreiber's face creased with astonishment, and Sara, staring at him over a report on a Bulgarian silk mill, muttered, "He's cracking up," and thought that she'd have her GS-9 sooner than she'd dared hope. "Something wrong, Max?" she called across.

"No," said Schreiber, jamming the card back into the enclosed envelope and this into the addressed one. "Just an old friend's remarriage." The use of the word 'friend' for Florence, who, at best, had never been that, made him think the marriage a good thing. He tried to remember what Peyton Chadwick looked like, but the only image that came to him was a moonlike object which, after a second, he realized was his picture of Mrs. Snooke's Timothy. "If he has Timothy's temperament, he'll last longer than I did."

"Christ," thought Sara. "The man's batty."

It was Tuesday, and Baggish was due back from Paris. Schreiber called Haus Stempel von Gode.

"Dr. Stempel *hier*," came the clear voice.

"*Ich möchte gern den Herrn Baggish bitte sprechen*," said Schreiber disguising his voice.

"*Nicht zu Hause*," was the response, and the phone banged down even more rudely than the words.

Schreiber picked up an informer's report. It was evaluated C-3—moderately reliable—and it came from a Chinese source which had heard that the Russians were planning a two-pronged attack on Germany through the Fulda Gap and Bavaria on July 4. Four or five such reports came in every month, and more before Christmas and Easter. "Americans are always afraid they're going to be assaulted while they're sitting on the can," was Joe McBain's interpretation of the phenomenon. "The informers get to know what's wanted and when it's wanted." Schreiber wrote a précis of the report, evaluated it himself, cited other documents in cross-reference and put the document in his Out Box. The phone rang, and Baggish's voice said, "Hello, Max. I just got back."

"Teddy," said Schreiber beaming. "It's good to hear your voice."

"Can we have dinner tonight?"

"Aren't you on the night shift?" asked Schreiber, for whom those weeks were barren ones.

"I've quit," said Baggish. "I'm leaving the job."

This announcement was more startling to Schreiber than Mrs. Carroway's. "Did you come into money?" he asked.

"Not yet," said Baggish. "It's...."

"Something happen in Paris?"

"I'll let you know at dinner. Let's go to Wiesbaden. We'll celebrate. May I pick you up at work?"

"Fine, thank you," said Schreiber.

"The car was great, Max. Thank you again."

"A pleasure, Teddy. I'm glad it brought you luck."

Baggish hung up without saying good-by. Schreiber had become accustomed to this abruptness, but, in a character which now held no mysteries for him, it constituted a backwash which made him less certain than usual of the stream.

At ten of five, Schreiber said, "See you tomorrow" to Charles and Sara, left the office, showed his AGO card to the M.P. at the gate, and crossed the street where Baggish waited in the little station wagon with Traudis and a stiff-looking German who with minor alteration in mien and costume could have passed for either eighteen or thirty-five. Schreiber frowned with disappointment at seeing them, but the disappointment was short-lived.

"Max Schreiber, Gunther Frötenhaelsch," said Baggish.

"Guten Abend," said Traudis with her enchanting, gap-toothed smile, as the other two shook hands.

"Hello, Traudis," said Schreiber. (He had called her this only in bed.) He climbed in the back with Frötenhaelsch, and exchanged a series of smiling nods with him for half a minute, indispensable German prelude to becoming seat neighbors.

"So you're a real American now, Max?" said Traudis.

"I don't follow," said Schreiber.

"You've got a car."

"It's a European car," said Schreiber.

"A fortiori," said Traudis. "An inverse form of *Coca-Colonizing.*"

"I didn't think of that," said Schreiber, and leaned his head against the window.

Riding along, he suddenly found himself at home with what struck him as old friends and a promising new one. "A funny thing happened to me today," he said.

"What's that, Max?" asked Baggish. He maneuvered the Fiat

past the smoking wreck of an immense truck near the entrance to the Autobahn. "Boy, that one got it."

Schreiber, whose eyes were closed, went on, not noticing that the others' attention was on the accident. "I learned that my wife re-married. A funny feeling that gives one. Made me feel as if I'm living the epilogue of my life, though God knows it's not been much of a life. In fact, I guess I've always thought of it as a kind of pro-logue. 'Something's going to happen,' I tell myself. 'Things are going to change.' I'm a time-traveler. I've always thought of where I'd be in a year or ten years. Some people wish they were in another place. Some wish they were another person. I've never wanted that kind of change. It was always the particular moment that depressed me, never myself, or the places I was in. Not that I consider that I'm such a hot-shot or that I've always liked the places I've been in. I guess to you though, I probably look like a space-traveler, leaving America for Europe as I have, but I'm not. Time's always been my way out."

They had been on the Autobahn since the middle of the speech, and the two Germans were trying to make something of the torrent of English, Traudis as an exercise in translation, Frötenhaelsch in more generous fashion. His English was largely a matter of vocabu-lary, and considering only this he was impressed by Schreiber's speech. The words "time," "space," "prologue," and "epilogue" eased his serious consciousness into the philosophic realm which was the one he loved. He had just come from an hour's entranced reading of Hölderlin's *"Andenken,"* and from the rolling free verse, he quoted twenty or thirty grief-spattered lines. Schreiber, half-under-standing, rode with the rhythm. "I've been understood," he told himself, and more than that; he felt that his prosaic self-examination had been sublimely transmuted.

When Frötenhaelsch finished the recitation, Schreiber said, "Thank you. That's what I meant. You've found just the right words for it. Won't you tell me a little about yourself now? It's so seldom that one meets someone who touches the right chords so quickly." Frötenhaelsch needed no push to discourse on such a subject and responded with a prodigality that carried them into Wiesbaden. Four hours later, Schreiber, back home, still full of the overdrive the expedition had kicked off in him, reduced the account, and then the whole evening, into the shorthand forms he used in his notebook.

Tuesday. Was picked up by Ted Baggish at 4:55 P.M. He at wheel. Traudis Bretzka in front. In back, Gunther Froetelmalsch (sp?) stud. econ. in Alfred Weber Institute. Approaches econ. via philosophy: "All modern accounting systems are filled with Kant. Problem of knowledge." Was ardent Nazi who converted to Western Democ. via term in English prison camp. TB's first shot at real night driving (His initials same as Traudis B's. Theirs mean disease, mine mean Military Supply.) Consequence, ride was occasionally tense coming back, but TB acquitted self beautifully. Half moon, pale gold over Autobahn. GF told about self—see above—going up. Way back, he and TB talked phil. in Germ. Understood most. Much about Nietzsche—Ger. late 19th cent. phil. GF had important sentence (from N.): "If man has character he also has characteristic experience which recurs again and again." Asked me what mine was. I said without thinking—in Eng.—"Infatuation." (This worked out to *Betörung* or *Verblendung*.) "Lorelei," said TB. "Not an experience," said GF. GF's experience was not seeing light first time, then seeing. TB's was backing out of situations due to feelings of inadequacy. I reminded him of his success at wheel, and he amended to non-mechanical situations. TBz claimed not to have one, then amended to "wouldn't reveal," woman's prerog.

Casino, pretty bldg. set in arcade, surrounded by park. Elaborate inter. Went in, signed membership card. Central room, high-ceiling, chandelier. Fancy, forty, fifty people at tables. Played roulette hour and half. Lost hundred-three marks. GF lost ten, the TBs won. We drank Rhine wines till late, in balcony, talked about gamblers.

Incident: TB fingering chips as wheel started was cautioned by croupier, put all chips down haphazardly and walked upstairs to table. Won eighty marks, sent up in velvet bag.

Incident on return: near sign which lists number of accidents on Autobahn (as you get off near Heidel.) big truck turned over on back. No one around, yet wasn't there when we drove up. Made me think—don't know why—of Mamma's brother Douggie who had heart attack on sales trip, died alone in hotel room. Found him on floor with scratches on rug where he tried to get up. Awful to die alone. TB drove me home.

3

Baggish's decision to quit his job had been prompted by a visit from Parsons a week before his trip to Paris. It was in Baggish's room at Haus Stempel von Gode. "I wouldn't ordinarily come to a suspect's home," said Parsons, "but this is a special case." A giggle flaked off his official seriousness.

"Suspect?"

"We've traced you out, Baggish-boy."

"Explain."

"No employee of the Department of the Army can submit, let alone allow to be published, material of any sort without initial clearance from the Command. When an employee publishes classified materials, material with classification higher than Restricted, he is liable to court-martial. In occupied areas, namely Germany."

"It's nice to pick up army tidbits," said Baggish, and from his armchair—Parsons was standing—he reached for a jar of peanut butter to make himself a sandwich. "What's it got to do with me?"

"We've read your little article. It's based on an official classified document which was traced to the office of one of your friends—" this word was drawn out with lewd shifts in pitch—"and you have been frequently observed at or near the desk where the document was—carelessly, I may say—kept. You're in warm water, dear heart."

Baggish explored his nose with a finger, and wiped the results on a sleeve. "A fig for you, Parsons. A fat fig for a fair fag." Parsons giggled. "What are you going to do about it?"

They exchanged evaluating looks. "You know I wouldn't do anything to hurt you, honey," said Parsons.

"I know that," said Baggish menacingly.

"But I think it makes us square."

"Ravenshit."

"I mean I thought you might want to reduce the payments." Parsons looked at the dark glacier moving across Baggish's face and sighed. "Oh well. Never mind. You've been real dear about it all. I'm going to report that you're a smart guy who guessed the right answers. But I better warn you that it won't stop there. You'll either have to quit the scribbling or the job, and resignation always looks better."

"That's fair enough," said Baggish. "Of course that means I'll lose my room at the Hotel."

"I'm just praying we'll get someone who's like you—or maybe even like me," said Parsons.

"But our mark payment arrangement still goes," said Baggish coolly.

After another, larger, body-shaking sign, Parsons murmured, "Until they cut 'em off me." On this, they shook hands.

The mail that day brought Baggish the insurance he needed to announce his resignation. Along with the clipping of his third article—on the possibility that the Russians would come through the Fulda Gap on Independence Day—came an offer to act as Special Correspondent for the *Times-Journal* and five affiliated mid-western newspapers. He was to be paid by the article, one hundred dollars for a thousand words, three hundred for longer articles.

The offer was embroidered with high praise for the first two articles, and the praise led Baggish to vault its tenuous security and write out a letter of resignation to the Major, one which concluded by praising the spirit and organization of the Staff Message Control, EUCOM, and acknowledge "with profound feelings of gratitude the assistance I received from everyone, and particularly from Mr. Benton Hoover, GS-4, my senior editorial clerk."

That night he wrote Ward to say he was coming to Paris: "I've got some business which involves looking over that group Eisenhower's heading," and, indeed, he intended to pay for the trip by doing an article on the shaping-up of the NATO headquarters in Versailles. He wanted to get away, however; it would be a cleaner break from his routine. Also, he wanted to sleep with Monique. He wrote her about his impending visit, told her to save him four days, and signed off "Birgitta, birgitta, Teddy."

4

The night after the expedition to Wiesbaden he explained his decision to quit to Schreiber. "A newspaper guy I know named Whitney has gotten into hot water over some article he wrote, and his paper is going to send him to Japan. He recommended me for his spot. I did a lot of newspaper work in college. It won't pay me much, but I won't have this damn night shift hanging over my head."

Schreiber winced at the name Whitney, and almost told Baggish that he not only knew about the case but was involved in it. He decided, however, that he didn't want his pupil to know of more blemishes than were visible. He contented himself with, "Must be a smart guy that friend of yours. I hear he's got a great knack for guessing the contents of closed envelopes."

"Yes, he's a shrewd one," said Baggish. "I hardly know him. Just met him in a bar a few times, and we got to talking about newspapers. I was really surprised when he sent my name in."

Schreiber considered the Neckar for a moment—they were sitting on the restaurant terrace at Neckargemünd—and then said, as if he'd hooked the wisdom from the stream, "I'm not surprised, Ted. I sometimes have a feeling about people, that they have a direction in them, some down, some up, some both. I feel yours is up, and it's right for you. Most of the people who have that direction show it so vulgarly in everything they do that it makes you sick. You aren't in there grabbing and punching; you're just working solidly."

Baggish took a huge swallow of Piesporter. "Poor dumb jerk," he thought. "What kind of crud can a man flop around in?"

Schreiber was talking about a fortune teller at a fair in Hazelton who had told him when he was eight years old that he was going to be famous. "It was nearly ten years before I let on to myself that that man's prophecy was no more nor less than sheer hot air."

"You know, Max," said Baggish in a tone less adulterated by self-interest than any he had used since he was a boy, "Why don't you save up leave and take a long trip, one that would really absorb you? You're too smart to just hang around here. I know you've got a big job, but a man gets stale in one place. I remember that you said you're a time-traveler rather than a space one, but if you go to places of historical interest, then you're traveling in time too, aren't you? I think you need to give yourself a chance, shake yourself up."

Schreiber suspended a dark spoonful of mock turtle soup at his mouth and smiled, partially at the sun caught in a net of cloud, partially at Baggish's remembrance of his self-analysis. "Who knows, Ted? Might be a good idea. I've got twenty-four days leave saved up right now. And I always did like history."

"You're far from old, Max. Who knows if your direction has even established itself yet."

"That's nice of you, Teddy," said Schreiber. "You've got a wonderful gift for saying nice things."

5

The notion of taking a long trip which Baggish put into his head became for Schreiber over the next few weeks a less-and-less unlikely, more-and-more attractive one. As often happens when desires are genuine, support for both the attraction and the likelihood came from all sides. Joe McBain and Anne Pendleton married in the Castle Chapel in the presence of nationals from twenty nations, in most of which Joe or his father had been stationed at one time or another.

Although he realized that he had been invited as an afterthought (at least the invitation had come by word of mouth from Sara two days before the ceremony) Schreiber was more affected by the occasion than some of the principals. Sitting with the Willeys in the last row of the chapel, he soaked up the gaud of medal and braid, flowers, silk, marble, and jewels before the altar where the Princes of the Palatine had knelt and married. Around him were the deputies of the Mufti of Jerusalem, General Franco, King Farouk, the Grand Duchess of Luxembourg, even a representative from the Soviet Consulate, and the chapel oozed with the babble of international power. Schreiber's historical palate burned with these spices, and Baggish's advice, which had at first seemed but the most offhand and trivial recommendation, now seemed an essential cure for what ailed him. After the ceremony, he went to the Special Service Library and drew out the six published volumes of Toynbee's *A Study of History,* along with *An Encyclopaedia of World History* for a list of the facts.

That night he settled down with Volume One and entered upon a magical experience. He had skimmed the one volume summary of the book when Florence selected it as a Book-of-the-Month Club supplement and hadn't liked it. Each evening for two weeks it had been his toilet reading, and though he was very tolerant of what he read while his bowels moved, he had written Toynbee off as a peddler of clichés, and the possessor of a smokescreen vocabulary and syntax worse than the worst legal brief. Now, however, with the handsome gold, black, and green binding of the Oxford University Press edition gripped in his hand, a glass of iced Pepsi-Cola by his side (he chose this drink because of the company's beneficent scholarship program), and Webster's New International Dictionary sitting on top of the historical encyclopaedia, he felt a revival of that scholarly passion which had borne up his old wartime study of censorship evasion. Nations, churches, tribes, battles, princes, poets, inventions, philosophies, the ten million phenomena which sluiced from Toynbee's pages made him reel with the pleasure of accomplishment, as if he controlled that which he learned, was master of what, under the binding, the historian arranged. He turned the pages of the volume slowly, as a gourmet turns those of a great cookbook, moaning now and then with excitement.

The reading agitated and fed his wanderlust, gave body, direction, and force to it. Each morning at the office, in front of the large map of the world which covered the wall opposite his desk, he spotted the towns and seas which he'd read about the night before: Sfax and Tarsis, Seville and Ploesti, Gujarat and Mylae became names in real space and real time for him, places where children grew and wars were fought. Once, while he was staring at the Gulf of Sidra, Sara asked him why he spent so much time at the map. "I'm becoming a citizen of the world," he answered, without conscious ego or wit.

Sara took this answer as she, and the other members of the group, took almost all of Schreiber's remarks and actions since the uncomfortable security rumble, as a sign that he was no longer with them, or rather, that his brief period of alignment had been but a lucid interval in a clouded, if innocuous career.

The second night of his Toynbee reading he went for a walk, dizzy more with his own accomplishment than Toynbee's. Along the river, his appetite for knowledge changed into one for food. He walked back to the Schnookeloch, a student restaurant on the Steingasse, and saw Traudis and Baggish at a table drinking beer and reading books. He went over to them, the sight of her increasing, if deflecting his appetite. When they saw him, they put their books away and smiled with what seemed to him relief.

"You and I never meet on your initiative," said Traudis, "yet we continue to meet. Can you explain that?"

"No," said Schreiber.

"You don't need to research that one," said Baggish. "You two meet like coal gondolas meet up with coal, or dugs with babies' lips. Ah, forgive, Max," he added gently, seeing Schreiber's perplexed distaste for the latter simile. "Sit down. We've been reading for want of things to say to each other."

"Theodore and I are incompatible friends," said Traudis. "You sit in the middle and be our Suez Canal."

This comparison also threw Schreiber, who felt as if he'd reached into the wrong drawer and come up with a pair of bloomers instead of a handkerchief.

"I was just going to call you, Max," said Baggish. "Traudis has a problem. She's got to go to an aunt's funeral up in Darmstadt this Saturday, and she doesn't want to spend the train fare. I told her that I'd drive her if I could borrow the car."

"Sure," said Schreiber. "Of course. I'm sorry about your aunt."

"Thank you," said Traudis.

"The problem is I can't take her. I've got the NATO assignment to get off."

"I'll be glad to drive you," said Schreiber, feeling his resolve yield under the pressures of opportunity and desire. "I've never been to Darmstadt."

"You're very kind, Max," said Traudis, hesitating over his name. "As always."

"It's my pleasure," he said.

"The Odenwald should be lovely now," she said. "I hope we'll enjoy it. We could stop for lunch in a little *Stube* in Gänsheim. It's almost Bavarian, lots of fat waiters and horrible singing."

"Sounds inviting," said Schreiber. "If unfunereal," he thought.

"It does indeed," said Baggish, feeling the Traudis-burden easing off his shoulders.

6

Saturday Schreiber called for Traudis at Haus Stempel von Gode. He honked the horn, a signal which drew Dr. Stempel out to the balcony in his undershirt. This spectacle caused Schreiber to crouch low at the wheel whence he issued only at a tap on the window glass. It was Schmigl.

"Herr Schreiber. What a rare pleasure. Where have you been? How are you?"

"Schreiber," screamed Stempel, leaning over the balcony to peer into the car. "Old Schreiber. I'll be right down."

Schreiber rolled down the window and shook hands with Schmigl, asked him how his studies were going, and evaded questions about his own frequentings and work. At the question "What are you doing here?" he blenched, and then pointed, for response, to Traudis, who was coming out the door followed by Stempel still in his under-shirt.

"Happy days are here again," was an equivalent of Stempel's teutonic blast as he crumpled Schreiber's hand in his own. "How we all wish that you had stayed with us, Herr Schreiber. Your com-patriot is a most difficult young man."

As if on signal, Baggish's face appeared at the first floor window. "Good morning, Max. All well, I trust?"

Dr. Stempel's face collapsed at the voice and he looked at Schreiber as if for protection.

"All well here," said Schreiber benevolently, puzzled, if pleased at the facial *Zusammenbruch*.

"We're off," said Traudis, and she opened the door, nudging Stempel aside with the handle.

"Good-by," said Schreiber to everybody. Only Baggish responded.

As he rounded the curve, Schreiber saw Schmigl and Stempel sneaking into the house. He asked Traudis what was wrong with them.

"Our Theodore," she said. "He's what's wrong with them." She put her arm around Schreiber's shoulder. "What a wonderful day. We'll have a good time."

Schreiber nearly drove the car off the road. "You surprised me," he said, recovering. She started to take her arm down. "No," he said quickly. "Leave it there. It reminds me of the way things used to be. I was just thinking of your aunt's funeral."

"Funeral?" she said. "Ah, the funeral. There's no funeral. It was just a way to get off with you."

"I see," said Schreiber slowly. "But what an overelaborate plan. You should have asked me straight out."

"Yes," she said. "As I practically did after Horstmann's party, only to find myself left out in the cold like a horse."

"Ted is in the plot, too?" he asked. "And I was thinking that you and he—well, I thought that Stempel might have been angry at him because of you."

"No no no no no," she said. "He just hates him. It's something chemical. Baggish moves in the opposite direction to him, and runs him down like a truck over a chicken. To me, though, he's very kind."

"That's what I thought," said Schreiber.

"A true friend," said Traudis. Under her arm, Schreiber's shoulder trembled. "Not as you were, Max. An intimate and—well, part of an arrangement. I admit all. I understand what you felt. I've thought about it ten thousand times since. You don't understand me, don't even want to, despite all your interest in me. Baggish understands, and Baggish forgives. You always think you're being used. You don't understand the passion behind 'using' someone. He does. Yet you are, in your way, an attractive man. One wants to be liked by you. It's important for me to be liked by you, understood and liked by you. I don't know why."

Except in the deadly hands of Florence, Schreiber had seldom felt the analytic scalpel in his interior. Clumsy as the probing was, the mere fact that Traudis thought, had thought and, apparently, would continue to think of him, made him feel that he had been far too harsh with her. Yet, for the moment he did not yield. "I don't really understand what you mean now," he said. "Are you accusing me? Are you telling me you're Baggish's girl and want to be mine? Why are you talking like this?"

"Stop the car," she said.

He pulled up on the side. They were in the Odenwald now, and
the sun passed through leaves to speckle their faces. Schreiber pulled
the emergency brake as Traudis' arms flung about him. She pushed
him down onto the steering wheel and kissed him.

"My God in heaven," he said finally. "What are you doing? Are
you batty?"

At this, Traudis' eyes widened, and kept widening until they
drew his into their orbit of suggestion. "Batty?" she said passionately.
"Batty?"

"Traudis," said Schreiber, pleading, "I'm forty years old. I can't
keep losing myself like a boy. And losing myself to something which
disappears as soon as I have it." The plea imposed an odd dignity on
the cramped struggle at the wheel. Traudis looked at him softly,
put a large, hard palm to his forehead and stroked. Her plum-black
eyes looked straight into his, and she whispered hoarsely, gently, "I
know, dear Max. I know. I hurt you terribly. All my German darkness swallowed you up. You can never forgive me."

In his hands, as tentative as a peach in the fruit inspector's, Traudis
was nothing if not an appeal to desire. He put his head on her breasts,
and rubbed it back and forth, kissing them through her blouse. She
took his hand under her blouse to her bare stomach and moved it
up and down. "Oh," moaned Schreiber. "Oh, oh." Traudis slipped
away, kicked open the door of the car, and then pulled him out.
Arm in arm, they walked into the woods, up a hill and then down to
a slot of grass by a twisted trickle of water. There, with the sun hot
on her, her eyes fixing his, Traudis removed her sweater, blouse,
brassiere, skirt, and underpants. Schreiber had never felt so excited.
"Oh life, life," he felt his insides singing, "Oh my life."

7

Twenty minutes later, as they drove through the Odenwald to the
little *Stube* in Gänsheim, Traudis talked to Schreiber for the first
time about her feelings and her past. It began, with a philosophic

prelude, but by now Schreiber realized that this was but the German way of saying, "I'll tell you how it happened."

"I've always needed some large idea to live by," it went. She linked her left arm in his right so that he had to risk steering with his left.

"I understand that," he said.

"When I was a girl I had the *Mädchengruppe*. I was a Squad Leader. I loved Hitler with my whole heart. It was a beautiful time; that can be said for it. Music, picnics, marches, flags. The seed of the future, that's what we were. Because of my need, I took to it very strongly. We never saw anything wrong. Once my father came home from Hamburg and said he saw a man with whom he'd played golf, a Jew, sweeping up the dock, but that was about the only odd thing I remember until the war. And the war itself wasn't so bad for a while. Sometimes it was wonderful. You can't understand that, can you Max?"

"I think I can, Traudis," said Schreiber. "I can understand it." The rust-colored image of Micheline Goupin slipped into the harsh, lovely face at his side. The double exposure led Schreiber to say further that he not only understood, but that he himself had felt somewhat the same about the war. Traudis was saying, "It ended in a second, as if someone had turned off every light in Germany with one switch."

"That's a fine way to say it," said Schreiber.

"The Russians were outside Stettin in '45. We heard their guns away off, but our troops marched through to stop them. We never thought, even then, that we'd lost more than minor battles. Except for some brutal, suicidal attacks."

"Propaganda," said Schreiber thoughtfully.

"Propaganda and ego," said Traudis. "Anyway, on the day it happened, I was just home from making bandages in the Stadthalle, when I saw German soldiers running through town. I'd never seen German soldiers running. We had all expected that there'd be an engagement on the outskirts, but there wasn't. My mother and I watched at the windows, watched them running past. Then a staff

car drove down our street through the soldiers to a square a block
away from us. A colonel got out and started yelling at the soldiers
to stop running and make a formation. They ran by him, and he
took out his gun and started shooting into the air, screaming like a
maniac. Then a little lance corporal came by and ran right into the
colonel, knocked him down. I don't know whether he meant to or
not. On his stomach, the colonel shot the man in the head. The
head was all over the street. My mother and I were screaming and
crying. And then my sister rushed in and said that the Russians
would be in town in an hour, and that there was a train leaving for
Hamburg in ten minutes. We each took a sack of things and ran
to the station. Everybody in the world was on that train. About
sixty kilometers from Hamburg, it stopped where the tracks had
been shelled. And we walked and walked to Hamburg, eating nothing, not sleeping. And when finally we got there, we heard that the
bridge to the west was going to be closed in an hour. We ran about
two kilometers to get through before the Russians came. Oh, it was
unbelievable. But the amazing thing was that somehow I felt that
everything that had happened was right. It was right that the soldiers
ran, and that the colonel was knocked down and shot his own
corporal, that we had to leave home and that the train didn't go
where it was supposed to. You see my big idea was all gone in that
first minute, and I guess my new idea was that the whole world
was wrong and so everything that happened had to be wrong. Do
you see that, Max?"

"Yes," he said. "I see that."

"And now," she said, and her arm detached itself from his, and
she looked out over the thick dark hills of the Odenwald, as if reading *The Prolegomena to Every Future Metaphysic,* "Now I want
to live for myself, not for a cause. I want experience, want to see
things. I want to be part of the world. I don't want to be put blind
into a house, to nurse children and cook for them. *Verstehst du,*
Maxl? *Du verstehst?*"

"*Ich verstehe,* Traudis. It's a natural desire, a proper one for you.

I want to live too. It may be too late to have a great career—I've no illusions there—but life is big and rich." Said in his ponderous German, the words had for both of them an awkward force which, at least, sustained them until the dark beer and thick *schnitzels* of the Gänsheim *Stube* restored them to more usual talk. Never before had they been, and never after would they be so close to each other.

8

After that day, which they came to call the "aunt's funeral day," Schreiber saw Traudis all the time. Every few days she spent the night in the Ritterhof, and now and then they took the car to their blissful slot of grass in the Odenwald. On weekends they began traveling around to "places of interest," and between sight-seeing, grand meals, concerts, and movies, they cavorted in bed.

For Schreiber, Traudis' revelations were very moving. It was more than personal sympathy for a human being's plight; it was an historical, general sympathy as well, one which an emotional world historian might feel for the decline of a favorite nation. In Traudis, Schreiber saw the corruption of a people's spirit by madness and tyrannical villainy, the collapse of lives, of families, of life's sweetness. From this sympathy, his love for her grew, and with it the desire to repair, to salve, to rebuild. Formerly, he had listened to her talk as a weary prompter listens from his pit to an untrustworthy prima donna; now everything she said enthralled him, sometimes as if he were an admiring fellow-artist. It was during these latter periods, that he seemed to feel that their needs dovetailed, that is, the needs beyond their transient ones. It was thus that the idea of a grand tour passed from him to her. They began to think of taking it together, and this possibility assumed the aspect of a solution to the difficulties of their lives. Indeed, the more they thought and talked of it, the more this solution to a disturbed past became an invitation to a brilliant amalgamated future.

One evening in October, Schreiber came back from work to find

Traudis on the floor looking at the big map of Europe and the Near
East which he had taken from his office. She was wearing one of
his white shirts; two buttons were undone, and she wore nothing
underneath.

She jumped up, put her arms around him as he started to take off
his topcoat, and said, "Let's go soon, Max. I wrote for visas today to
all the places we might go." Her eyes were like lit matches.

Looking into them, Schreiber had a vision of the two of them,
Traudis and himself, a slimmer, harder version of himself, lying in
huge white beds in rooms looking out over blue seas. Traudis, breathing hard and flushed, looked as if she were already there, gulping
salubrious air and exposing her body to the sun. "We're practically
on our way," he said smiling, and touched her inside the second
button.

It was a month before they had actually worked the trip out. He
had now accumulated nearly thirty days leave; he requested a month
starting in the middle of December, and after a puzzling delay, the
request was granted. He was told to leave a copy of his itinerary with
Parsons of C.I.C. "New regulations for civilians in Intelligence,"
said the Colonel in charge of the office, looking at Schreiber as if he
had forgotten to put on a tie.

"As soon as I work it out, sir," said Schreiber.

"Naturally," said the colonel.

He and Traudis planned the trip in one long session, sitting on
the floor in front of the map, drinking white wine. "First stop,
Belgrade, *nicht?*" said Traudis, her face sharp with excitement at
the wonderful prospects. She drank the wine more to contain than
to raise her spirits.

"How long does it take to get there?" he asked. "I assume we go
by train."

"Absolutely. Even in dollars, the plane is impossibly expensive."

Schreiber smiled tenderly at her consideration of his pocketbook.
"About two days. Eight hours to Munich, four more to Salzburg,
eight more or so through Austria, and another ten or twelve to Bel-

grade." On a piece of his notebook paper, Schreiber wrote, "Belgrade —two days."

"How long in Belgrade, would you think?" he asked.

"A day," she said. He noted the time on the paper. "It might be better to go to Trieste and sail for Athens," and the largesse and freedom which such a choice meant for her brought stunning colors to her face. Schreiber felt the grand tour would offer nothing as beautiful. "Athens, through the Aegean to Istanbul, then Aleppo, Damascus, Jerusalem. Alexandria and Cairo on the way back. We'd better see American Express about hotels and tickets."

It was the first suggestion of an agency, of anything which was to come between themselves and whatever lay behind the map, and going down to the American Express Office the next day committed them to a labyrinth of detail only at the end of which they would travel. Visas—for Schreiber fairly easy, for Traudis, a month's assault on fifty offices, German and foreign—tickets, reservations, currencies, inoculations, and then instructions left at the office, books returned to the library, baggage, shopping, and then, one day, they were ready, the preparatory ritual just falling short of exhausting their desire.

At three o'clock one freezing January morning, they stood in the Frankfurt *Bahnhof* whelmed in mufflers, overcoats, galoshes, and wool caps, surrounded by bags, laden with tickets, currency, and an itinerary whose complexity and length helped weigh the unreality of the actual departure with enough burdens to make them know they were really off. Schreiber touched her face with his gloved hand. "It's hard to believe," he said. Traudis nodded, her eye on the track where their train was to pull in.

In the second class compartment, Schreiber, stretched out on one of the seats opposite Traudis on the other, looked out the window and thought of the long evenings back in Rye and Noroton, where, after dinner, he would reread the mail in the living room, drink, and listen to the radio and to the clicks of Florence's rings as she turned the pages of the Book of the Month. They had stopped going to movies, because he liked to leave bad ones, and Florence didn't;

she sat rigid with excitement through them all, darkening at any disparaging comment during or after the film. With one couple they had played bridge, but Schreiber was an unsure player, and after Florence had frowned at a mistake, he became less and less sure, so that he picked up each hand fearing that his cards would be good, and that he would have to bid. He thought of all this now as if he were visiting a museum.

He looked at Traudis, asleep under the overcoat he had bought her, and then reached over and touched her hair. "Good night, my dear," he said.

She stirred and mumbled that she was very sleepy.

He folded his overcoat over her, put his head back against the window, and tried to imagine what Belgrade would be like. He remembered that the Danube was there, and that if nothing else worthwhile happened on the trip, at least he'd have seen the source of the most beautiful piece of music in the world.

PART FIVE

CHAPTER ONE

I

In December, the *Times-Journal* suggested that Baggish do a series of articles on the growth of German industry since the end of the war. The suggestion appealed to him more than the five others he had followed through—examinations of the Bonn Constitution, Adenauer's cabinet, the neonationalist parties, university life in the postwar era, and Germans as tourists—and for a while he tried to discover the nature of the appeal. As a hunting dog at the edge of the wood senses the quarry before he has picked up its specific scent, so Baggish found in the suggestion an invitation which went beyond itself.

Gunther Frötenhaelsch got the necessary information for him. "I'm looking for a typical industrialist," Baggish told him one day over the *schnitzel* which was to be Gunther's reward for his research. "Not one of the great tycoons, but someone who, since the end of the war, has cleared, say, a million marks for himself. He should be over fifty, but not much older, young enough to have spent a decent fraction of his life in the *Hitlerzeit*—"

"Do you mean indecent fraction?"

"—yet old enough to have half his business career before him. He's got to have a family, and, if possible, I'd like to have him live within two hours train time of Heidelberg."

It took Gunther three days of looking around the Alfred Weber Institute files before he submitted a name, but Baggish shook his head. "This pigeon only has a son. Americans think of a family as at least one son and one daughter."

"You take no chances on extinction," said Gunther, slapping up a jawful of *Kalbfleisch* to which Baggish's generosity had extended.

The second suggestion was also turned down. "The children are too young," said Baggish. "The man married late and so isn't typical. I want the sole important differences between the German and American business man to be nationality, economic outlook, and business practices."

The fourth choice proved acceptable, although Baggish said that he must see for himself. "He's a widower, and that may be better than what I was thinking of. But we'll have to see."

"You're more finicky than a eugenist, Theo."

Baggish's choice was Herr Wolfgang Kammerbusch, the owner of a large paint factory in Höchst, an industrial suburb of Frankfurt. Before and during the war, Kammerbusch had managed the factory for I. G. Farben; after the *Zusammenbruch,* he managed it for the Tri-Partite Farben Control Division of the Allied Military Government. In 1948, with the approval of the Control Board, he bought out the Farben interests. His personal fortune was estimated at two to three million marks and the capital value of the concern was close to fifteen million. He was fifty-eight, a widower with two children, a son, Hermann, now known as Ulrich, twenty-nine, the company's Director of Sales, and a daughter, Herthe, twenty-three, a student of Slavic Linguistics at the University of Frankfurt. A second son had been killed in the African campaign, and Kammerbusch's wife had jumped from the roof of the factory the day after she learned the news.

"That's the story," Gunther had said. "Bruno Flasdieck knows the son slightly. He seems to be reasonably intelligent, although he is not of course in Bruno's circle."

Baggish addressed the following letter to Kammerbusch that evening. It was in English:

December 8, 1950

My dear Mr. Kammerbusch:

I am a foreign correspondent for the *St. Louis Times-Journal* and the Northwest American Newspaper Alliance. I have been assigned to write a series of articles on German industry in the Postwar period. It has been suggested by certain responsible people that as an important and progressive industrialist of this period, you would make an excellent subject for one of the articles. I would, therefore, very much like to interview you at your earliest convenience.

May I thank you in advance for your cooperation.

Sincerely yours,
Theodore Baggish

Post Scriptum: I shall not be able to make an appointment before December 11 or after December 18. (I have to be in London and Paris for an indefinite period.)

T.C.W.B.

Three days later, he received an answer (in German), as follows:

11 December 1950

Most honored Herr Correspondent Dr. Baggish:

Thank you for your letter. I shall be happy to see you any time. Would you come to lunch with me in my house, 80 Bieberpelzallee, Frankfurt/M this coming Saturday at one o'clock? I shall try to answer any questions you may wish to put, and I will myself take you through the plant.

Respectfully yours,

and it was signed under the secretarial typescript, "W. P. Kammerbusch."

2

It was the first snow of the year, and the American plows were out on the Autobahn; Baggish cursed behind one of them half the way to Frankfurt. The Fiat's window wipers moaned with the labor of clearing off the plow's snowy wake, and the little car trembled with the wind. "Like Lincoln on his mule," thought Baggish.

In Frankfurt, there was no snow. Baggish drove along the river to Bieberpelzallee, turned up a short gravel drive to a gray stone house which made no claim on the world but that of unabashed presence: "I'm here. I'm large enough. None of your business how I look. I cost more than you do." A bewintered strip of garden led to a bridle path and a garage which showed the backs of a Mercedes and two Opels. Parts of similar houses showed through rows of cedar. "It's not Versailles," thought Baggish, "but it's here, definitely here. And now."

It was two hours later, while sitting with Kammerbusch at a large window giving on the bridle path where Herthe Kammerbusch cantered up and down a two hundred yard stretch, that Baggish drew his first easy breath since driving up the gravel path. It had been a trying lunch: the food was thick, creamed, deprived of its native flavor, yet disdainful of artificial ones. Herthe had been ill-at-ease and listless, her brother arrogant and suspicious, Kammerbusch enigmatic. Now he hulked over Baggish, his round face, smooth and gray as cleft rock with eyes that shifted with the secretive movement of hatching cocoons. His body was a caricature of health, a swollen chest, tiny stomach, legs like huge splinters of the trunk. He had walked Baggish around the house, and kept staring at the impassive face, wondering how young this peculiar American was. Baggish seemed young only at first sight; his walk, gestures, and expressions were fifteen years older than their elements, and sensing this, Kammerbusch overcame an initial distaste for him.

"Stuffy, but not too bad," he said to him in the drawing room where they sat after the house tour. "It was von Brenneken's, the old Bourse President. He didn't survive the troubled era."

Baggish followed Kammerbusch's talk with difficulty: there was a sort of rasp in it which was neither dialectal, colloquial, nor a sign of toughness or rudeness. "He was not one to bear up under privation and depletion. Not," he said, indicating the mahogany curve of a Bechstein grand piano whose surface carried the reflection of a harp from the next room, "that you visitors have borrowed everything." Baggish allowed a twist of the mouth for this. "A little pleasantry," said Kammerbusch without the rasp, so that Baggish knew that its source was authority and assurance, and that Kammerbusch had a limited supply of these strengths. The knowledge made him feel easier.

They both watched Herthe riding outside. Kammerbusch asked Baggish if he rode.

"Not since the war," said Baggish, stroking his back.

"You were a soldier then?"

Baggish inclined his head.

"I hope that you have lost whatever bitterness you may once have had."

Baggish smiled and said that after such a dinner it was difficult to feel bitterness about anything.

"Our cuisine is not extravagant," said Kammerbusch, with the rasp. "It's intended to maintain, or even strengthen. Simplicity is the motto, although if there are personal dietary problems, we adapt to them." Baggish winced, remembering the frizzled veal and creamed broccoli devoured in religious silence by the three Kammerbusches. This moral theory of the household cuisine led Kammerbusch to discuss what Baggish had ostensibly come to hear, namely the account of his business career, his factory, his workmen and their living conditions, the early restrictions and present freedoms as embodied in the Bonn Government's "progressive taxation policy," and his ideas for the development of his plant which, he hoped, would be supervised by his son, "as I am not as strong as I look, and have done the best part of my work in digging out from under the war."

As he talked, more and more grandly of his hopes, his eye cantered in miniature after his daughter, who, now and then, glanced in through the windows as she rode. "All to the good," thought Baggish, observing this paternal absorption. Meanwhile, he detached facts from the discourse and noted them on a scratch pad. "Magnesium Chlorates—30,000 gr.t. '48, 36th.—49, Silesian imports cut 12% after Belg. fr. collps," a long string which he would only need to yank at occasionally in the sort of general, reflective article which was his stock-in-trade. Kammerbusch plunged into the statistical mysteries of his growth, and his eyes now ceased their paternal voyagings and paid tribute to the exultation he found in his triumphs. His language became cryptic, and Baggish hardly made pretense of note-taking now, only watched the gestures and probed the center of the man whose future was to be, he felt, a part of his own.

Suddenly Kammerbusch stopped in what seemed to Baggish the middle of a sentence. Herthe had dismounted, given her horse to a gardener, and come toward the house. Kammerbusch looked drained and his eyes twitched with fatigue.

"I'm afraid I'd better go now, Mr. Kammerbusch," said Baggish. "You must be very tired after a hard week and then this long interview."

"You're considerate as well as attentive, Mr. Baggish. I do get tired now more quickly than I wish."

"I only hope that you'll let me come for at least one more talk. American journalism is, as you may know, personal journalism, and I know that a fuller picture of you and your family would be valued and appreciated by our readers. And then, I myself would very much like to know you better."

Kammerbusch evaluated this slowly. "I should like to know you better also, Mr. Baggish. There aren't many men of your generation who come to this house—despite my son. Ulrich has always associated with either much younger or much older men, and consequently he too is not typical of this most interesting generation of yours. When can you come again?"

Baggish stifled the impulse to say "tomorrow." "The day after tomorrow," he said, looking into Kammerbusch's eyes until he felt that an agreement had been formed with him. It was as if a river had forced a channel to the sea. They rose and walked to the door where they found Herthe in her riding clothes.

"Will you show Mr. Baggish out please, my dear?" asked Kammerbusch after a deliberative pause. "I'm very tired and I know he'll excuse me."

"I shall be attentive to him, Poppa," said Herthe.

"Thank you again," said Baggish to Kammerbusch. "I'll see you in a couple of days." He walked to the door with Herthe and explained. "We didn't finish our talks. I'm going to come up Monday."

"I suspected that something like this might happen," she said. "Do you have an hour to throw away now?"

3

They drove to Frankfurt and went to a small café on the lower level of the bridge opposite the cathedral. They sat by the terrace overlooking the Main and giving on a still lower terrace where boys and girls in shorts were doing gymnastics. "It's a *Turnverein,*" said Herthe. "I used to belong, but these were juniors then, and I don't know them. The café is pleasant. I may be presumptuous in taking you out here, out of the context of my home. There, however, I see you surrounded by familiar objects, and it's difficult to form an independent judgment of you. In one sense, you seem familiar, in another, an invader."

"I'm glad that you want to form a judgment," said Baggish. "Perhaps I feel the same way. A year ago I had never been in Germany and never spoken German. Yet sitting here with you, talking, and looking at the river, I feel not so much that I've been here before, but that I am where I'm supposed to be."

The gymnasts had lined up in two squads and were playing a tag game. Watching them as they ran faster and faster, their voices rising in serious excitement, Baggish and Herthe felt themselves a unit, a barely divided singleness. Their talk was affected by the rhythm of the games. The apple wine they drank emphasized the sympathetic emotions, and as they talked they swayed slightly back and forth, toward and then away from each other.

"There is something almost cinematic about sitting here with an American newspaperman at this place. I've been here so often, though never with a man except my brother. I must ask you a question that concerns me, but should not worry you."

"Yes?"

"Are you married?"

"I'm single."

"Another thing," she said. "At dinner I noticed that you looked appraisingly at me, and that you've now stopped. Do you think me ugly?"

Baggish thought for a while and then answered. "I found you unusual-looking at first. Your hair has an odd, neutral color, and your eyes seem sometimes quite large, sometimes very small. Your gait is unusual. Nonetheless I couldn't remember you when I looked away, and then, when I saw you riding, you moved away, and I found I could remember you. Now I like the way you look."

"That's enough for now," she said. "Nothing must be rushed." Both of them, however, were very sure that this thing would be.

Herthe took a bus home, and Baggish drove to Heidelberg as fast as the Fiat would go. He went into the Schwarze Loch, sat at one of the tables and drank six glasses of beer, three more than he had ever taken at one sitting. Back home, at Haus Stempel von Gode, he slept the sleep of the blessed.

4

On Monday, Baggish drove up to Bieberpelzallee again; this time he was to stay overnight. In the afternoon, Kammerbusch took him to Höchst and had a foreman show him around the factory. It was huge, brown, spectacularly ugly, and much more than the making of paints seemed to be going on. When Baggish asked Kammerbusch about this, the industrialist said, "Yes, we have a number of incidental products which we haven't really done much with yet. But we're hopeful." Baggish informed Kammerbusch that diversification was a key factor in the continued growth of American industry. "At first, it was but a stop-gap to destructive taxation: then it was seen as a new stage of industrial organization."

"Yes," said Kammerbusch gently, "we have tried to keep abreast of some of your developments. We have been living under a government tax tent for a while, but we too are waiting a time when we must expand on our own. Now here," and he waved to the window below, "we have turpentine, varnish, thirty or forty gum, oil, and coal products waiting to be packaged and marketed. What we lack is a spirited sales force to carve the markets for us. For ten years, we Germans simply commanded markets, commanded sales, commanded prices. We lost the habits of persuasion." Hands laced, he stared past Baggish's head toward the bellowing sound of litharge blending with zinc oxide in a thousand-gallon vat. The noise seemed to soothe him, like good winds to a sailor. "It's too bad, Herr Baggish, that a bright young man like yourself has had so little business experience."

"There are a number of roads to the pinnacle," said Baggish. "Who knows, if some day, men of my experience in publicity might not command very large positions with expanding business organizations."

"May I say that I have been thinking myself that such training would be an excellent thing in our field?"

"You know," said Baggish, "my trip to England has been put off indefinitely. If you permitted, I might be able to stay an extra day or two in Frankfurt."

"I've been meaning to invite you," said Kammerbusch, "and was only afraid that your engagement would necessitate your departure. Could I ask you to call Herthe at my house and make arrangements with her?"

"Nothing could be pleasanter," said Baggish.

5

An hour later, at the Kronberg Zoo in Frankfurt, Baggish and Herthe were watching the daily performance of the elephants, a circular dance, trunks to tails, with stops and reversals signaled by the cracks of a trainer's whip. "Ha ha ha ha," laughed Herthe, head back, her eyes like little blue fish scooting around a bowl. "How wonderful when monsters are delicate." She pointed to the hippo pool thirty yards from the elephants where, shining in the cold sun, the great black hunk of flesh hauled itself out of the water, and waddled to within five yards of his monstrous neighbors, his ears twitching madly as if telegraphing signals to auxiliaries hidden back in the bush. His wee, moronic eyes took in the galumphing capers. Then he turned his back to them, and, almost at the thundering periphery, deposited the fetid roughage of his last digested meal.

It was a stunning sight. Baggish felt his insides toppling. He roared, held his sides, pounded himself on the chest, bent half to the ground to hold himself. The spectators glared at him, frigid, unamused, revolted by this complementary exhibit. Herthe grabbed him by the scalp and dragged him off to a bench. He put his head against her sternum and laughed and laughed, bouncing up and down against her. "What a beast," he managed through his groans. "What a critic." Another look across at the great mass of dung charged his battery once more, and he guffawed maniacally. An old man, passing, halted to stare at him.

"Ah, you're a delicate one," smiled Herthe, and she took a handkerchief from his pocket and passed it over his face. "What an eye for subtleties. Debussy must be your meat. Hah. You should be dropped into some Congo wadi with a knife in your teeth. You could catch alligators for lunch and laugh all day in the sun. What a shock you are, Baggish." The rebuke was followed by her raising his head by the ears and kissing him full on the mouth.

From the corner of his eye, Baggish saw the old man's cane shaking at them. Still kissing Herthe, he raised a gloved fist at the man, who hopped off as if chased by tigers. "We're a display without the aid of bars," he said to Herthe, and kissed her again. "You are for me," he said after this.

"I feel well-disposed myself," said Herthe.

"This is new for me," he said, meaning his laughter at the hippo. "Will you forgive me?"

Taking the remark in a more natural sequence, Herthe said, "Don't be mushy, Theodore. We have been given to each other. How could you have felt this way before?"

"True," conceded Baggish. He really did enjoy this odd wire of a girl in a way he had never before enjoyed a human being.

6

To dinner at Bieberpelzallee that night, Baggish brought a magnum of Sekt, the German champagne.

"Ah," said brother Ulrich in the closest approach to smiling his repertoire of frowns permitted. "Is this a courtesy of the American newspaper world, Herr Baggish?"

"You will call me Theodore when you hear why I've brought it," said Baggish, ignoring the barb.

"Suspenseful," said Ulrich. "It must be an illustration for the article, 'German Industrial Family Dines at Home on Champagne and Oysters, Courtesy of U.S.A.'"

"You know my son's fine wit by now, Herr Baggish," said Kammerbusch, "and have, I trust, learned to ignore it. Tell us what I hope will be your good news."

Baggish reached for Herthe's hand and raised it to his lips. "This is the good news," he said.

Astonishment rearranged the drear map of Ulrich's face. Kammerbusch leaned back in his chair, touched a napkin to his forehead, and, after a few seconds, asked, "Are you sure that you had not met before Saturday?"

"Not in this world, Poppa," said Herthe.

"We met, we talked, we looked, and that was enough," said Baggish.

"Not quite enough," said Ulrich. "A few other things are involved."

"One of them is not you," said Kammerbusch quietly.

"I understand that," said his son, and he put his napkin on the table and left the room.

"He'll survive," said Kammerbusch. "But that is incidental at the moment." He looked at them closely. "Are we to call you an engaged couple?"

"That's up to you," said Herthe. "It describes our relationship adequately enough."

"I'm sorry there's no ring," said Baggish. "I don't much believe in that custom."

"I hope you believe in certain others though," said Kammerbusch. "You know that a relationship with Herthe involves you in our life, our position here."

"Of course," said Baggish. "I'm a strong supporter of noncommercial customs—and, of course, certain commercial ones. Marriage is in the books for us."

"A pleasant surprise, Poppa?" asked Herthe.

"Strangely enough," said Kammerbusch, "after the first three hours, I thought something might come of it. I miscalculated the time, but can you blame me? I don't know American methods. I'm in hopes of learning some from my son-in-law."

"I'm somewhat newer and faster than most," said Baggish. "You mustn't use me as a yardstick. I'll be glad though to share what I know with you."

They drank some champagne, and then Baggish and Herthe took a walk in the garden. It had turned very cold, and the color in Herthe's face, as they passed under the lights, stirred Baggish in a way which made him see that fortune had kindly let his needs converge. "Or perhaps," he told himself that night as he undressed in Herthe's room (a separate bed had not been made up for him),

"It's just that a strong passion converts what it sees into what it needs."

That night, Baggish slept for the first time in his life without feeling that the morning lay at the foot of his bed waiting for him to fill it.

7

Baggish's first article on Kammerbusch appeared in the *Times-Journal* and the affiliated newspapers just before Christmas. It took up a full page, a mass of print islanding a picture of Kammerbusch and Baggish in front of a gigantic separator in the Höchst plant. The article centered about the new German industrialist's conception of work as the sign of both his own worth and his country's rehabilitation, the government's benevolent view of this conception as embodied in the tax laws, and with the sense of business adventure which was rooted in disillusionment with ideological politics and any other "intangible force." The article was reflective and general, but there were numerous details culled from Kammerbusch's personal experience, financial problems, and relations with the occupying powers. A description of the snapshot of his dead son on the office desk, "a constant reminder of the futility of mysticism," concluded the piece.

"A splendid job," Baggish's editor had written. "Let's have more," and he enclosed a two hundred dollar bonus.

Kammerbusch too was impressed by the article, and when Baggish suggested that the series might well be a splendid entry into the American market, "or, at least, into some more fruitful arrangement with the American producers," Kammerbusch heard his innermost desires articulated, and with this young stalwart near him, he no longer felt his respectful terror at the famed, holy cartel which, at Farben, had been the great shadow on the junior executives' thinking, blocking them from any but day-to-day thoughts.

"Have you any friends in the American business and financial world, Theodore?" he asked.

"I make friends easily," said Baggish, and he moved his hand from the page to reveal the picture in the middle which testified to the claim, and exchanged smiles with his future father-in-law.

Before the second article appeared a week later, Baggish had been taken into the business as Director of Foreign Sales and Special Assistant to the president. Kammerbusch himself worked out in Bonn the legal questions involved with this ennoblement of a foreigner, and the still more difficult dispossession of Ulrich at a family dinner. The last was more difficult and succeeded only when Baggish told Ulrich that he hoped that he would accept a position as head of the German branch of an investment office he was thinking of starting in Europe to take care of all the new American capital which lay around waiting to be gainfully employed.

"A brilliant idea, Theodore," Kammerbusch had said. "Do you know anything about this business?"

"I've bought a book," said Baggish, smiling. "And with the help of people like Ulrich and a small capital outlay, which will, I suppose, have to wait"—here he smiled at Kammerbusch—"a little while, I think we can move in."

"And we thought Hitler had plans," said Ulrich, but in the face of this family tornado, nearer to a smile than usual.

The second article amounted to a three thousand word puff for Kammerbusch paints, the factory, the production methods, the managers, workers, and owners, and an impassioned account of the manner in which such a firm constituted the sort of obstacle to the "swelling aggressiveness of the Russian bear" that the British Navy constituted for Germany in the earlier part of the century, a bulwark, therefore, for the United States.

This elaborate piece of apologetics brought some celebrity to Baggish. It was briefly cited in one of the larger American news magazines and picked up by the *Frankfurter Neue-Zeitung*. Baggish was interviewed by the newspaper, and on the strength of the interview, was invited by HICOG to give a series of lectures on American and German industry in the Amerika Häuser all over West Germany.

This was not the end. After a month's tour, Baggish had written enough lectures to make up, with his other articles, a small book. He spent two weeks giving it a Lippmannian varnish, having Gunther Frötenhaelsch check his figures and add others, and sent the manuscript to a New York publisher.

He was not particularly surprised when the publisher wrote that he and his colleagues were delighted with "the little treatise" and would make it a feature of their Spring List.

CHAPTER TWO

I

Raja went up to Europe twice a year to get talent for the club. His itinerary, at any rate, was always arranged with this in mind, but there was another motive for his going, and it was this one which accounted for his excitement even now in this, his sixth trip to the continent.

Raja knew that without Beirut for base he'd be lost, but he also knew that without his trips to Europe and the acts he brought back from it, Beirut would be the interminable blank page it had seemed to him before he'd started leaving it.

The club was the focus of Raja's double view, and its formation had been, as its continuance was, the center of his life. It was not his wish to make it a European club any more than he wished to see Beirut Europeanized, but he did want to make it like nothing else in either Europe or the Middle East.

Raja had never felt wholly comfortable in Damascus or Cannes, Baghdad or Estoril, Alexandria or Paris: the Middle Eastern towns lacked Beirut's gleam and comfort, the European ones lacked what Raja thought of as the permissive ripeness of the East. For Raja, Lebanon was a jewel hanging between the massive equivalences of Europe and Asia. Once, in his early twenties, Raja had gazed at the world maps which were the mural decoration of his father's hotel lobby, and had had a geographical-historical flash: he saw the two continents as mirror versions of each other, Japan and England as the two earlike islands depending from the heartland and controlling their respective seas with navies, China and France as the great centers of literature, manners, and cuisine, India and Italy as the southern sources of romance, Germany and Russia as the centers of heady, dangerous mystiques, the Balkans as the turbulent Arab States with Austria as Turkey, and alone, unmatched, unmatchable, the jeweled pivot of Lebanon. In this flash, his mission had begun.

For Raja, the expeditions to the resorts and cities of Europe were pillaging ones, the spoils of the West for the enrichment of the East. Though he was far from being a scholar, he was aware of the wry twist this gave more general history.

The sixth trip was the first he had taken by boat. It was his father's idea. "First of all, it's cheaper," he'd told Raja in the hotel lobby where he sat most of the day. "But the main thing is that with the boat you have time to prepare yourself for the change." His father had gone up to Europe for twenty-three years before the war to sell brocades and had always been mindful of "the change." He would not believe his son's claim that he did not recognize such a thing.

Raja had said, "It's ridiculous. I can fly to Rome in a few hours, and it takes five days by boat just to get to Venice."

His father, smiling and rubbing his fine gray hair—of which, at sixty, he was somewhat ashamed before his son who was entirely bald at thirty-five—said, "You'll find it a totally different experience. You relax as never before. You get to know people better than you would in almost any other tranquil circumstance. And then, there's time for reflection." Knowing Raja's weakness, he returned to the second point. "I always met at least one charming person on the trip."

Raja went to bed the night before the sailing with special excitement. The suit which Mohammed Yusef had made up from the Portuguese wool which he'd brought back from his last trip was hung above his bed, the notes for his final instructions to Mama

Tagari were on the table next to a bowl of figs and a picture of Mario
Lanza, and all over were the leather bags, packed with luxurious
items which constituted Raja's personal raid on the world's arsenals
of production.

He was the last person to board the *Enotria,* the new, white, five
thousand ton Italian liner on the Middle East run. Papa Tagari had
just put the last of the bags in Raja's cabin when the gangplank
began to lift, and he had to jump the last foot to the pier. Raja
leaned against the first class rail and waved to him below.

The sun going down at his back sank gold plummets into the
bowl of mountains and the white crescent of shore where, through
the palms of the Avenue de Français, Raja could see the northern
wall of the club. When the boat moved out and he could see it no
longer, he went down to his cabin.

Washing up in his undershirt, and staring at the whales of flesh he
so detested, he began to feel an uncomfortable swaying which soon
began yanking at things in his stomach. He found the bottle of
dramomine pills in his coat and swallowed two with some bourbon
from an American flask. The yanking did not stop, and he began
to sweat. He opened his belt and lay on the bed staring at the blue
walls of the cabin. "The change," he said out loud, and thought
angrily of his father lounging in the hotel lobby. Terrible upheavals
threatened his insides, and he had a feeling that the boat wasn't
shielding him from the sea, but opening him to it. He put the pillow
over his head and, moaning, managed to get to sleep.

He awoke at a rap on the door. "Signor Yonakim? Are you all
right?"

"Yes," said Raja. "What's the matter?"

"Dinner is being served, sir. Would you prefer something in the
cabin?"

"I'll be out in a few minutes," said Raja. He felt better now, and
although he noticed the swaying, it did not disturb him. *"Mal de
mer,"* he thought. "A European disease."

His dinner partner was the Belgian Chargé d'Affaires in Damascus, a hulking, dour man who totally ignored Raja after quizzing him in Arabic about the *"Qu'ran"* and finding out that he was a lapsed Maronite who considered the book a barbarian poem and, furthermore, that he had discarded his classical Arabic with his schoolbooks. Raja had made his usual efforts at geniality, but the lifelessness of the dining room and the ugliness of the inquisitorial face across the tablecloth depressed him. He saw no one of interest in the room. There were some Iraqi pilots, a large table of three Italian couples who seemed to be eating each other's whispers, two old men whom he'd seen in his club and remembered as Italian tobacco people from Ismir, and a handful of people whom—so depressed was he—he didn't even bother to classify.

He left before dessert, walked around the deck three or four times and stared over the railing at the second and third class passengers on the main deck till he was chilled. Then he went into the salon, a bright, half-moon of a room with green and gold lounges spaced luxuriously around a red bar and brilliant with marine mosaics on the walls. A man who looked like Mussolini until he put a violin under his chin led two other musicians through French and American popular music and selections from German operettas. It was a mournful place until the room began to fill with people from the other classes. Smoke, talk, and drinking familiarized the atmosphere for Raja.

To his surprise, a couple of the people who came in from the other classes were Americans, one a fattish fellow of forty or forty-five who was sitting with a young priest, and, across the way, a young fellow of twenty-five or -six who was speaking French with a waiter. Few Americans traveled the Middle East line who weren't businessmen or diplomats in first class. Raja's interest was roused, particularly by the young man who had the sort of open face which Raja liked in most of the Americans who came into his club, the fliers stationed at Dharan or Bahrein who came in on leave, or the salesmen and legation people, many of whom lived in his father's hotel. Raja sent his waiter over to ask if the young American would

have a drink with him. As the American started over, Raja decided
that perhaps his father had been right after all about taking the
boat.

2

In Damascus Ward had sat next to a group of Syrian-American
businessmen in a night club. They were on a State Department–
sponsored tour of their native land, but behaved even less like their
ancestors than the most extravagant caricature of an American
tourist could have. They spoke only English—though boasted to
Ward of knowing the "lingo"—smoked large cigars and were flam-
boyant tippers. Like Ward, they stayed in the Hotel Orient Palace,
the gloomy first class hotel of Damascus. In the night club, they
watched a spectacular belly dancer conveying odd parts of a remarkable body into unexpected areas of the room. One of the American
Syrians remarked, "Largest belly button I ever saw. You could stick
a silver dollar in it" and another said, "Ten to one it would give
you change." Now, sitting on the main deck of the *Enotria* with
a copy of *Eminent Victorians* in his lap, Ward laughed out loud.
Raja, watching him unseen from the first class railing, called down,
"What's the gag, Robert? Let me in on it." He came down the narrow iron stair.

Ward told him the exchange and Raja laughed till his face was
limp, then called a steward, handed him a thousand lira note and
asked for his deck chair from the main deck. "More sun and better
company down here," he said.

"Thank you," said Ward sourly. "Though I won't be much company for you. I'm just about to go to sleep."

"I won't interfere," said Raja. "I'll just wrap me up in a blanket
and sleep too."

"You're a great noninterferer," thought Ward. "Fine," he said, and
turned away, eyes closed. Up until this Lebanese fag had started
trying to take over his life, his trip had been a great success. It had

satisfied, or better, it had exhausted his wanderlust. He was not only ready, he was eager to get back home, and home meant the States, and that meant settling. God knows, he was ready for that.

In Paris, it had taken him a month more of Juliette to discern her shoddy materials, and then his father's princely check arrived— "for your last fling, son"—and he'd headed for Rome and Athens, Constantinople, Baghdad, Teheran, Damascus, Jerusalem, and Beirut. He'd swallowed six of the seven cities of wisdom, and he was full.

Two days ago, the *Enotria* had stopped in the seventh city, Alexandria. Ward's original plan had been to get off, go down to Cairo for the day, see the pyramids and then take the next boat, the *Tarsus,* to Brindisi. But in Beirut, he had changed his tickets. He decided to spend a couple of hours in Alexandria and call it a day, but even this turned out to be too generous an allowance. He'd walked past half an acre of fly-bitten bums to the statue of Mohammed Ali and then said to himself, "The hell with it." He bought a picture postcard and a little monkey toy for his sister's baby, and walked back to the boat. On the gangplank he wound the toy up; it came to pieces in his hand, and he threw it into the harbor. "That's it," he told himself. "That's the end."

He also threw in the water a piece of paper on which Raja had written the names of the twenty "best spots in town." "I'd love to show them to you myself," he'd said to Ward, "but old Raja is *persona non grata* in this burg. I staged a private little show or two for old Farouk; and people never forgive you for certain kinds of favors you do them. You better watch it too, my boy. These Egyptians are crazy, and right now they're jumping Americans like bugs. Don't carry a camera around, and be careful."

This warning played a small part in the abbreviation of Ward's plans, but mostly, he knew, it was just general satiety, the sort he'd felt in lesser degree back in Tours the day he'd first seen Juliette. Now it was the real article. After a woman in Baghdad had thrust the bruised stumps of her little boy's arms into his face and crooned the one Arab word Ward had learned, *"Baksheesh,"* into his ear, he had canceled a tour through the ruins of Chosroe's palace. That night he had gone to see an old Rita Hayworth movie and, unlike the be-fezzed and burnoosed audience, he had understood, been repelled, and then calmed by it. "I've got traveler's indigestion," was his analy-sis. "I need home brew, even the worst." It was that night he decided that going home and putting his European capital to work was the thing to do.

The clincher had been Raja. For a couple of days he had bought Ward drinks and meals in First Class. This turned out to be the groundwork for an amazing invitation which he'd extended yes-terday: How would Ward like to be Master of Ceremonies in his Beirut nightclub? There'd be a good salary, most of which he could bank, as he'd have first-class room and board at Raja's father's hotel, the pick of any girl at the club, the use of a new Buick or Mercedes-Benz, and, if he stayed two years, an expense-paid trip to Europe. Ward reeled with surprise, he had a moment of temptation, shameful temptation as he regarded it after, and then refused, telling Raja of all sorts of plans, none of which he'd formulated up till then. "In America," he'd said, "if you're going to get something out of a career besides a living, you have to start young. I'm twenty-five, and I've got to get back while the getting's good."

Raja said that he understood perfectly, and Ward thought that he had seen the last of him. Indeed, last night, he had collared the other American on board, the fat lawyer from Heidelberg who turned out to be a friend of Ted Baggish (the sole thing Ward found to recommend in him), and Ward had paid for his own drinks at the bar.

Yet here the fruit was again. If it hadn't been that they were a day out of Venice, Ward would have walked off, but Venice was going to be the end anyway, the end of Raja, the end of this endless boat trip, the end of Europe, the end of Ward's apprenticeship. He could hold out till then.

He went to sleep in the January sun, smiling, half-aware that

Raja was watching him, but not caring, feeling generous and not averse to letting the poor fruit enjoy an inexpensive pleasure.

3

Schreiber spent much of the trip sitting in a deck chair at the stern, watching the gulls plunging for garbage in the ship's wake. The gulls and the Mediterranean were not enough to distract him from those topics which he wished to avoid, but which, like the stiffening nausea that had controlled his first hours on board, threatened constantly to overcome him. Sometimes, lying in the cold sun across from the huge, snoring bulks of an Austrian couple from Graz, he made sorties into his study of history: at Alexandria, while porters in sneakers blasted the air with what were surely blasts at man, God, past, present, and future, he remembered something about a lighthouse, a library and colored illustrations from his grammar school geography book of the Temple of Karnak; passing Crete the next day, while the Dominican who sat at his table explained that what he took for clouds was really snow on Mount Ida, he remembered a free-standing staircase, some vases decorated with a serpent woman, and the word "thalassocracy."

He salvaged from this some happy moments by contrasting the times when he couldn't tell Crete from Cyprus, or from Madagascar, for that matter. The salvage job brought him, however, to the forbidden image of Traudis crouching over the map and planning the trip with him, the trip which he was ending by himself. He shook it off, went up to the first class bar and had a martini with Raja, the manager of the Beirut nightclub who was always there extinguishing his own marine thoughts under the bright mosaics.

"The first and last time I go by ship," he said.

Schreiber had heard this before. "Why didn't you get on a plane in Alexandria?"

"I am *persona non grata* in Alexandria," said Raja. "They don't like Raja in Alexandria."

Schreiber didn't like Raja on the *Enotria,* but there were no better
companions, and long stares at the blue jewels within blue jewels
of the famous sea made him sick. Such sickness would lead to the
familiar sickness of the sea, and he would stagger to his little cabin
where his cabin mate, a young Maronite priest who worked in palae-
ography at the Sorbonne, would be stretched out in equivalent
miseries on his own bunk.

"Thirteenth trip I've made," said the priest when they were both
at dinner with the bearded, Spanish Dominican, "and I still have
no fortitude at sea." They spoke French together, the Dominican
ludicrously, the Lebanese very well.

"The calmest of all seas," said the Dominican who was returning
on it to Spain after six years in Palestine, where, as he said, "My
congregation disappeared over night. Imagine, God planting me in
the middle of No Man's Land." He ate well, despite his troubles,
and, at the table talked happily about literature with the Maronite
and politics with Schreiber. His political hero was General Franco.
"He brings soul and iron into the state," he said. "You don't strangle
Stalin with guns alone, or with butter. You must show him more
than the back of your hand. Franco shows him two iron hands
clasped together in prayer." His literary hero was Lope de Vega
whom he compared to Shakespeare by stretching his arms wide and
saying, "Lope. A shelf of books," and then, spacing his fingers
an inch apart, "Shakespeare. One little book." "Yes," he said to
Schreiber. "You English don't know the world. I shall show you
though, *cher ami.* You leave the *Enotria* a new man. *Lo que será,
será,* as Don Juan has it." He smiled through his beard. He was really
a young man, as they learned when he showed them his beardless
passport picture. "Surprised, yes? First thing I do when I find the
shore is shave the beard. You're lucky, *mes chers.* If you knew what
we have to give up for the order," and he flapped his gown as they
rose for their after-dinner walk on deck. "Look," and he grabbed
a handful of the black wool. "Hot in summer, cold in winter. But
God restores. God makes it worthwhile. Yes," he said again to

Schreiber. "Listen to me, and you get off the boat a new man."

It was the *Enotria's* third voyage and consequently there were no movies. "Next trip," said the purser, a dark, movie-star type who did favors with the hearty considerateness of royalty. "How about music? What will you have? Lehar? Menturicci, put on the *Lustige Witwe* records. My favorites," he told Schreiber as they sat in the stiff red leather chairs of the second class lounge under the loudspeaker. The music started, blaring and scratchy at once. *"Komm in meinen kleinen Pavillon,"* sang the tenor. *"Ich bin eine anständige Frau,"* sang the soprano. *"Nun, gehen wir ins Maxims,"* sang the chorus, and the purser called, "Menturicci, *ancora,"* and he and Schreiber smoked Italian cigarettes and listened till ten o'clock. "You are enjoying the trip?" he asked Schreiber anxiously between the second and third repetition.

"Yes," said Schreiber.

"I'm happy. It's very important, the first fifteen trips. Say good things about us."

"I have no influence."

"No matter. It's the growing of sentiments, the people's feeling that there is something fine, and this begins by a few words of mouth from the passengers of the first fifteen trips. The opening impression spreads around the world. There are graphs to show this proved."

Music at night, Raja in the afternoon, and gull-watching the rest of the time. Wrapped up in his deckchair blanket, he had a vision of Traudis and Tiberius driving together over the desert. What had happened in Beirut was absurd, a record playing backwards, all the sounds present but disordered beyond sense. But what happened, happened. The sea played with his melancholy, joined and augmented it. It was like sitting in front of a fireplace in winter, feeling oneself sink into the dying coals. Traudis and Tiberius: what were they about? He had half a mind to go back to Florence, and then he remembered that it was too late even for that. No, he thought, big fires burn out quickly. She'll get tired and come back. He could hardly distinguish in his dazed view of the sea whether he meant Micheline or Traudis. These people were unfortunates, broken-up by wars and terrible handicaps; they needed what they took; he didn't. He'd had enough of them, enough of strange places, outlandish languages, murderous hatreds, seasickness, garbage, the Near East, Europe. If the trouble blew over in Heidelberg—he had a feeling it might not, but if it did, he'd save some money and then go back to the States, out West somewhere, and open a general store or buy into one, become an inconspicuous part of an inconspicuous place. Then, remembering Traudis' note, he knew that he wouldn't have the strength.

"Dear old Max," it went,

No future going back home, and no point in going on with you. We were satisfied for weeks, and for months before that. That should be enough; everything has its term. I'll see a different type of life now. Why not with this old friend of yours? He's wise, rich, and he thinks as I do. You and I never thought alike, much as we did together and much as we liked each other. You've got too much American in you. The black man doesn't. You're all *thing* and *place* and *time*. Category, pigeonhole, business. I can't cut the flow of my life to fit such patterns. But you're a good fellow. Keep in touch with me—I'll let you know where. This is the best way for it.

Always yours,
Traudis

4

In Salonika he and Traudis had slept in a six-by-eight bed next to a French window which looked across the bay at Mount Olympus. They'd had a day there, seeing the Byzantine mosaics and the shops, driving in the mountains where Alexander the Great had been born, drinking a yellow resinous wine by the water. Breakfasting in bed on Turkish coffee, *croissantes,* butter, and jam, they had regarded each other, mouths full of the hot sweet, as the containers, if not the substantial matter of each other's euphoria. For Schreiber, it was the moment he would remember best, one which, years after, lying in a lonelier bed, he would reconstruct as the bomb-shattered, stained glass of Wells Cathedral was reconstructed, the assemblage of colored fragments retaining the vividness if not the shapes of the original window.

This was the best memory, the one that would calm him to sleep. The other memory originated in Beirut a week later. He and Traudis spent a few hours of their first night in Beirut in Les Nuits De Paris, Raja's nightclub. It had, according to the concièrge at their hotel, the best floor show in the Middle East. They were sitting at a table, surrounded by other tables filled with American Air Force men, an assortment of international salesmen, and Near Eastern businessmen, tête-à-tête with the ladies whom Raja provided. Schreiber, looking at Traudis, saw her staring quizzically at something behind him. He turned, felt, and then saw a dark hand blazing with diamonds on his shoulder, and heard a voice saying, "Hello, Max."

It was Tiberius. Tiberius in a tweed suit from Saville Row, so redolent of wealth and confidence that Schreiber could neither call him by name nor, in one sense, identify him, even while he felt, deep inside himself, that he knew him better than he knew himself, recognized inside himself the accumulation of Tiberius-feeling, sinister and familiar, lethal and unabating. It was externalized for him in the flashes of diamond, which so fused with the black hand that the hand itself seemed the source of the light. For seconds Schreiber blinked at it before he said, "My God. Is it really you?"

Tiberius smiled sternly as if enjoining the separation of the waters. "Who else?" He yanked a Raja-girl out of her chair at the next table, and drew the chair up between Schreiber and Traudis. "Where shall I begin, Max?"

"Does he know German?" Traudis asked Schreiber. *"Ich bin* Traudis Bretzka," she said, holding out her hand.

"Tiberius Fitch," said Tiberius, holding out his own hand until she shook it with hers. "I can't speak German. French."

"Good."

Schreiber was seeing in Tiberius, Micheline's rust-colored face, a tropic island in a black sea. "Yes," he said dreamily, "What have you been doing? What are you doing here?"

"I can tell you quickly, or I can tell you till I never catch up with myself," said Tiberius.

"Quickly," said Traudis.

"I've been running for six years, you know Max, since I went over that little hill with French lint sticking to my coat. I've been in Marseilles, San Sebastian, all over Spain. I did money work in Tangiers, ran a statistical service in Conakrey. Who knows? Everything. I can hardly remember. I'm a great one for not remembering. You're the first thing I've bothered looking back at in years, Max."

"That's nice," said Traudis. Schreiber too had felt himself warm to it.

"I hit it big three years ago, and I'm very big now. I'm running a fleet of oil trucks for Ibn Saud. I'm richer than Rockefeller. You need money? I'll give you half a million. You need a job? Anywhere in the East you want to go. I've been in the Kremlin, China. I had a talk with Chou-en-lai. I'm big. I'm so big, I can't remember how small I was the day before yesterday." A trumpet call shook the narrative and a blue spotlight picked up a man in tails walking up to a microphone. "Let's get out of this fleabag," said Tiberius. "I know a good, quiet place."

Outside was a pumpkin and magenta Cadillac convertible. Tiberius opened the door for them, and drove down the shore line to a glass-domed restaurant leaning over the Mediterranean. It was lit by small tapers and the almost full moon. "Nice?" he asked. He led them through the darkness to a terrace, where a waiter in tuxedo bent as he saw them. "Nice to see you, Monsieur Fitch," he said in English. There were three other patrons, each at a different table, well-spaced from each other, and concentrating on their plates. Tiberius ordered in Arabic, and they found themselves in front of platters of tiny shrimp cooked in sweet, clear wine and served on circles of Eastern bread.

"Are you happy, Max?" Tiberius asked.

Schreiber felt the wine-soaked shrimp melting into his stomach. "Yes, I am," he said.

"I too," said Traudis, and she looked at Tiberius in a way which, had Schreiber had the least inkling of what was to happen, would have led him to take her out of the restaurant then-and-there.

But that was it. That was the only clue he could have had, and that one depended on an unwritten history and an invisible sequence. Afterwards he asked himself, "When did it happen?" In the day-and-a-half they had left in Beirut before sailing time, he was with them almost all the time. That Tiberius did not leave them, except when they went off to their hotel—he had a permanent suite at the St. George—seemed to Schreiber more natural than if he had seen them only at meals. Tiberius belonged to them, and despite the initial shock of seeing him, Schreiber felt that this was right. Time habituates opposites to each other; old enemies are usually easier to be with than new friends. But for Schreiber, that was it: Tiberius was around, and no pressure was exerted by or on him. They talked easily together, mostly about what they saw and ate. Only occasionally did Tiberius mention his excursions into the jungles, seas, and cities of the East. The mentioning was skillful: Tiberius knew the *farceur's* maxim that of the two people in the farce, the one who kicks, and the one who gets kicked, it is the latter who gets the laughs. Portraying himself as a victim even while he reeked of power and self-assurance, secured him not only sympathetic laughter, but impassioned absorption from both the man he had wronged, and the woman who would be the means of his wronging him again. On the terrace of the St. George swimming pool, in the glass-domed restaurant, at the Roman ruins at Baalbek, where he drove them the next morning and where in the Temple of the Sun he lectured them, sweetly and modestly, on the layers of conquest which showed themselves in the broken columns, or in the bazaar behind the giant clock which divides the new Beirut from old, Tiberius led and taught, listened and smiled.

And on the second night, instead of Traudis, Schreiber found her note on the bed. She had not taken her clothes or her luggage; her toothbrush was in the rack, a pair of nylon underpants hung drying on the bathtub. The room insisted on her return, and until an hour before sailing time, Schreiber was sure that she would come and sure that he would say nothing about her absence unless she talked of it first. When she didn't come, he packed her clothes in her bags and left them with the desk clerk, explaining that Madame had changed her plans and would pick the luggage up in the next few days.

Even in the taxi, he thought that she might be waiting for him on the ship.

5

Of all possible confessors, Raja seemed the least likely to Schreiber. Why he opened up to him instead of, say, to the young American who had said he was a friend of Teddy Baggish in Paris, he could not figure out. (Except that Ward seemed a strangely mixed-up person: for instance, he claimed to know Baggish well yet had thought he was a Midwesterner, and had all sorts of funny notions about him which Schreiber didn't bother either to pay attention to or contradict.) It began when Raja told him that he thought that he'd seen him in the club the other night. "Weren't you with that oil man, Fitch?"

The pain of admission had led to the confidence. In ten minutes Schreiber confessed that the fellow had run off with his girl.

"Lousy whores, these bitches," sympathized Raja. "I'd sooner trust an Egyptian. Well, I suppose it'll feel good to be getting back to Heidelberg."

Schreiber said that he didn't really look forward to it now. Not only had his girl gone, but his best friend there was moving up to Frankfurt. Also, he'd had a notice in Istanbul from his Colonel that a Reduction-in-Force was planned and that his job might only have a few months to run. "I suppose I can always get another," he said.

"I'm a lawyer, and the Army's never had an easy time getting trained personnel, but I don't know. I don't feel entirely easy about it."

Suddenly, while Schreiber spoke, Raja had another flash. He saw in this fat American the Western counterpart of himself. More than that, he saw a Western companion, or maybe a shadow, a capable, disengaged, unaggressive shadow, part drifter, part romantic, displaced, uneasy, available; and he made his offer.

"It may sound sudden to you, Max, but I've got what might be called a sporting proposition to make you, something in which you could be of help to me and by which you might be helped in turn. I'm losing a key man in my operation in Beirut. He's the emcee of my show, but his main job is keeping the talent up to snuff, the personnel on their toes and off their asses. The money's not bad, you get a room in the hotel and all the meals you want there. If you sign up for three years, I'll take you along the next time I come to Europe to get the acts. Beirut is a great place, an easy city to live in, and be let alone in. I think you'd like it." Schreiber sat blinking, a fish pulled into the air. "Think it over, Max, will you? You can have all the time we have left on the boat." In a few hours the *Enotria* was due in Venice.

Schreiber felt something click into place; and the click said, "Why not?" The arguments which rose in his head after he'd heard it, beat themselves to death against a closed door. What was he going to do with his car and all the other things he had in Germany? There he knew people, he knew the language, he was at home, one westerner with other westerners. Suppose he went to Beirut. He might see Tiberius there, or even Traudis, might see them together. What did he know about being an emcee in a night club? He'd never said a word in public: he found night clubs puerile.

All this perished in front of the "Why not?" He'd go to Germany, clean up his affairs, pack the rest of his stuff, sell, or give the Fiat to Baggish, join Raja somewhere and head back with him. It was simple. He'd learn Arabic. If he saw Tiberius, he would wait till he apologized before speaking to him. As for Traudis, who knows. She'd get tired of mooching around the desert, she'd get tired of trying to keep up with Tiberius, of being treated like a piece of lint. She'd come back to Beirut, and he would be waiting, ready to start up again. If he'd learned something in Europe, it was that every day brought enough to live for. You lived in what came up. That made you what you were.

He'd give it a try. Three years. He could survive three years in a coal mine, a submarine, a trailer camp. He'd taken Bucceroni that long, and Florence longer than that. Why not Raja?

"I don't know how much use I'll be to you," he said, "but I'll give it a try. It sounds like a generous arrangement to me."

His fat palm was lifted and patted by Raja's fatter one. "We're going to make it together, Max. We're going to have us one fine time. One real ball."

"Why not?" said Schreiber. "I don't see why not."

6

The *Enotria* sailed up the Grand Canal at four o'clock in the afternoon. The sun leaned into the water, puddling the colors from the loggia, palazzi, domes, and towers. Schreiber had never seen anything so beautiful. Everything seemed to be detached from its home color and shape, drifting into an airy, rainbow amalgam. It was like the melting of a good emperor's heart.

"The whole damn city is sinking right before our eyes," said Raja at his elbow. "A few centimeters a year, right into the canals."

"Oh no," said Schreiber. "I hope not. What a loss."

"Loss of the worst smelling burg in the history of the world. And these people complain when they go East. They can't tell violets from Shinola. Come on. Let's push off this trap." He yanked at Schreiber's arm, and then pointed to his overnight bags. Schreiber, reflecting on the dissolution of this flaming jewel, picked them up slowly, and followed Raja to the Purser's deck where the custom's men sat.

Raja went up to them, then came back to Schreiber and said, "We're in the clear. Let's head off."

Schreiber followed him down the gangplank, the bags banging against the ship. He had the odd sensation that he wasn't returning to Europe but leaving it. "Funny," he thought. They stepped into a gondola, and he sat back, breathing hard.

Moving slowly up the canal, he looked all around him at the city, the old queen of Europe, and then, while Raja was busy admiring the gondolier, he whispered, "So long, dear heart. So long, dear, dear heart."